D1399613

IF ONLY
WE COULD DRIVE
LIKE THIS
FOREVER

Elisabeth Harvor

Penguin Books

Published by the Penguin Group
Penguin Books Canada Ltd, 2801 John Street, Markham, Ontario, Canada
L3R 1B4
Penguin Books Ltd, 27 Wrights Lane, London W8 5TZ (Publishing & Editorial)
and Harmondsworth, Middlesex, England (Distribution & Warehouse)
Penguin Books, 40 West 23rd Street, New York, New York 10010, U.S.A.
Penguin Books Australia Ltd, Ringwood, Victoria, Australia
Penguin Books (N.Z.) Ltd, 182-190 Wairau Road, Auckland 10, New Zealand

First published by Penguin Books Canada Limited, 1988.

Copyright © Elisabeth Harvor, 1988.

Canadian Cataloguing in Publication Data

Harvor, Beth
  If only we could drive like this forever

ISBN 0-14-010383-X

I. Title.

PS8565.A69I47 1989   C813'.54   C87-094822-9
PR9199.3.H37I47 1989

British Library Cataloguing in Publication Data Available
American Library of Congress Cataloguing in Publication Data Available

"Not that the story need be long, but it
will take a long while to make it short."
—Henry David Thoreau

If Only We Could
Drive Like This Forever

Elisabeth Harvor was born in southern New Brunswick of
Danish immigrant parents. Her stories have appeared in
*The Hudson Review, The New Yorker, Saturday Night,
The Windsor Review* and a number of other magazines
and journals. They have been anthologized in *Best
American Short Stories,* 1971, as well as in several other
collections, including three of the Oberon annuals, *Best
Canadian Stories,* and in *More Stories by Canadian
Women,* Oxford University Press, 1987. Her first story col-
lection, *Women and Children,* was published by Oberon
Press in 1973.

Harvor has taught writing at Concordia University and
is currently teaching in the writing program at York
University.

IF ONLY
WE COULD DRIVE
LIKE THIS
FOREVER

Elisabeth Harvor

Acknowledgements

The author acknowledges with thanks the Canada Council and the Ontario Arts Council, who provided funds while this book was in progress.

The following stories have been published previously, in somewhat (and, in some cases, very) different form: "To Supper in the Morning and To Bed at Noon" in *The Fiddlehead*, Summer, 1987; "Heart Trouble" in *The New Yorker*, March 12, 1979, and in *The Penguin Book of Modern Canadian Short Stories*, 1982; and parts of "The Age of Unreason" appeared in *Saturday Night*, *Journal of Canadian Fiction*, *Best Canadian Short Stories*, 1977, and *The Penguin Book of Canadian Short Stories*, 1980.

*For Finn and Richard
and for Terence Byrnes*

Contents

Contents

To Supper in the Morning
and to Bed at Noon

When Arthur woke up it was dark and the rain had stopped. It was unearthly quiet, the way it sometimes was after a late-day rainstorm, as if the rain had rained all the noise out of the city. He didn't think his mother could have come back yet—he had a sense of the dark apartment spookily lying beyond his bedroom door. He wondered if it was true, what Margo had said, that their mother had a new lover. He himself had seen no signs of it. He couldn't even remember when it was that she'd last been involved with someone. He did recall that she'd been in love with one of her patients, a Frenchman from Morocco, all one winter and spring, and that for three or four months after it was all over between them there had been an uneasy stillness in the apartment, like a held breath.

He stepped out of his room, expecting darkness, but then saw from the brightness of the hallway that all the lamps in the living-room were blazing. When he got there he found his mother sitting curled up on the low sofa in her good dark suit, warming her chilled fingers around a mug of hot tea. She called out, "Hello, Arthur," in a calm-enough voice, but it seemed to him that her grey eyes, above the grey-glazed mug, were guarded, over-bright. He thought, let's all just hope and pray it isn't another Moroccan.

He walked over to the armchair in front of the windows, dropped into it. "I fell asleep. Didn't even hear you get back."

"Just got here about fifteen minutes ago."

The rain hadn't only rained all the noise out of the city, it had rained all the energy out of their voices. Arthur looked out the window, down toward Budapest Park. It wasn't quite night. The sky was a sky-after-rain colour—a high, cold-looking green. Here and there lights were coming on down on the lakefront. He felt too tired to yawn. A fashion magazine with a vacant-faced girl on its cover was lying on the coffee table. "Margo forgot her magazine," he said to his mother.

"I think she'd already read as much of it as she was planning to. . . ."

She'd probably already be back in Kingston by now. He wondered if it was raining in boring little Kingstontown, too. In any case, he pictured her walking across the campus at Queen's in the rain, her parka hood hauled up over her hair like a rainhood, her mukluks damp, the hem of her long skirt droopy from being dragged over the misted wintry grass. She was the one person who aroused in him an emotion too complex to name. Maybe he loved her, maybe he hated her; he'd be the last to know either way. The strongest memory he had of her from when he was small was of the time she and two of her little girlfriends had devoted a whole afternoon to tormenting him. One of the questions they had kept asking him over and over again was, "Are you pregnant?" Finally, bewildered and worn out, he had whispered yes, and this had led to at least an hour of their shrieking and pointing at him and pretending to vomit.

"How do you think the visit went this time?" he asked his mother.

"Not bad. Pretty good, really. She seemed more open this time. More forthcoming." She turned to him, her eyes bright with some preoccupation he planned to ferret out. "Isn't that how she struck you too, Arturo?"

"Oh, sure," he said. "More forthcoming, more upstanding,

more outgoing...." Sometimes he wondered what Margo would think if she could hear them talking about her like she was a weekend guest who'd overstayed her welcome. "The fact of the matter is, she's a normal person," he said. "You worry about her too much; she's no more neurotic than I am and I'm basically pretty normal although I'm too proud to admit it. Except, of course, for when I'm feeling totally insane. Which might be ninety percent of the time, actually." He made himself stop. *God*, how he loved to talk about himself! It was pathetic.

His mother looked like she was a million miles away. He felt a need to get her attention. He picked up the fashion magazine and displayed it in front of his chest. "I ask you: is this, or is it not, the dumbest face you've ever seen?"

"She doesn't look burdened by worries, or even thoughts, I would have to agree."

"She doesn't look like she's been burdened by a thought *ever*," said Arthur. "All the lights on but nobody home." He dropped the magazine to the floor, picked up his copy of *Shakespeare Survey 33*, opened it to the article on *King Lear*. And after a moment said, "Hey, listen to this. It's talking about how in *King Lear* the world has been turned upside down—men carry asses on their backs, children become parents to their parents, people go to supper in the morning and to bed at noon. Sounds like your life, when you're on night duty. To supper in the morning and to bed at noon."

"Yeah," she said. "Pretty absurdist."

Arthur closed his Shakespeare book. "You remember that girl I was talking about at breakfast-time? The new girl? The one who sits down at the back with me in English?"

His mother nodded, her eyes on his. "The Scots lass," she said.

"Yeah, but her dad is Norwegian. I know this because we got into a conversation after school today. Isn't that weird, though? That we both have mothers who come from Scotland? Her name is Pippa. She told me she used to see me last year sometimes, before she even decided to change schools, walking down Spadina. She told me she decided then that I must be a very enigmatic person."

"If she thinks you're enigmatic, it means she's crazy about

you," said his mother. But now her eyes were filled up with a distracted look. He thought of asking her—if he asked, he would ask sharply—"Is something the matter?" but instead said, "Yeah? I *thought* it might mean that."

His mother lifted her straight fair hair, which had recently started to go white at the temples, over the collar of her suit-jacket. "What does she look like?"

"Blond hair to about here." He pointed two fingers at his shoulders. "Glasses. She looks good in them, though. Very nice eyes, not too big. Why do people think big eyes are beautiful anyway? They give me the creeps." And not waiting for her to reply he said, "Anyway, about Pippa. This is going to sound superficial, but it's her best quality, along with her eyes and her personality and her smile—absolutely sensational legs."

His mother's smile was fleeting; then there was a rasp as she crossed one hefty black-nyloned leg over the other. She extended this leg straight out and bounced it up and down a little, lightly, absently, from the rounded plump fulcrum of her bent knee; studied it with a small wistful smile. "Unlike my own. Which are . . . colossal."

Arthur shot an uncomfortable glance at his mother's legs. He tried to look judicious. He tried to study them without actually looking at them. "Not colossal," he quickly said. "Just a little on the heavy side."

"Mr. Tact," said his mother. She set her tea mug down on the floor beside the sofa and worked her feet out of her high-heeled sandals and lifted them up to the sofa, then drew both feet and legs in under the dark protection of her skirt. She said, "Listen, I'm going to have to ask you for a favour. I want you to stay home from school tomorrow morning."

"This is a favour?" But then he remembered that his class with Pippa was in the morning. "What *for*, though?"

"I have to go to the hospital for an examination. An intestinal thing. They're going to have to sedate me, and so they want me to bring somebody with me."

He stared at her. "When did you find all this out?" He felt like a jerk when he heard how mean and suspicious his voice was coming out, but it seemed to him that whenever things started to go really well what always happened was that one of his parents would spring something on him.

"This afternoon. I had an appointment with Hopwood."

"But what's the big rush, though? I thought it took a long time to get something set up at a hospital."

"It's Mike Hopwood's day at the G-I clinic tomorrow; I just turned out to be lucky."

"What's this thing called that you're going to get done?" He couldn't seem to squeeze the cold dubiousness out of his voice; he thought, *Jesus, I'm starting to sound like Dad.*

"Colonoscopy. They go in with a long flexible tube and look everything over." She coughed drily. "All made possible by the wonder of fibre optics," she hoarsely added, her voice dry as a reed.

He relented a little. "Are you worried about it?"

She rose with a powerful spring, took off for the kitchen. The effect was startling to Arthur, like seeing a white-faced, golden-haired ship's figurehead pop up out of a jack-in-the-box.

But it was too quiet out there—as of course he had known it would be—and after a minute or two he got up and followed her. She was standing with her back to him, her hands gripping the wing handles of the faucets, pretending to look out the window. He came up behind her and hung a cautious arm around her shoulder. As she let her head fall against him he could feel the tumult inside her, like hundreds of little pistons pumping up and down deep in her shoulders. Usually he kept things formal between them (to this end he always made a point of calling her "Mother"), but now, out of anxiety, he went back to one of the endearments of childhood: "Aw, Mumsie—don't worry, okay? Everything'll probably turn out to be fine. And then you'll laugh at yourself for having got all bothered and anxious."

The hospital was an older, more elegant hospital than the one where his mother worked, and its basement hallways smelled of disinfectant and baked linen. Orderlies and sleepy-looking women with raincoats caped over their uniforms were yelling things out to each other.

"Sweetheart!" a big orderly with evil sideburns was yelling at a pert little nurse with horn-rimmed glasses. "I *told* you you shoulda come to the Bahamas with me!" Early morning camaraderie, Arthur guessed it must be. Every member of the staff in rude and heartless good health. He, on the other hand, was feeling jittery. His stomach threatened to heave. He could feel his chest getting constricted from the cheerful horror of the place.

On Dr Hopwood's floor they had to walk down a long corridor to reach the Gastro-Intestinal clinic at the far end. As they hurried toward it Arthur caught a glimpse, in a small bright room, of a wizened little nurse sitting filing her nails beside a tray of syringes. Then they passed two women wearing lab coats over their slim skirts and blouses. Doctors? Lab technicians? The taller one, whose legs were too skinny and who had a horsey but nevertheless beautiful face with deep-set angry eyes was saying, "Yeah, well. But that, in effect, was what I *did* say. I said, 'Listen, buster, if you want to get your jollies out of hurting *me* . . . ' " Everything about her accent and delivery was old Tory Toronto. Doctors, Arthur decided.

He had to wait in a little alcove off the G-I clinic. Twenty minutes, his mother had said. After twenty-eight minutes had jumped by on a hospital clock that looked like a school clock, he could feel his unease heightening. He stood up, looked around at nothing. Sat down, but then right away got up again. Was she really going to be okay? What if she wasn't? He decided he couldn't wait here for one second longer and he took off in the direction of the room where he'd seen the little nurse filing her nails. But the room, when he got to it, turned out to be empty. On a white enamel table sat a clear plastic tray of syringes. Beside it was a small tin tray that looked like a tray from a cafeteria for dwarfs; it had some swabs on it, and also a couple of bottles—one of them a bottle of nail polish, dark and viscous as blood. The room smelled sickeningly of polish remover.

He turned back, came to a door he pushed open in time to be greeted by the sound, far below him, of the impersonal crash of institutional cutlery. It sounded like whenever they got too big a pile of dirty dishes down in the kitchen they would dump them onto a conveyor belt that would rush them off someplace to be smashed so they wouldn't have to be washed. Cooking smells came up to him: breaded scallops, codfish cooked in milk. I'd puke, he thought. I'd puke if I had to eat pig swill like that. He drew back into his own quiet hallway at the same moment he saw, down at the clinic end, the door his mother had been ushered through being shoved open. An East Indian nurse emerged, peeked round into the alcove, then turned to gaze down the hallway. "Mr. Blakely?" she called out to him.

He hurried toward her.

She waited till he reached her, then spoke in a mournful, soft British voice: "Your mother is ready to go home now."

"Fine," he replied. *His* voice, he wildly noted, had come out sounding truly ridiculous—a sort of hushed croak.

"Did you come to the hospital by taxi or by private car?"

"We brought our car."

"Will you be doing the driving, Mr. Blakely?"

When he nodded she looked worriedly reproachful, as if she had known him for years and therefore knew him to be unreliable. She said, "I was just wondering, because your mother is certainly in no condition to be doing any driving herself."

Arthur didn't like the "in no condition"; it made his mother sound like a drunk. And so he replied in a dead, formal voice, "That's why I came along with her. It was my understanding that she would be receiving a certain amount of sedation." He stood miserably hunched, his fists rammed into the pockets of his lightweight windbreaker; and his jaw felt painfully stiff, as if any future smile he might smile would come off looking tight and false to the point of lunacy.

"We had to give her more than the usual medication," the nurse told him. "Some of the colon areas were fairly inflamed."

What did she mean by inflamed? Was it a euphemism for cancer? And what did she mean by fairly? Did she mean very? Her words made him recall being a little boy and screaming —it seemed to him now that he'd screamed it hundreds of times—"I wish you would die!" Sometimes he'd screamed it at his father, sometimes at his mother. (But most often at his mother.) "What sort of medication?" he hoarsely inquired.

The nurse looked startled. "Valium for relaxing the muscles. Demerol for the pain."

This gave Arthur the fear that when his mother was wheeled out she'd be sitting pigeon-toed in her wheelchair, her head lolling idiotically off to one side; but she came out looking normal, just a bit sleepy. The athletic-looking nurse pushing her chair was the perfect plastic type he hated himself for tending to go for. She had a deep tan and short, sun-bleached hair; she must just have got back from a holiday somewhere. Spring skiing in the Rockies, maybe; she had the narrowed, measuring eyes a skier gets from squinting against sprays of snow-mist. She flashed a quick cold smile at Arthur, then pouted at the clouding-up sky beyond the hospital's small-paned tall windows. "We'd better put your hood up," she said to his mother. "It looks like it might rain out there." And she shot up the zipper on his mother's slate nylon parka, then yanked up the hood and tied its drawstrings into a tight, skin-pinching bow under her chin.

It struck Arthur then—and not for the first time either— that hospitals were humiliating places, much more humiliating than school even. In fact, driving home in the car and re-hearing the sound of the nurse's snappy manhandling of the nylon parka—a sound that had grated on his nerves as much as any screech of chalk on a blackboard—it occurred to him that a lot of hospital words were interchangeable with school words: examination, tests, a good report. He thought of asking his mother, "Did the doctor give you a good report?" but instead asked her a more careful question: "Did Hopwood say anything to you—after the examination?"

"Wasn't there."

"Wasn't *there*? What's that supposed to mean?"

"Called in sick. Lorca did it."

"Who's Lorca?"

"His partner."

"Okay, then. So what did his partner say?"

"That his partner would be getting in touch with me."

"Hopwood will be getting in touch with you," said Arthur.

"Right." She had turned her face away from him. He couldn't tell whether she was looking out the window or crying. After a while he thought she might be asleep, but he wasn't sure. He cleared his throat. "I'll be having a real easy day at school today. Only two classes—Art and Frog."

No answer. He hated French; it was the only subject he regularly failed in. Which was weird, because Margo was the exact opposite—the world's most ardent Francophile. Frogophile. He had nothing against the French personally, of course, apart from—but was this personal?—their devious gushy language, but Margo and his parents were all such gung ho Frogophiles that the prospect of joining them in their passion for speaking the language made him feel worn out before he could even open the first page of his French grammar.

His mother heaved an emotional-sounding sigh.

"Are you awake?"

Still no answer, and so they drove on in more silence. Street after grim residential street in the fitful late-morning sunshine. Feeling lonely, he wound down the window so he could smell the lake. He remembered that until he was four or five years old he had believed Lake Ontario was the ocean. He could still recall the amazed sadness he'd felt the day he had learned it was not. He quoted to himself: "Nero is an angler in the lake of darkness." It was one of the lines he liked in *King Lear*. But it wasn't a lake of darkness today. Quite the contrary; it was hurting his eyes with its fish-sheen glare of light.

At their apartment tower he parked at the front entrance, then reached over and gave his mother's shoulder a shake. "We're home!" he called in the low but hectoring singsong he remembered his parents using with him when he was a kid and asleep in the car at the end of a long family trip home in the dark.

With a sound somewhere between a grunt and a cry she twisted away from him.

Arthur was assailed by a feeling of exasperation tinged with a sensation that hovered between tenderness and amusement. This must be what it would be like to be the parent of a whiney little kid. He shook her shoulder again. "Time to get out, Mother."

"No," she moaned and she curled away from him in a deeper commitment to sleep. "I don't want to."

"Hey, come on now. You've got to come up to the apartment. The nurse said you had to go straight to bed."

A few minutes later, sitting on the edge of her bed, his mother sleepily drew off her parka, then crawled between her sheets still dressed in her shirt and jeans. Her windbreaker was lying over the seat of the chair by the window. Arthur picked it up and caped it over the back of the chair. He wondered if there was anything he was supposed to do for her. "Do you want me to pull the curtains or anything?"

She made what sounded like a moan of assent and so he went over and pulled them. Then he went out to the kitchen and poured himself a glass of milk to have with his salami sandwich. Dessert was a bottle of beer and a muffin. He agitated the beer in his mouth like toothpaste-water—something he used to be fascinated watching his father do, years ago, when they were all still living together.

As he turned into his school street, feeling the exaggerated shyness he always felt after he'd missed a morning of school, Arthur was confronted by a noisy crowd scene: fifteen or twenty people finishing their lunches in the cold sunlight, out on the balustraded main stone stairway. Right away he saw that Pippa was among them, leaning back on her elbows, the sun transforming her spun-looking fair hair into the brainless big mop of a girl in a comic strip. She was laughing in what looked like a very admiring way up at a jock named Wade Maloney who was crouching sleekly toward her, *his* hair slicked back, and her feet were shod in flat grey suede ankle boots, the kind that looked like they'd been copied from the ones the Fool always wore in Shakespeare's plays. Arthur made a wide arc to the left of the stairway and then ran down the steps to the west wing's basement entrance. Once inside this utilitarian cavern he made straight for the hissing, steam-heated boys' washroom, located in the cavern's north end between the tunnel to the boys' gym and the janitor's office. His relief at finding it empty was so great that for a moment he mistook it for happiness. But his hand trembled as he drew his comb out of his pocket and started to comb his too-long brown hair. As he combed he cursed Maloney, but he wasn't exactly overjoyed with himself either. You should get your hair cut, he told his reflection. You look like a goddamn hippie. He wished he'd worn another shirt too; he could have wept when he saw what a putz he looked like in this one. But no more time for regrets; the bell for first class was going off.

His school had recently adopted a class-rotation system, called the "tumbling timetable," and as a consequence Arthur was forever having to stop and ask himself, what week is this? Which way has the timetable tumbled? It was what he had to ask himself now, standing blankly in front of his locker. Then he remembered it was Art. He grabbed his spattered lab coat and plastic bag of paint tubes and took off at a run for the studio on the third floor.

Art passed, then a spare. In French, Mrs Fischer—who, although she taught French, was actually German—handed back the corrected French tests. A lonely-eyed, good-looking blonde in her thirties, she was not a popular teacher. She was a test-freak, that was why. Every day Arthur's class had to spend the first twenty minutes of the period scribbling answers to test-questions while Frau Fischer sat and stared out toward the bare park, deep in her lonely Teutonic thoughts.

He had failed, by a fairly wide margin. Not a surprise. Across the bottom of the second page Fischer had written,

"Disappointing work, Arthur. I know you can do much better than this." Maybe so, but he couldn't bring himself to care one way or the other; the image of Pippa laughing up at Maloney had sucked all the breath out from under his heart. If only his mother hadn't asked him to drive her to the hospital. Because Maloney (though a dumb jock) was nobody's fool.

When the period was over Arthur went out into the clear air (no sign of the rain the cold nurse had predicted) and sat on a stone wall to the west of the school's main entrance to watch for Pippa. He had some bad moments, fantasizing her walking toward him with Maloney, but at last she came dawdling along with another girl in the shadow of the arched stone portico of the school's northwest wing. They had their heads bowed over a letter Pippa was holding. They kept bumping into each other as they walked, and because of this he was sure their legs were weak from the shrieky pleasure of laughing. He couldn't bear it when two girls got together to snicker over a letter some unsuspecting person—probably a guy—had, in hope and innocence, written. But supposing the guy was Maloney? Even so, he decided. Even Maloney deserves better than this. Arthur was suddenly finished with Pippa. She was too young, she smiled too much, she was too easily impressed, she was a giggler. He stood up, pulled on his coat, picked up his books. He only turned back for one sorrowing farewell look at her. But as she stepped out into the cold sunlight she looked up and saw him and turned and said something to her friend—a short girl in a navy coat who immediately took off in a run across the frozen grass of the playing field—then came walking on alone toward him, the letter clasped to her breast. Was she going to show it to *him* too? He would refuse to read it.

But she greeted Arthur shyly, with her unsure eyes, as she approached him. She wasn't biting her lip, but her eyes had that look girls' eyes get when they are biting a lip, and her hair seemed to carry a silvery glow and crackle deep within it, like a pale bonfire; seemed to electrically brush the shoulders of the grey-and-white ski cardigan she was wearing over her thin blouse and jeans. The cardigan's buttons were engraved acorns, made out of silver. By way of saying hello to her, Arthur reached out and pulled on one of these cold silver acorns with a finger and thumb. Shyly, he jiggled it a little. "Hello, Pipster," he said.

She looked up at him with her light grateful eyes. "Pipster! Sounds like trickster. But this is no trick, Mr B. This is news of homework in English." She handed him the letter.

He let go of the silver acorn and opened the paper out. He saw a numbered series of questions. He studied them without seeing them. He was looking at her name: Pippa Fjeldahl. She had printed it in three different scripts at the top of the page. "Well," he remarked in a voice barely above a whisper. "Thanks a lot." He refolded the paper and slid it into his shirt pocket.

"You weren't sick, were you?"

"No. I had to take my mother to the hospital."

"Oh," she said, and although her voice dipped with concern, something that looked like an uneasy pleasure seemed to stand, sharply withdrawn and watchful, far back in her eyes. Maybe she didn't get along with her own mother. "Is your mother sick?"

"They don't know yet. They had to do some tests."

"I hate hospitals." She spoke with passion. "*Hate* them."

Arthur said he hated them too, and as they started walking together up the cracked sidewalk bordering the playing field he found that his attention, which was ordinarily completely engaged by the female portion of the student population, had shifted and fixed itself on the faces of his own gender and was methodically searching them out for expressions of admiration and envy. He noticed that it didn't seem to upset him at all to discover that his happiness was contaminated with triumph. Why not? Triumph was sweet. He also didn't seem to be feeling overly upset by the fact that his laughter was too ready and false sounding. In fact when a not-completely spontaneous laugh caused him to take in a great lungful of mud-and-ice smell, the smell became instantly dear to him, in spite of his nervous false laughter; it gripped him in the

entrails and announced itself as a future trigger of memory—
as a smell he would associate forever with this first day of
walking with Pippa in the open air.

Arthur's mother was lying propped up on one elbow in her
bed, reading the paper and eating from a green glass bowl of
yoghurt. Sunlight—lakelight—flooded her room. She lifted
her spoon in greeting.

"Hi, honey."

"Hello." He sat down on her bed in his coat. "How ya
doing?"

"Not too bad. Sore though. But at least they didn't put a
hole in my gut."

"You really don't trust hospitals very much, do you?"

"I just hope you and Margo never have to go into one."

"That'll be the day. I don't plan to get sick ever—I'm such
a healthy young dude. And Margo wouldn't have the *time*."
But mention of Margo made Arthur feel he ought to try to be
a bit more entertaining. He said, "You should have heard
yourself this morning when you were all drugged-out out in
the car." To demonstrate, he threw himself down on the end
of her bed and jacked his knees into the fetal position—with
his big blade of a nose and last year's too-short black coat he
was hopeful he cut a reasonably comic figure—and theatri-
cally moaned, "No! I don't want to!" And was rewarded by
her half-amused, half-uneasy laughter. He got to his feet and
stretched, then gazed with a certain hesitant longing at the
phone. "Are you planning on using the phone in the near
future?"

When she shook her head he went over to her bureau and
unplugged the phone. An armload of bright summer skirts
and a pair of grey pantyhose had been dumped over the back
of the chair by her window, but her bureau was unusually
tidy. Her silver-backed hairbrushes and a matching hand-
mirror were lined up on a silver tray. The initials J.J. (for
Jean Johnson, her name when she was a girl back in Scotland) were engraved on the back of the mirror. He said, "I'll
turn on the news for you if you want."

"Thank you, Arturo."

He turned on her radio, then securely closed her door behind him and went down the hall to his own room, the phone book and the phone hugged to his chest. He also securely closed his own door. He even went back to it and locked it. Ordinarily she wouldn't come into his room without knocking first, but you never knew; she might decide that undergoing a medical procedure gave her special privileges.

He plugged in the phone and sat down on his bed with it held in his lap, still in his coat. Then he pulled the homework sheet Pippa had given him out of his pocket. Fjeldahl. He looked it up in the phone book. There were only two Fjeldahls listed and one of them was way out in the Beaches. Quickly, before he had time to change his mind, he dialed the downtown number.

When Pippa came on the line there was a kind of bored fall in her voice that made him feel tense. He said, "I was wondering if maybe we could go out somewhere tonight, maybe to a movie or something." He told her the name of the repertory house he had in mind, which happened to be in her neighbourhood.

She said she couldn't. But now it seemed to him that he could hear disappointment in her voice. She said her mother's younger sister was visiting from Scotland with her two little nieces, and that she'd promised to babysit for her the next two nights. "I'd be free on Sunday night, though."

"The one I was thinking of is one you've probably already seen—*Being There*."

"Oh, I'd love to see that. I never did get to see it when it first came out. It was on in Glasgow, just before we left for Canada, isn't that crazy? I've been wanting to see it for years."

"*Great*," said Arthur, and his voice—in his ears but he prayed not in hers—sounded truly feeble with surprise and pleasure.

"And listen, you don't have to come get me. I'll meet you there."

"Okay. How much ahead of the movie do you think we should meet?"

"Fifteen minutes."

How easy all this was! He could have been asking girls out for years! He was wondering if he regretted that he hadn't when Pippa said, "I wish it was Sunday night right now."

His heart took a leap. Before the conversation, imagining it going well, he had only pictured himself feeling relieved at the end of it, not inspired. He ran a hand through his hair and dropped his voice commandingly low. *"Be* there," he said.

At a party Arthur finally located well after midnight there was an older girl who smiled at him and patted a place beside her on the brown plaid sofa. But after he sat down next to her she just kept smoking in a weirdly private way that made him regret having burdened her with his presence. He had to content himself with pretending to feel much more curiosity about his surroundings than he was really feeling. There was the sound of conversation and occasional protesting low laughter coming from a room he took to be the kitchen. Someone had tacked up a length of sand-coloured fabric with little greenish and black tribal figures woven into it. Not much of a party, but he was willing to give almost anything a chance for an hour or two. He couldn't decide whether this proved he was an optimist or desperate.

Before she had even finished her cigarette the older girl stood up, stroked her hair back behind an ear with the fingers of one hand, massaged her midriff with the heel of the other. "Gas attack," she said, smiling a brief but sweet smile down at Arthur. He returned her smile, thinking to himself, what a flake, and then must have looked like he was planning to get up too, because she held the long-fingered hand with the cigarette in it out toward him in the hostess gesture that says, "Don't get up—stay there," and then padded over to the African curtain and drawing it back with the same graceful motion she'd used to draw back her hair, she stepped through to the other side.

Arthur roused himself and made his solitary way down a dark hallway to look for a toilet. He passed by a bedroom with burlap curtains at its small-paned dark windows. There was a phone on the bedside table. Maybe on the weekend he would phone Margo and talk to her about taking their mother to the hospital. Or maybe there wouldn't be any need to. Maybe she'd get a good report back from Hopwood. This wasn't the first time she'd had a cancer scare, after all. She'd had to get a lump taken out of her breast a long time ago, back when he was starting grade nine. But *shit*, he thought, I wouldn't be a woman for *anything*.

Sometime later—but it was still dark out—he found himself walking up an ice-blistered alleyway behind some people who'd been at the uneventful party. They were strangers to him and the moon was low at the wrong end of a windy cloud-streaked sky. Their dark coats and one regal girl's street-length black cloak (was she a holdover from hippie days?) were swaying slightly with the motion of brisk walking and the pre-dawn wind. There weren't any leaves on the trees yet, but Arthur was reminded of the big surfy sound in the leaves of the trees near a summer cottage his parents used to rent down East, near Cape Tormentine, when he was a boy. He remembered the whole family swimming in the wide warm river after dark, a river made even warmer for Arthur by the fact that he'd peed in the part he'd kept dog-paddling short, gasping laps back and forth in. Margo, at fourteen, hadn't swum half as much as the rest of them; she only took quick groaning little dips and then flashed up out of the black water, hoisting herself with a shimmy up onto the wharf where she then affectedly reclined, waving away the mosquitoes with the tip of one of their mother's cigarettes. With her childish ruffled bikini and a bathing cap that looked like a white bonnet, she made Arthur think of a self-centred little baby waving its pacifier. But afterward, when they all started climbing up the cold sandy path to bed, Arthur had held on tight to his mother's hand because Margo had been transformed from a ridiculous smoking baby into a majestic evil alien, striding ahead of them up the sand hill in the moonlight, their father's navy trenchcoat swingingly caped like a king's cloak over her shoulders, her head eerily small in her shining moonlit white cap.

Arthur ran down into the subway in a cloudy dawn, but when he climbed up, only half an hour later and hatching a sneeze, it was into a world that looked like it had been exposed for hours to windy morning sunlight. It was a light that sobered him up quicker than a cold shower would have done, because he was at once struck by the realization that he ought to have phoned home to tell his mother he'd be late. An image of her sitting smoking and crying at the kitchen table rose before him with such clarity that he took off at a run, whimpering curses under his breath.

At six-thirty in the morning, the grey-tiled plaza was deserted. Only the gulls were awake, wheeling and mewing in from the lake, hoping for nourishment from shopping centre garbage. But there was none of it; it had all been blown away by the wind or swept up. The venetian blinds of the pharmacy and the metal blinds of a store called Folklore were pulled down, and the curtains of the café were drawn shut. A store called May-Hee-Ko, Folklore's rival, had a row of squat figurines on display in its window. With their swollen grim mouths and their tubular clay arms folded tight across their baked clay chests, they had, in the glaring light of this ice-glazed April morning, a primitive competitive look. Every locked-up restaurant and blank-faced store had its newspaper doormat.

Inside the polished lobby of his own building, also deserted, Arthur tore past the elevator and lunged through the swinging door to the stairwell. He had a snivelling speech at the ready, and taking the six flights of stairs two steps at a time, he rehearsed it: "I'm a jerk, I'm a rat, I deserve to be shot." He burst into the apartment with it, his head already turned toward the kitchen table. But his mother wasn't at the kitchen table, and in fact the whole apartment was steeped in silence. The end of the short hallway that led to the bedrooms, which at this time of day was ordinarily dim, stood in bright morning light. An image of his panicky mother, driving up and down the streets of the parents of people he barely knew, blubberingly making a spectacle of herself as she desperately searched for him, took possession of him and made him feel wild with rage and humiliation. She had done this one night when he was eleven or twelve, and he had lived all these years in dread of her doing it again. He slammed the door to the hall closet and swung into the living-room. Her white-striped grey dressing-gown had been flung inside-out over the back of the sofa. A corner of the fashion magazine with the idiot model on the cover was pinning down a corner of the dressing-gown. All the lights on but nobody home, he remembered saying to her. He was almost seventeen, for Christ's sake! But when was *she* going to grow up? He snatched the magazine up from the sofa and pelted it at the rocking chair, immediately setting the chair to rocking back and forth like a rocking chair in a haunted-house movie. Then he took off down the hall to look into her room.

And saw that she was still at home after all, sound asleep. A band of sunlight the width of a folded-up blanket was lying across the bottom of her bed; the light blue curtains were still open, showing the morning sky. The drugs must still be having an effect, then; ordinarily she couldn't sleep unless her room was totally dark. He couldn't see her face, because like everyone else in his family, she always twisted toward the wall and hauled the sheet up over the top of her head and slept hooded like a bedouin. He stood in her doorway a moment, listening to her breathing, then crossed into his own room and lay down on his bed.

He was feeling too keyed-up to sleep himself—parties sometimes did this to him—but he thought he might just lie back and rest for a minute or two. But in doing so, he at once slept. And sleeping, at once dreamed. He was in a park close to where he'd lived with Margo and his mother the first year he was in high school. It was a winter evening and the park was deep in snow. He was following the park's lamplighter, an extraordinarily tall and skinny, stoop-shouldered old man. They were making their way from lamp to lamp, but instead of lighting the lamps (there would have been no point in lighting the lamps because the lamps—of the vintage and incandescence of the lamps of the storybooks of Arthur's childhood—were already yellowly glowing) the old man was putting them out. Puzzled as he was by this, Arthur felt he should try to help out, and in fact offered to, but the lamp-lighter would not tolerate any interference, and so Arthur was reduced to merely following him from lamp to lamp, feeling incompetent and foolish and sad. He woke up startled, almost frightened. Who was the patronizing old lamplighter? Not anyone he knew. And what did the dream mean? He couldn't decipher it. He felt foul-mouthed, bleak; in desperate need of water. The roof of his mouth was parched; the cruel, persistently bright morning light hurt his eyes. He stumbled down the hall to the kitchen and drank three tumblers of polluted Lake Ontario water from the tap, which water, dioxin-tainted though it was, quenched his thirst. Next, he decided to make himself some toast. But when he opened the breadbox it was empty. After a consultation with the kitchen clock, he decided to walk to the store. It would be eight o'clock by the time he got out on the street; the Korean grocery should be open by eight. If he walked far enough west he might even run into Pippa. (Out walking her dog. Out walking her nieces.) He wrote a note, which he taped to the door of the fridge:

7:45 A.M. Gone
out for a walk.
Also to buy bread.

Three little guys of about seven or eight were playing a game of catch with a football out on the plaza when Arthur returned from the store, a loaf of raisin bread tucked under his arm. The smallest one was jumping up and down like a maniac, screaming at one of the older ones, "Sock it to me, Brucie baby! Sock it to me!" And when Bruce pelted it to him he caught it in a knock-kneed catch and then, hugging it gleefully to himself, started to jump up and down again yelling, "Ah loves ya, Brucie baby! Ah loves ya!"

Arthur had to smile to himself. Where did they learn to talk like that? From listening to over-the-hill Hollywood actors pretending to be friendly to each other on TV talk shows? They were too young and innocent to know how corny they sounded. Will I ever have a kid? he wondered. He remembered being a little kid himself—playing Superman with his

mother's nurse's cape. He remembered lying on his mother's
and father's bed and playing with his mother's hairbrushes—
playing they were silver Volkswagens; playing they were buf-
falos in the moonlight.

As he was passing by the door just before his own apartment door he heard a phone start to ring. It was picked up on
the ping of the second ring. It made him wonder if his mother
had heard back from Hopwood. Wondering this, he felt an
intense fear of talking to her. He hoped she wasn't still asleep,
though. He wanted her to be awake, but he didn't want to
talk to her. How could that work? She could be on the phone.
But not talking to Hopwood.

But the first sound he heard, stepping inside the apartment, was the sound of the shower. It was a sound that
speeded everything up for him; it was like a flash rain moving in over a forest where every stealthy step forward on dry
twigs might, up till the moment of the rain, have alerted a
pursuer. He hauled off his boots and stowed them swiftly in
the hall closet, then raced sock-footed down the hall to his
room. He was already throwing himself into the business of
tearing off his clothes before he even reached his bed. He was
breathing like a runner. He plunged into the bed still dressed
in his socks and undershorts.

But his room felt too hot. He beat his heels up and down
on the mattress to bounce the blankets off the end of his bed,
then hauled the sheet up over his head.

He heard the shower stop. His heart jumped to his throat.
Then silence. Then the bathroom door opening and closing.
Then a tap on his door.

"What *is* it?" he moaned. "I'm almost asleep!"

His door was pushed open but not, by the sound of it, all
the way. "Just thought I'd say hello."

His answering hello came out in a morose-sounding
croak.

"I guess you just got home."

"Right."

"I saw your note."

He said sternly, "Good."

"Thanks for getting the bread."

"You're welcome." But then he took pity on her. "Listen, Mom, I'm really beat. I'll talk to you later, okay?"

"Okay."

Was her voice too light? Too hurt? His body felt stiff with the strain of trying to hear if she sounded like she'd been crying. "Good night, then," he said, and already he seemed to be holding his breath, primed to listen again.

"Good night."

He couldn't tell how she was feeling at all, but a little while after she'd padded off, clinky breakfast sounds started coming from the kitchen. Faucets being turned on and off; the sound of cutlery; the radio, turned low, playing dance music.

Now I'll be able to sleep, he told himself. But for a long time he couldn't. There was too much commotion outside. It sounded like all the little children in the neighbourhood were now playing down there in the plaza—at least a dozen of them right under his window—yelling out to each other the shrill happy commands of one of the games of a holiday morning.

Heart Trouble

The doctor is still at breakfast when Maria arrives. She can hear the sounds of cutlery and breakfasting voices as she steps into a vestibule that smells like a field of hay, and then a slight fair man with prominent tired eyes comes down the hall to greet her. But his voice when he says, "Hi, there, I'm Don," sounds even enough. An American voice. "Come in here and find yourself a chair. I'll be with you in five minutes."

So she goes into the first room on the left of the hallway and sits down in a big brown velvet chair and tries to read the titles on the spines of Don's books. There are baskets everywhere—the source of the hay smell; they are grouped on tables and lined up along the tops of the low bookcases; they are hung on the walls like the shields of not-very-warlike tribesmen.

She is reading from *Food Is Your Best Medicine* when Don comes back. He's carrying an open notebook in one hand. He tosses it onto a low table and then sits astride a tooled hassock in front of her chair. His knees come close to touching hers and when he says, "Hi, Maria," the hassock sighs.

She considers asking him, "Do you find it cold up here? Did you come up to Canada because of the war?" But she only says, "I can hear you don't come from here."

"I come from Kentucky." And, after a short silence: "Well. And what brings you here, Maria?"

"Psoriasis." She rolls up the left sleeve of her blouse and holds up her elbow for him to see. "I have it other places, too. Knees. Scalp. Base of spine. I feel like a leper."

But Don is looking at her face. "You also have a heart murmur," he says.

"How can you tell that?"

"From your nose. There's a cleft at the bottom of it."

"I thought you used the eyes for diagnosis."

"The eyes, too," he tells her, hitching the hassock closer. "Let's have a look at them."

Maria takes off her tinted glasses and Don fits over his head what appears, in Maria's blurred vision, to be a sort of belt with thick rectangular lenses in it. Then he holds up a little wand of light and shines it in her eye. She wishes she'd remembered to brush her teeth when she got up, but all she did was get into some cotton clothes (the friend who recommended this doctor told her not to wear synthetic clothing) and then washed two apples to eat as breakfast on the way over.

Don looks into her eyes for a long time and makes some notes. "There's weakness in the liver and the kidneys and the heart," he finally tells her. "Also the pancreas. Also, your lymph glands are backing up. In fact, you're on your way to having what is known in iridology as a lymphatic rosary."

What else can be left? "What can we do about all of that?" she croaks up at him.

"We're going to have to detoxify you." He makes some notes for her on three little slips of paper, telling what to eat and in what proportions, showing her which foods are yin and which are yang, and telling her that she is yin too, very, very yin, and that she will have to give up dairy products entirely. "Also, I don't want you to drink much."

"That's no problem. I only drink at parties and then only in very small amounts."

"Oh," he says. Then he smiles. "But I wasn't talking about alcohol. I wouldn't want you to have any alcohol at all. Not with your liver in the shape it's in. I was talking about water. All you should have is two cups a day, maximum. Your kidneys are overworked." He stands up, ready for the next patient. "I'm glad to see you're wearing natural-fibre clothes," he tells her, patting her shoulder. "That's good."

Maria is invited to a party where she meets an architect named Mitchell Kincaid. They stand talking to each other the whole evening, while Maria holds a glass of tonic water with a slice of lime in it. Mitchell's wife goes home early. She seems to be high on something. She walks past Maria and smiles a smile so sweetly eerie it's unearthly. The smile seems to go right through Maria; this is the way an angel might smile, she thinks, or a psychotic person. The person smiling it doesn't connect to you in any way; the smile is utterly pure and self-sustaining.

Mitchell says he can tell Maria is a very open person. She's pleased but knows it isn't wise to be. In her experience, the people who tell you you are open invariably end up telling you you are hard. "I don't think I'm so very open," she says.

"What I mean is, I can see you are not a hard person."

"I can be a tough person."

"Tough is not the same as hard." And then: "Women have sometimes told me that I'm emotionally too demanding. I'm talking about younger women—women who are, you know, quite a bit younger than you are."

The next morning, Mitchell phones her and suggests he come over to give her a yoga lesson. She says that would be wonderful, great. He asks her if he can come over after supper. She says no, she'll be busy, but she'll be free almost any night next week.

Mitchell says that next week is going to be terribly busy for him, but when Maria suggests Tuesday night he does agree to that. Then he says, "My wife knows much more about yoga than I do; maybe she should be the one to teach you, maybe I should bring her with me."

There is a pause and then Maria says, "Oh, okay. If you

like." So when Tuesday arrives she doesn't know who is coming, both or neither or Mitchell alone. No, that isn't true; he will come alone or he won't come at all. Still, at supper that night she says to her sons, Tom and Andy, "Some people I met at a party last week might be coming over tonight. A husband and wife. They're going to teach me some yoga. Maybe just the wife will come, maybe just the husband. Maybe both, maybe neither. It was all left very vague." The boys say they will be up in their rooms and they hope they won't have to come down and say hello or anything. Maria says, "Of course not. I just wanted to let you know what might be happening." After this she relaxes a little. It's always important for her to cover herself with them—especially with Andy who, ever since the breakup of Maria and her husband, Norman, has been very anxious that his mother not be rejected by men. Last winter she went out for a while with a man named Al who was very unreliable about coming anywhere near the time he promised to come; she still has a whole cupboard filled with bottles of wine Al brought in apology.

Mitchell arrives half an hour late, and alone. They will be needing a blanket, he says, and Maria tells him she has an old camping blanket somewhere upstairs. As she's walking along the upstairs hall, she can hear Mitchell walking along the downstairs hall to the kitchen. She can hear where his feet stop. Coming down with the blanket she meets him on his way back into the living-room. "This is very rude of me," he says, "but I've been reading your appointment calendar." He looks awfully pleased. Looking for other men's names, she supposes. (Only Eddie's name is there.)

"And what did you find on it?"

"That you go belly-dancing."

"Oh, that was a terrible experience. I was so unco-ordinated. I only went to one class."

"Who was the teacher?"

"I forget her name. Some glamorous blond shrew, very impatient."

Mitchell squats and spreads the blanket out on the floor. "And who is Eddie?" he asks her.

"Eddie is my boss," she says in a voice whose softness does not at all alert him to her love for Eddie; in fact, he even smiles.

"I want you to lie down on your back."

She steps out of her shoes and onto the blanket. "You don't want to have a beer or something? Before we get started?"

"Let's just do the exercises first. After we're finished you can make us some tea."

When he has her positioned on the blanket he starts pacing around her. "Relax. Let your legs go limp. Close your eyes." He paces some more. "This is called the corpse position and it's very relaxing," he tells her.

She smiles but keeps her eyes open. On the sofa she sees what looks like a pedlar's bundle. "What's that?" she asks him.

He opens it. It's his yoga pants, tied up in a T-shirt.

"Do you want to change? The bathroom's at the top of the stairs."

He sprints up the stairs but doesn't go into the bathroom; instead, she can hear his feet running into her bedroom. She thinks of the mess in there and then does close her eyes.

When he comes down again she can feel him easing himself onto the blanket beside her, feels him put a hand on her belly. "Now, I'm going to teach you how to breathe," he whispers.

Andy comes down the stairs on his way to the basement to watch TV. "Oh, hi," he says to their two prone bodies. "Did you do the wash, Mum? Did you put it through the dryer?"

Mitchell stands. "You should get up for this one," he tells Maria.

"It's done," Maria says to Andy. "Bring it with you when you come up." Mitchell takes her hands and pulls her to her feet.

After the boys have gone to bed Maria and Mitchell sit across from each other at the dining-room table and have their tea. Mitchell talks with the speed and desperation of a man who fears he might be thrown out at any minute. Maria doesn't say much. When she does tell him something about herself he responds vivaciously—an odd word to describe a man, she thinks, but the right one. In fact there is an over-vivacity in him that suggests some fundamental lack of attention.

He tells her that yoga is important to him because he has asthma. He tells her about a co-op he lived in when he studied architecture at the University of Toronto; he talks about politics, about his work.

Finally she says, "Mitchell, listen, I'm going to have to ask you to go now—I'm dead, and I have to get up early tomorrow morning."

In the kitchen he puts his arm around her and she puts her arm around him, and on their way out of there his shoulder hits the wall phone and the receiver pops from its holder and falls to the floor. "Oh, that happens all the time," she says in an apologetic voice as they bend down together for him to pick it up. They continue with their arms around each other to the door. His kiss grazes her cheek, and she doesn't offer more of her face to him than that. He runs from her then, out into the mild wet night. She thinks that his speed announces his hurt; thinks, I won't see him again. In bed she has trouble sleeping.

When she gets home from work the next afternoon Lowell, the spring-water man, is parking his truck in front of her place. "I've bought myself a still," he tells her. "To make water, not whiskey. There's a distilled-water craze in this town. I kept getting all these calls from people who wanted to know if I could deliver distilled water to them, and so I started asking, "Why does everyone want distilled water all of a sudden?" And it turned out they'd all been to see these same two guys—two brothers, actually—who take samples of your spit and your urine and then send them off to a big computer down in California and in a couple of weeks the computer people send back an equation that tells you everything about the state of your health."

"And then the two brothers put you on a diet of distilled water?"

"Yeah. There's an ideal equation to aim for. One equation for Caucasians, one for Orientals. And then these two guys—

Walter is the one I went to—detoxify your body with certain foods and minerals. They say they can even cure cancer this way. The thing is, you have to drink an awful lot of water. Half, in ounces, of your body weight in pounds. For a big man it could come up to three quarts.''

"I've just been to see a man—and this man is a doctor—who believes people drink too *much* water. He sees the kidney as an overworked sponge.''

"He must be macrobiotic. The macrobiotic people could put me out of business.'' He lines up the bottles of spring water along one wall of Maria's long kitchen.

Before he leaves, Maria gets the phone number of the two brothers.

The next day she puts in a call to Mitchell at his office. When she says, "Mitchell, hi, this is Maria,'' he says "Who?'' and she has to say her name two more times before he will acknowledge he knows her.

Yet when she invites him for lunch at her place the next day he accepts quickly enough. She tells him she can get an hour and a half off from work, and he says he can do the same. Then she says that she has been thinking about the other night and that she feels she was too elusive. But then she found him too intrusive, she says, so it wasn't a simple thing.

"Too *what*?'' he asks her.

"Too instrusive.''

"And you were too what?''

"Too elusive.''

"Oh,'' he says. "Well.'' He yawns. "You know how it is.'' He yawns again. *"C'est la vie,''* he says.

After Maria has put down the phone she can feel herself blushing. It was silly of her to try to discuss something like this on the phone. Still, she has finally asked a man over. She goes upstairs and picks out the blouse she is going to wear and washes it by hand with sweet-smelling soap.

At lunch they drink the wine Mitchell brought. It's a cheap one, Maria has noticed—during the winter with Al she became an expert on wines. She pours herself only a little bit, remembering Don, and when she goes into the kitchen for the salad she fills the rest of her wineglass with water.

After they've finished eating, Mitchell talks about women he has known. He tells Maria that the last woman he was involved with was a poet; he even mentions her name. It's a name Maria knows, although she doesn't know the poet's work. She is familiar with her face, though, from the jacket of her latest book. In the book photograph she had dark blond hair and was standing with her fists plunged into the pockets of an old embroidered jacket, the wind in her eyes. Mitchell says that the poet turned out to be a very hard woman. Maria wants to talk about Eddie, but she doesn't want to mention his name. She says, "For a long time now I've loved a man I work with. Unrequited love. He has five children and is moderately happily married."

They carry their plates and wineglasses out to the kitchen and Maria runs hot water down on them. Then Mitchell tells her that he was first attracted to her because of her eyes. Maria is surprised by this, because her eyes are small. Small and sweet is how, in a kindly mood, she would have described them to herself. "Your pupils are so dilated," Mitchell says. "There's some new evidence out now that people with dilated pupils are very open people. . . ."

Women, he means. She says, "My pupils are always dilated —it's because I'm nearsighted."

"No more nearsighted than I am. And look at mine."

She peers at them. They are sceptical pinpoints. She lifts off his glasses, takes off her own, tries his on. His glasses are very strong; his face swims before her—amoebic, pale. Only his hair is the same—a bushy gold sphinx shape. "You look sort of distorted," she whispers.

"I *am* distorted," he assures her in a low voice. He's standing close to her and they're both smiling. He puts his arms around her and she rests her head on his shoulder. But she can't make any more moves toward him than that; when he kisses her she can't open her mouth to him. She feels irritated with herself. When she invited him for lunch she considered the possibility that they might go to bed together (at least to the extent of anxiously putting fresh sheets on her bed), but all she can do now is massage his arms as he stands with his hands on her hips. And say, "I like you, Mitchell." It sounds tepid, even to her, but it's the best she can do; she isn't even sure it's true.

He drives her back to her office on his way to his own. He has an odd car for an architect—a great raft of a car, battered, heirloom of an earlier decade. The door on his side doesn't work, so he goes in on her side and hitches himself over to the steering wheel. They drive in silence through the Beechwood woods, then pass a street that runs down to the lake. Mitchell says that his partner lives on the lake. Maria met Mitchell's partner at the party where she met Mitchell. "Do you know who your partner reminds me of?" she asks him. "My ex-husband. He's dark too, and he has the same kind of drawn, delicate face. We're the same height, but I always felt I was bigger than he was." The way she really sees Norman is as a small handsome boy with a beard. "I always felt clumsy beside him."

Mitchell smiles. His face looks whimsical in profile; he has a great, beaked nose and a quick, wry smile.

"And so now I like men who are bigger than Norman," she tells him. "I like men with big noses," she adds. This is the truth—part of the truth—but it's also a strategy. She believes herself to be a sensible woman about men's looks, and as a sensible woman she believes she can like the looks of any man she comes to like.

Mitchell reaches over and takes her hand. And Maria at once feels she's been devious. She doesn't even know if she likes this man. She only said what she said to soften him, because he seemed angry. When they get into heavier traffic she withdraws her hand.

Mitchell starts talking about Liz, his wife, and about Liz's sister, who he says is a bitch. In what way, Maria wants to know, and he tells her some of the things this sister has done to Liz. What about some of the things *you*'ve done to Liz, Maria wants to ask him, but considers this would seem, under the circumstances, a curious question. Instead she asks him (suddenly seeing the light), "Do you think *I'm* a bitch?"

He is cleverly, judiciously slow to answer. Yes, all in all, he rather does think she has the potential to be a very difficult and demanding woman.

She feels worried; she doesn't know how much of this is true. She thinks, I don't suppose we'll see each other again after this, and she starts to hope that they won't.

After a month on the macrobiotic diet, Maria still doesn't feel much better. She's sleeping better, but her skin is still as afflicted as ever and she's having pains in her arms. She phones the California-computer brothers and makes an appointment with them. They are "camping out," one of the brothers tells her, in a private house in the east end of the city. Maria goes there on a Saturday afternoon at the beginning of August. The house turns out to be a little white cottage with green shutters and a walled garden. The garden has a gate with a latch. A tall bald man opens the door to her and leads her into a dining-room. They sit across from each other at the dining-room table and he asks her some questions and makes some notes. A tent-style business card gives his name: W. B. SPAULDING, NUTRITIONIST. Balding Spaulding, thinks Maria, and she decides this must be Walter, the brother Lowell saw. Mr Spaulding gives her a tiny paper cup to spit into and then hands her a bottle for her "other contribution." The bathroom is upstairs, he says, first door on the left. When he has been given both specimens he carries them into a sun-room off the dining-room and sits, with his back to her, at a card table cluttered with jars and bottles. She closes her eyes. After a while she hears him go over to the sink and wash everything away. Then she hears him sit down at the card table again. One of his knees is jiggling, and in tandem with its jiggling she becomes aware of the beating of her heart. "How many children did you say you have?" he asks her. His back is still turned to her and this gives the conversation an ominous cast.

"Two."

"A boy and a girl?"

"Both boys."

"How old are they?"

"Thirteen and sixteen."

"They live with you, do they? You're responsible for them?"

She answers yes to both questions.

He gets up from the card table and goes over to a sink and washes his hands, then comes back into the dining-room. He sits down at the table and transfers the test numbers onto another sheet. Then he looks up at her. It's the look she's been waiting for—the knife. "You're in rough shape, girl," he says.

"In what way?" she asks him. She feels frightened and also, in a way that surprises her, very angry.

"In several ways. First of all, your salts are so high I can't measure them. Forty is the highest number for body salts and yours are higher than that. Your body is too acid. It is also throwing off one hundred times the number of dead cells that it should, and this, translated, means it's dying faster than it's rebuilding itself. But the big thing to worry about is your uric-acid reading. It puts you smack in the middle of the zone for a major heart attack. You could drop dead at any minute, it's that bad."

There is a long silence. Then she says, "I hope that hearing all this isn't going to make things worse—for my heart. If it's in the shape you say it's in."

"I believe it's best to tell the truth. And besides, there's some good news. There aren't any cancer cells anywhere in your body. So! Think positively!"

That night, Maria is alone at her place. Tom and Andy are staying over at Norman's, as they always do on Saturday nights. After supper she thinks of putting on one of their records, but the thought of the effort it will take to climb the stairs to the record player makes her feel weary. And what would be the point of putting on a record anyway? She would put it on and then not even hear it, out of worry. She is too worried even to cry. She just wants to stay downstairs, move slowly, husband her strength, keep warm, for it is surprisingly cold for summer and the eaves of the row houses up the hill have been hit by a low, golden fall light. She goes out into the hall and gets her shawl and pulls on a pair of Andy's ski socks. Norman would be shocked to see that the ski socks are still out here in the hall in midsummer. He has a much more housewifely sense of the seasons than she does, and when they were married he was always after her to wash and put away the winter clothes early in March. Now that he no longer lives with her she doesn't do this, and on the shelf above the coat rack there's a pile of ski tocques and scarves and mittens—a hilly wool banquet for moths. If she dies tonight, or any night this summer, this will become known about her: the state of this shelf, other shelves—the extent to which she was unable to cope with her life. Of course, Norman is right, in a way—to everything there is a season and all that—but he was rigid about it too. He used to want Tom and Andy to talk to him at suppertime, to be funny and profound with him, because suppertime was the only time it suited him to try to be close to them. As far as she could see, it never worked. But here she is, also out of season, maybe even dying. Does she want to die? Part of her must want to; why else should she be in the state she's in? But oh, how hard it will be for Tom and Andy if I should die, she thinks. Odd how I feel so certain of that; they're the only ones whose love I feel sure of. I'm the one they tell their dreams to, I'm the one who loves their jokes, I'm the one they feel free to yell at. I'm necessary to them.

The last time Maria remembers going out with Norman—a long time ago now—they went to the ballet. (Norman loved the ballet, but Maria, who loved it when they were first married, had come to dislike it.) Maria brought two oranges along in the car with her to eat as supper on the way over. After she had finished peeling the first orange and was ready to section and eat it, Norman suddenly flung out his arm and hit it down to the floor of the car, where it rolled crazily around in the grease and fluff. "Why can't you do things when other people are doing them?" he yelled at her. "There's a time to eat and a time not to eat! When will you learn that?"

Two weeks after the visit with Walter Spaulding, Maria makes an appointment with her own doctor, Dr Mildred Hardy. Dr Hardy wears her white hair in a bun and has pinned a silver spray of heather to her flowered dress. She has very high young breasts for such an old woman. Maria believes that Dr Hardy is a very conscientious doctor. Not too free with medication but fond of stuffing Maria's pockets with grandmotherly little gifts—mainly samples of medicated shampoos and creams—and she's also fairly open to unorthodox medical information. Still, she is a woman whose ways were forged in a particular medical climate—she went to medical school eons ago when she was in her forties —and her training is still very much with her. Maria dreads making the confession that will prove her lack of faith in Dr Hardy, but by this time the computer in California has sent back its coded report and Mr Spaulding has translated it for her and she feels she has new reason to be worried on her own behalf: cholesterol in the danger level, uric acid in the danger level, and she has, or is on her way to having, a possibly fatal disease, lupus erythematosus.

When Maria tells Dr Hardy about Don and the computer brothers, Dr Hardy only asks her how much they charged her. Maria says that Don was free and that the brothers charged forty-five dollars for the two visits. Dr Hardy looks out the window and says she can think of better uses for forty-five dollars than having her spit sent off to California. After this she talks about medical fashions. "Tongues used to be what they looked at," she says. "But nobody looks at tongues anymore."

And then she tells Maria about a dress she saw last week in a store on Rideau Street—an exact replica of the dress her mother made for her the year she graduated from high school: the same voile, the same sleeves.

"The blood tests will take a week to ten days," she says when she is saying goodbye to Maria. "I'll call you when they come in."

According to the blood tests the computer wasn't all right

and it wasn't all wrong. Maria's cholesterol is high, and so is her uric acid, but the important thing is she doesn't have lupus. Dr Hardy sends her to a dermatologist for her psoriasis. The dermatologist is a flushed, eager young man with smudged glasses. "I can only give you something to control it," he says. "As I'm sure you know, there's no cure for it. Although in Toronto now they're treating people with black light. And swimming in the Dead Sea is supposed to be very good for it—if you ever find yourself in that part of the world. And sun, if you can get some. It's been a terrible summer, though, hasn't it? All this rain."

On Saturdays Maria always goes shopping for the week's food at the Byward Market with her friend Deedee. One Saturday afternoon in September, while waiting at home for Deedee to come, she falls asleep. She wakes up to the sound of the door slamming. The kids, in and out. When she comes downstairs to watch for Deedee, she sees she's already coming up the front walk, hunched up in a tan nylon windbreaker belonging to Lennie, her husband; her hair is braided to one side in a fat fair braid with a bow of blue yarn tied around it, and she is frowning and smoking.

"Hurry up," she says by way of greeting Maria as she steps into the living-room. "I have to pick up the kids at my mother's at four o'clock."

Maria draws on her jacket and hits at her pockets for keys and money. Then she and Deedee step out into the weak sunshine. Walking out to the car they bump into each other.

"I had a nap. After an afternoon nap all creatures are sad."

Deedee doesn't answer and Maria wonders if she heard her. But she must have, because once they are in the car and on their way, Deedee, in a voice whose explosiveness suggests a certain angry incubation, says, "Do you know what I wish? I wish you'd get over Eddie, that's what I wish. That is what's sad."

Maria sighs. "In a way I suppose I don't belong in this

century. There's this hopeless, impossible love. Also, I don't own a car. As you may have noticed."

"Actually, I think you're kind of trendy. A woman of our time."

"Thanks a lot, friend. How am I trendy?"

"All this chasing after cures."

"I'm in pain, Deed."

"Give up dreaming of Eddie and run three miles a day and your pain will vanish, I guarantee it."

"Do you run three miles a day?"

"I'm not in pain."

They drive past the street where Maria's office is. Eddie's car is there, parked at the deep-shaded end of the street. The street looks like a street in a movie; it has that air of false peace.

Maria takes Andy (who has had the flu) for a visit with Don. It's mid-fall by this time—clear, cold brilliant days—and the pains in Maria's arms are worse than ever. Whatever they are, they can't be rheumatism. Don has moved to a community clinic with a sign on the door that says MEDICAL CARE IS A RIGHT, NOT A PRIVILEGE. In the waiting room there are notices of abortion-referral services and clippings about diet and smoking, and there's an article headlined BEACH BOYS GET VD BUT NO TENSION HEADACHES.

Don looks into Andy's eyes with his iridology light. When he's finished he says that Andy has a very good constitution. "Much better than yours," he says to Maria. "Your mother probably had the flu when she was expecting you."

"Am I finished now?" Andy asks them.

Don tells him he can go.

After Andy has left, Don says to Maria, "Don't be too panicky about all of this. You were a long time getting into this condition; you can expect to be a long time getting out of it. You've had years of using tar paste and cortisone cream; you've had a lot of X-rays, you've taken sedatives. . ."

Maria bows her head. She's thinking of all the junk she's

taken, also of all the nights she drank herself to sleep with hard liquor and tap water.

"Every day I see people who are desperate to make themselves better after years of eating wrong and not getting exercise," Don tells her. "But they don't know how to go about it —there's so much conflicting advice."

"And they've got to the point where they're afraid to trust their instincts?"

"They've got to the point where they don't *have* any instincts."

It's time for her to go. She can feel Don is going to hug her goodbye; she can feel him priming himself to do it. They stand up at the same time, and Don hugs her and she hugs him back. When she's getting her coat from the coat rack out in the hall she thinks how inevitable that was, how it is all part of the scene here—the waiting room that looks like an old lady's parlour, the nurses in their jeans and old sweaters, and on the rack two coats that she guesses must belong to the nurses: two broad-shouldered, eroded fur jackets.

The first snow comes, and with it comes a windfall: Norman, who has sold the house they used to live in, shares the profits with Maria. She thinks of taking a trip. She has never wanted to go to Florida, but Florida is the closest warm place, so that's where she decides to go. She plans on leaving right after New Year's.

On the afternoon of Christmas Eve, she goes downtown to the Byward Market. It's a warm rainy day, and the air of Christmas carnage she looked forward to (the fragrance of torn tree bark, the slashed sound of bells) is partly undone by the rain and by the fleet of hearse-black panel trucks parked at the mouth of the market and stocked with flowers. She is looking at the daisies—she wants to buy several bunches of yellow ones—when she notices that a young woman buying flowers from the neighbouring truck is watching her. Maria smiles at this woman—she thinks she must have met her at some party—and the woman smiles reservedly back. Then it hits Maria, what party they met at: the woman is Mitchell's wife. They seem to turn away from each other at the same moment then, each one devoting herself to the buying of flowers.

In Florida, Maria dreams of her father. In the dream he is still alive and living in the house Maria was born in. She wants desperately to get to see him. She is walking across a great field of high grass, then comes to a trench that stretches the whole length of the field and is very deep. She looks down into it and sees that if she ever fell down in there she would never get out again. But she leaps across easily and continues on her way. When she gets to the house it is completely closed up. She rings the bell three times and at last sees her father, looking as if he has just been awakened from a deep sleep, coming to open the door. He looks sad—she can see him and his sadness through the walls of the house—but she doesn't think his sadness has anything to do with her. In parts of this dream her father is Eddie.

Maria writes a letter to Tom and Andy, and a postcard to Eddie and everybody else at work. She writes pretty much the same thing in both. She describes the beach (how white it is) and the long, antlike lines of promenaders moving "in nineteenth-century fashion" endlessly up and down the shoreline in their overcoats. "The wind," she writes, "blows in from the Gulf of Mexico and is bitterly cold; there are a few shell collectors, no swimmers, a few joggers wearing gloves."

The best part of her day is the night. She takes a long walk on the wet sand every day at sunset. She seldom meets anyone, and when she does it is almost always a solitary soul like herself. Her heart has a rule of thumb for the few people she does meet: if the dark figure comes toward her at a walk her heart goes on alert and her arm presses her shoulder bag tight to her side, but if the figure comes at her in a run her heart and arm don't respond at all. All a thief would have to do, she thinks, is jog. When the sky is completely dark and all the little hotels along the beach have turned on their lights, she hurries back to her room. She makes herself supper and tea, and after supper she takes a long bath and then lies on one of the big beds and reads. She keeps the door to the balcony open so she can hear the waves coming in on the beach. Two nights it rains, and she stands awhile out on the balcony with her winter coat tied on over her nightgown and looks down at the rain falling into the garbage pit and the parking lot and the ocean. She thinks about Tom and Andy, who are staying with Norman, and wonders what they are doing. She wonders if Tom has borrowed Norman's car and driven out into the hills to go night-skiing. She tries to imagine him skiing at that latitude, in the fierce cold, under stars, but has trouble with it. Instead, she sees him lying on his bed, reading. Andy she imagines watching television. Norman is reading the paper. Maybe there is even a storm.

She takes a taxi downtown to a health-food store. The day is cold and grey. The taxi-driver says that this winter is even worse than last winter and everyone thought last winter was terrible. In the store, Maria buys almonds and peppermint tea. When she is paying for them she notices a flyer announcing a talk by a man named George someone. He has a saint's face—a saint's or a fanatic's. According to the flyer, he is a physiotherapist who worked with the American Army in Vietnam, where he learned some Oriental pressure techniques from the Montagnard tribesmen. When she gets back to her hotel room she phones his office and makes an appointment for the following day.

The next morning is almost warm, feels almost like a real Florida morning. And George, when she meets him, doesn't look fanatical at all; also, he looks too young to have been in the war. He takes her into a treatment room and gives her a pale green hospital gown and a pair of pale green shorts, then leaves her alone to change. She is puzzled by the shorts but then guesses they've been offered in case she's come without panties. Or maybe this is just the decorous South.

When George comes back into the room she warns him about her skin. She always feels she should do this whenever she has any kind of treatment because she wants to prevent herself hearing the other person's shocked intake of breath when he undoes the ties of her gown.

"I've seen worse cases than this," George says in his warm-sounding drawl.

"I've also got quite a bit of pain in my right shoulder," she tells him, and after he has worked on her shoulder for a while she says, "A physiotherapist I went to back home said that the karmic meaning of pain in the right shoulder is resentment, that maybe there are people I need to forgive."

"Maybe you need to forgive yourself." And then he talks to her about herbs and tells her how he cured a baby's colic by feeding it bottles of catnip tea. He also has iridology equipment and he looks into her eyes with it. "Liver," he says. "Also heart."

He also recommends some books to her, one of them a book on herbs, which she sits out in the sun and reads that afternoon. For nervousness it advises red sage, skullcap and catnip. It says that one great cause of nervousness is novel-reading. Later that day a cold wind comes up; it makes her feel like she has a bad toothache in her right shoulder. The next day is no better, and that night, when she's taking her pre-supper walk along the beach, she admits to herself that she wants to go home. She goes up to her room and phones Air Canada's toll-free number in wherever it is—she guesses it's in Miami—and, to her amazement, is able to get a flight out of Tampa first thing the next morning. Then she goes down to the desk and says to one of the boys there, "I'm checking out tomorrow; I can't stand the cold," and the boy says, "I don't blame you." All the way back to her room she thinks, That was easy, that was easy.

The day after her arrival back home Maria gets a phone call from someone out of her past—although more out of Norman's past than hers, a former secretary of Norman's named Elaine. Elaine tells her that she has cancer; she's had six operations and chemotherapy and cobalt and her hair has fallen out and now she wears a wig. At Elaine's mention of the wig Maria is suddenly able to recall her face and along with her face her straight shiny brown hair. Elaine says that the doctors cut slits in the soles of her feet and shoved tubes up them and then shot dye into the tubes and finally were able to locate the cancer in some lymph nodes in the back of her stomach. She describes each of her six operations, how long they took, how long she was in hospital. Maria wants to ask her what made her suspect she had it, but Elaine distracts her by asking her if Norman got married again.

"He's living with someone, but I don't think they're married."

"I heard that he was," says Elaine.

"Well, maybe he is; he's free to—we got a divorce." But she's thinking, he would have told me, wouldn't he? He would have told Tom and Andy.

Elaine says that there are a lot of young people who come to the cancer clinic, kids only nineteen and twenty.

That afternoon Maria makes two appointments—one with a doctor Dr Hardy suggested might be able to help her with the pain in her shoulder, one with an herbalist.

The herbalist's name is Monsieur Lamarre and he looks like Maria's idea of a chef—big belly, benign smile. "Bad circulation," he says when she has described her symptoms. "I have here herbs to clean you out."

"I was afraid there might be something wrong with my liver," she says in a tense, husky voice. "I was afraid of cancer."

"There is no cancer anywhere in your body. It is your heart I worry about—the angina. You must be very careful of this. Is there heart trouble in your family?"

"My father died of a heart attack. My mother had one too."

Monsieur Lamarre checks Heart on his questionnaire.

"Diabetes?"

"Both sides."

"Diabetes, both sides, *oui*. Nervousness?"

She smiles.

"Nervousness, *oui*," says Monsieur Lamarre. "*Oui, oui, oui, oui, oui.*"

They both laugh. Then Monsieur Lamarre leans back in his chair and gazes at a blue-white spot of sunlight on the grey linoleum floor. "You have not had an easy life," he says, and she wants to cry out to him, *Oh, that is true!* At the same time she recalls all the times she's been abnormally lazy, has let her life go sliding by. "You are a hard worker," says Monsieur Lamarre. "Of course, it is hard when a person does not have someone to care for her. I am not just talking about sex; I am talking about someone to really love you and care for you. You do not have this in your life at this time." He doesn't look at her when he says this; he doesn't need her eyes to acknowledge that what he says is true. He believes in his own clairvoyance.

The doctor recommended by Dr Hardy is young, but he has stern, hypnotic eyes. He asks her to get undressed. "This is the hardest thing I'm going to ask you to do." His voice surprises her, it is so kind.

She stands naked before him.

But he looks into her eyes. "Your pupils are fairly dilated," he says.

"They're always dilated. I think it's because I'm nearsighted."

"You see nearsightedness as a cause. I see it as an effect."

"What is the cause, then?"

"When you were a little girl, something made you open your eyes too wide. You tried to see everything and you ended up not seeing very much. My guess is that you let people push you around."

He paces around her, frowning; she feels like a horse, or a slave on the block—his look is so shrewd and total.

"You would believe almost anything anyone told you," he tells her. Norman used to say that too (Norman, who was always bossing her around).

"Also, you keep your knees locked."

"Oh, do I? Why do I do that?"

"Fear," he answers in a light voice.

"Of what?"

"Someone was always at you when you were small, wouldn't let you be." He kneels to her knees to unlock them.

She starts to cry.

"That's right. Cry."

"But I cry easily. Always have."

"But do you cry right? Do you cry with your body? Or are you just crying up in your head?"

"I cry as quietly as I can, usually."

"Well, yes, that's what I see when I look at your body. A tremendous stillness. You've stilled your body so much. It's as if your body is saying, 'I'll be quiet, I'll be good, I won't have temper tantrums, I'll work hard, I'll study hard, and I'll think, think, think.' You must get very, very tired of being so good all the time."

It is a moment before she is able to answer him. When she does she says, "I do."

A Sweetheart

On the way over on the ferry, Kathryn wondered if she should warn Alec about her mother. They were sitting in the old black Plymouth Alec had bought for himself two weeks after coming out to Canada from England. They were the front car in a row of farmers' battered cars and trucks and so had a ringside view out over the water. The only barrier between them and the river was a long, low-slung length of rusty old chain threaded through arched openings in the squat posts that had been nailed to the splintered front deck of the boat. Probably better not to warn him, she decided; once when she'd tried to warn a girlfriend about her mother, the girlfriend had reproached her later and called her mother a sweetheart and a living doll. So she only said, "My mother is English too."

When he didn't respond she added, "She loves to sing." Has a lousy voice though, she longed to tell him. But she did not. Instead she cleared her throat and said uneasily, "She's crazy about the songs from *My Fair Lady*, so tonight we'll probably have a singsong."

Alec said that that sounded like fun.

She threw him a distrustful, appraising look. She said warningly, "She'll probably make quite a fuss over you."

Alec said he never objected to having a woman make a fuss over him.

"Too right," said Kathryn, giving him a light punch in the arm. It ended with their getting into a mock-wrestle; they didn't stop until Kathryn, sneezing violently, collapsed against his shoulder. Then, as if they were tired, they gazed out over the dark autumn river. Kathryn said, "I think I might be coming down with the flu."

Alec said he knew a good cure for the flu.

"What's that?"

"Get you drunk. Get you plastered."

"Is that what they recommend back in the mother country?"

The mother country—he smiled to hear it called that.

Kathryn said that when she was small she'd thought the mother country was a country where only mothers lived. Mothers manned the streetcars. Mothers delivered the mail.

Alec smiled down at her with an expression of almost sappy affection. It made her want to squirm away from him in embarrassment. He stroked back her hair, said he wished he'd known her back then.

Kathryn had quickly to list some things—about herself, to herself—that she didn't approve of, in order the keep from feeling guilty for being so critical of him. She was too shy; she was sexually inexperienced; she was too critical; the top part of her body was too matronly but her legs were too short and too fat, like a fat toddler's legs. Sometimes when she stood naked in front of her full-length mirror she felt like the top part of her body was mother to her legs.

Alec, still smoothing down her hair, drew her head to his shoulder. She ordered herself to calm down, and after a few minutes of listening to him talk about his work she was able to relax and even to feel somewhat bored. It was because of his voice; he had a knack for making it go incredibly dead. Which in a way was appropriate, since "dead" was a favourite word of his. But then with the British, everything was dead this and dead that. There were a lot of things he was dead keen on; for example he was dead keen on going out to see her parents' reclaimed nineteenth-century house. And then there were some things he found dead boring. Just as long as she didn't turn into one of them, she thought, feeling some embarrassment about her job at the bank. She stole a covert look at his profile—the hooked nose, the lank dark hair, the way he was staring out over the water as if it was making him angry. He was really incredibly handsome, although some of the other tellers at the bank found him too stocky and short. It was true that when he came in at lunchtimes to visit her and she was wearing her high-heeled sandals, she did seem to tower above him, but today, since they were both wearing sneakers, they were the same height.

Alec was saying he didn't think he always wanted to be an engineer and build bridges. He was considering going back to school to study architecture, he said. In his soothing drone, he told her that his great interest was the restoration of old houses.

Kathryn said she didn't always plan to work at the bank either. She referred to it as the boring old bank. She said she might go on to university someday herself. She didn't really mean it, though: her dream was something quite other than this; her dream was to have a child and to have that child trust her above all people and to live with the child and its father and to sleep every night with the child's father in a big double bed with the fall (or summer or spring or even winter) rain beating on the bedroom window pane.

"Still," she said, "I don't mind working at the boring old bank all that much. But what I really like best is not living at home."

He did smile at that.

Kathryn was feeling very drowsy by the time the ferry rounded the bluff at Cape Stedman. The smell of the Plymouth's upholstery brought back memories of trips in her parents' car, years ago: the smell of hard-boiled eggs and bananas. But the sight of her parents' house high up in the trees made her sit up. "There's the house," she said. "But you can only see the top part of it."

Above a high bluff of maple and cedar trees they could

glimpse the four chimneys and the black roof with its four gables and the top storey with its eight tall casement windows set in stone. There was the first touch of fall on the bluff's foliage, and the deep river, near the island's rocky cliffs and small shale beaches, was a clear polar green. The house's top windows, blank and bright with the afternoon light, seemed to be sending signals out to the people on the boat. We rule this wood, we rule this water.

Alec and Kathryn got out of the car. The sun was shining down on the small distant house up in its high bluff of trees. They walked to the boat railing and then stood pressed tight against it, looking southeast and up, toward the house. The sun burned their faces but the wind was cold—nipped their noses, fingers. Kathryn, who'd drawn her sun-streaked fine hair up into an untidy windblown bun, felt small and pleased and desirable; she felt held in the excitement of living in a cold clear-aired northern country; she felt in love with the little islands with the spruce and birch trees on them. She loved the wind-bitten headlands. Her short legs were hidden by her black corduroy trousers. Her big breasts looked smaller beneath her navy nylon windbreaker. She was glad Alec was so handsome; she was glad he was standing with his arm tight around her; she hoped the men who ran the ferry were looking down on them, from their glassed-in wheelhouse above the cars and trucks and roped-on lifeboats. She breathed in deeply and, breathing in, was sure she could smell the golden decay of autumn in the trees of some of the little islands that were bobbing by the ferry. Out here in the middle of the bay the water was darker, an intense dark blue —almost black—in its windblown central channel. The ferry's engines sounded different too, in the fall—more heavily chugging, more insistent, a deep mechanical throbbing behind a sound like the constant flushing of six toilets on both sides of the boat.

"Your house is disappearing," said Alec. And it was. Now only its chimneys were visible above the big bluff of trees.

"Going, going, gone," said Kathryn, and by the time the house had disappeared completely—the bluff seemed to have bobbed up and down until it had bobbed itself up to cover the house utterly—it had lost all its power. It seemed like a summer house then, lost up in the woods, a place belonging to people who lived somewhere like Massachusetts; old people; old crippled rich people; people who hadn't come north for ten, fifteen years; an abandoned house, forgotten, gone to seed in the woods. From here you couldn't believe that there was a road in to it or that it was only a six-minute drive from the village of Point Castile.

Ten minutes later the ferry was starting to swing in a wide arc, starting to churn and tread water, preparing for its advance between the weathered grey breakwaters of the Cape Stedman landing. The breakwaters looked spectral, like two halves of a burnt-out flooded church. Between their windward and leeward grey walls they were piled high with grey boulders. Their nave was an aisle of still water. The ferry came flushing and churning in between the breakwaters, shaking up the wharf-images and creating a commotion among the gulls. The deck-hand—a freckled, complacent boy Kathryn recognized from weekend crossings on the ferry—sprang forward to throw a heavy rope out to lasso the nearest post of the pier; then, looking obsessed, began his impressive high-speed spooling of the rope around its sister post on the prow of the boat. There were the little squeaks and adjustments of a ferry being berthed at a pier. The deck-hand spiked the ramp of the wharf with a long, finned spear, which looked to Kathryn like a harpoon, to guide it into a better alignment with the ferry.

Alec's car was the first car over the ramp. Being a passenger in the first car made Kathryn feel awkward. She waved a shy wave to the perspiring deck-hand as the car eased past him, but he only stared back at her as if he had never laid eyes on her before in his life.

Then they were on the road to Bellwood Beach, a road that climbed and clung to the wooded coast for nearly a mile. From the plateau of the first long hill they glanced back and saw the ferry, small in the bay below them; a little white sled with a glass box on top of it, already starting to sled its way back to Port Charlotte across the cobalt-blue water.

As they got closer to the house, Kathryn started to feel the old familiar knot in her stomach. It was the old coming-home knot; it made her feel restless and apprehensive, as if she might need to throw up. She could feel her legs getting damp inside her black corduroy pants. A briney female odour was coming up to her from between her corduroyed sun-warmed thighs.

Coniferous trees—dark pines and spruces—were growing close to the south side of the highway. They were part of the bluff she and Alec had looked up at from down in the bay. But to the north of the road were long sunlit pastures, sloping far back to small, low-lying farms and grazing cattle. After ten minutes of driving they had to swing south, into the woods, then sharp right onto a private gravel road for the final tree-shaded part of the journey to the stone house.

And then it came into view, looking like a manor house in some country where a chilled aristocratic northness was dis-tilled in the air—Sweden, say, or Scotland. Alec swung the car up the gravel crescent of the driveway, brought it to a stop just west of the formal front entrance. As he and Kathryn disembarked in the strong fall sunlight, Kathryn found her-self feeling a little groggy and disoriented, like a tourist about to pay her respects at a shrine. The air, even this far inland, smelled of the fine invigorating salt sting of the Bay of Fundy, seemed to carry some memory of the foggy morning still in it—into the sad, clear-aired afternoon.

The house was flanked by small groves of pines and blue spruces, and by formal mounds of blue lupins and delphini-ums. The sun gave a haze of importance to all of it—above all to the speared flowers and spruces.

As she opened the front door to them, Kathryn's mother seemed to be totally caught in the grip of the painful bright-ness of welcome. She clasped Alec's offered hand in both her hands. Kathryn, hanging back, felt embarrassed by the inten-sity of her mother's greeting of Alec; thought, he will think I've never brought a man home before in my life. This in fact was the case, but it caused her some pain to have it so clearly announced. It seemed to her that she was forever vowing to act womanly when she was with her mother, but that it only took two seconds for her mother to do something that would make her start to act resentful. At the same time she was feeling oddly proud of her mother—of her petite, freckled fairness; of the pearls in her pierced ears; of the way she was immaculately dressed—tailored white shirt tucked into new-looking tan dirndl skirt. Only her white ballet slippers looked grubby. Her feet looked veined and blue from the cold in them.

In the sunny living room Kathryn's mother linked arms with Alec and squired him over to the glass doors at the back so he could look down over the long lawns and gardens. Kathryn, tucking her shirt into her black trousers, followed behind.

It was a different sunlight back here; it felt like a different season. There was a breeze spinning the round yellow leaves of the young leafy trees; the air seemed more balmy. Kathryn's father was down on his knees in the garden, pulling weeds from one of the flower beds. When he looked up and saw them, he rose, wiping his hands on his canvas gardening pants. Then he came walking up the garden path, a greeting that was more like a question than a greeting in his thoughtful grey eyes. He stepped inside. Shook hands with Alec; affectionately embraced his daughter.

Kathryn asked him if he'd been out working down on the boats earlier; she said she'd seen one of the dories pulled up on the beach when the ferry had sailed by the bluff.

He said no, he'd been working up on the roof. "Come out to the front and I'll show you what I've been up to." And leaving Alec and Kathryn's mother still standing looking out over the back garden, Kathryn and her father crossed the sun-blocked front hallway and walked down the shaded stone steps and out into the bracing sunlight at the front of the house. They turned and peered up at the patched part of the roof. While they were studying his morning's work, Kathryn's father asked her if she'd known Alec long.

"A couple of weeks. He keeps his money at the bank. He always stands in the line for my cage. That's how we got to know each other." Remembering how she'd first seen Alec, hesitating beyond the roped-off section of the bank's lobby and then picking her out from a whole row of tellers, made Kathryn throw her father a quick anxious look. She loved her father and wanted him to like Alec, and so it puzzled her that she should at the same time be longing for him to say something disapproving.

They had their tea in the back garden. Kathryn's mother fixed all her attention on Alec; asked him endless questions about England and his work. Alec said that he'd been talking to some of the engineers down in Port Charlotte and that they'd told him there were big expansion plans for the land beyond the townships west of the harbour. "Shopping malls," he said. "A new hospital. But most of that won't be built for years down the road yet. For some of the developments they're projecting as far ahead as the 1980s."

Kathryn sat gazing out over the garden, trying to imagine what life would be like in the 1980s. In 1983 she would be the same age as her mother was now. It was hard for her to picture it. She could imagine herself in the future easily enough, but she could not imagine herself being older in it. She saw herself sitting out on a bleak modern terrace. She was seated on a streamlined white modern chair while she entertained a circle of people at a futuristic round white table; a robot holding a square metal tray was pouring tea for her blank-faced modern guests from a pot with a short utilitarian spout.

The garden, meanwhile, had cooled down. The afternoon was casting long shadows across the long lawn and gravelike mounds of the flower beds. Presently they had to go into the house to fetch jackets and sweaters. "We're nearly a mile in from the ocean," Kathryn's mother said to Alec, and she linked her arm through his. "But we still get our share of chilly sea breezes."

When the supper was over, Kathryn's mother announced the singsong. Sitting on the white-painted piano bench, Kathryn's father sorrowfully, skillfully played; Kathryn's mother, a pearl-buttoned cardigan caped over her shoulders, sang "The Rain in Spain" and "All I Want Is a Room Somewhere." Kathryn, her fair hair combed and still darkly damp from a pre-supper dip in the river, sang a low quavering version of "The Skye Boat Song" and then, in a surer voice, "The Red River Valley"; Alec sang a sexy slow Cockney version of "The Ballad of Mack the Knife" in the professionally wistful voice Kathryn associated with British popular singers. Together they all sang marching songs and sea shanties.

When it was over, Kathryn's mother laid a tanned hand on Kathryn's bare arm and said in a poised low voice, "Come out to the kitchen and help me get the coffee."

But out in the kitchen her mother's eyes scanned Kathryn's face with a perplexed diagnostic sorrow, apparently very disturbed by what they were finding there. Her mother could be an intensely earnest person, but it was an earnestness in the service of false things, in Kathryn's opinion. Etiquette, for example. About the real disasters, although she could publicly be as horrified as the next person, Kathryn suspected her mother was secretly cavalier. But she was not cavalier about the disaster she apparently hoped to avert at this moment, and so Kathryn understood that it must be a disaster of etiquette. At the same time, there was something so stern and, in the weirdest way, so heartfelt about her mother's earnestness, that Kathryn could not stand within the range of its searching gaze for long without feeling that she might soon be obliged—and very much against her own better judgment —to totally alter her concept of good and evil.

Her mother was saying to her, "He's a lovely man, your Alec. A real darling."

Kathryn did not want to respond to this and so she only stared moodily out at her mother. She feared that almost anything her mother might say to her now would make her start to cry—that the only thing protecting her from it was the fact that she was keeping herself alert with distrust.

She watched her mother turn on both the hot and cold taps and then rinse her hands under the mixed blast of water. She watched her shake the droplets of water from her fingers and then dry her hands, finger by ringed finger, on an embroidered white cloth. She watched her turn to look at her. Her pale blue eyes seemed to have absorbed some of the cold of the September evening. "You wouldn't want to lose a man like that. Not a man of that calibre," she said.

Kathryn felt distaste for the *calibre*—for the calibre of this conversation *too*—but cornered, answered, "I guess not."

"I should think not," said her mother. "But you will, if you act vulgar. The way you were swinging your hips when you were singing! You have to try to be worthy of a man like Alec. You wouldn't want him to be ashamed of you."

"I don't believe he's ashamed of me."

"Believe me, dear little Kathryn, I only want to help you." Her mother was still staring at her with her terrible, earnest gaze. "Men are more fastidious than women, you have to understand that. Now that you have . . . a sweetheart, you will have to take care not to act crude."

Kathryn despised the word sweetheart. Having had it said to her, she felt the need to be alone and ran up the stairs to the bathroom. In the company of tall glass flasks stocked with eggs of beige soap and stacks of snowy towels that smelled like they'd been laundered in a subtle French scent, she peered at herself in the mirror, used the toilet. After she'd flushed it she could hear an echoing flushing down in the bay—the ferry making its final trip across the river for the evening. She crossed the hall to her bedroom to look out the window.

Down in the black bay the ferry was making an odd spectacle in the night. No part of it seemed to be connected to any other. The wheelhouse was a lighted guardhouse looking down over a darkened fast-moving prison; below it the lifeboats, illuminated by powerful hooded lights, were white wooden hammocks hung from chains; below the lifeboats the paddlewheel, also lit up by a visored light, was a waterwashed antique mill wheel for tourists. She stood watching the whole show sail past the point where she and Alec had got out of the car to stand at the rail and look up at the house. She recalled herself looking up—small and happy in the bright light. It made her feel spooky, as if back down on the boat she'd also looked puzzled, trying to catch sight of herself up here at her own bedroom window.

Running back down the stairs, she met Alec on his way up. They swung hands, kissed lightly. "We better make plans to get away from here tomorrow night, or we'll end up spending the evening playing Scrabble."

Alec, squeezing her hand tight, whispered, "Too right."

All the way through the clam chowder the next night at supper Kathryn kept waiting for Alec to make his announcement that they'd have to go out for the evening. But he didn't. Judiciously breaking his French bread into careful chunks, he talked about former wars—World War I, Korea; said World War I was a farce.

Kathryn's mother looked startled. But she was quickly able to convert her surprise into awe. "You know a lot about politics, don't you?"

Now, thought Kathryn, he'd better say it now. But her mother was leaving the table to fetch the dessert. When she came back into the dining-room with it—a heaving hot apple pie on a china tray—Alec said, "That looks sensational, doesn't it, Kath?"

Kathryn glanced at it and then quickly up at her mother. "Alec and I have to go out tonight. We've been invited to visit some friends of his over at Brewer Creek."

Her mother sat down. She was holding her silver pie-trowel upright in her right hand, like a bibbed King Henry VIII holding his meat-knife clenched in his fist. Her eyes were as blank and sunstruck as a gardener's. "Friends?" she asked. "What friends?"

"Friends from his office," said Kathryn, and under the table, Alec's sockfooted foot crept across to her bare foot and firmly capped it, like a consoling hand.

The rest of the meal, under the constraint of Kathryn's mother's unhappiness, they talked about music. Kathryn said that her favourite song was Bobby Darin's "The Ballad of Mack the Knife."

Alec smiled at her. "That's not really a Bobby Darin song, you know. In point of fact, Bobby Darin stole that song.

From Bertolt Brecht.'' The way he pronounced Bertolt Brecht sounded exaggeratedly German. "From *The Threepenny Opera*," he said. "From *Die Dreigroschenoper*."

It seemed to Kathryn that it restored her mother to see her daughter being put in her place. She won't mind my going out so much *now*, she thought.

But now Alec was looking impassive—not there, almost. He had withdrawn his foot from Kathryn's foot; that withdrawal was like the withdrawal of the eyes and the attention of someone at a party who has caught a glimpse of someone he would rather talk to, and Kathryn started to feel frightened that he wouldn't be able to get up and leave once supper was over. She was worried that if they didn't make their getaway fast, her mother would invite herself along for the ride. Or that she would detain them for so long with coffee and conversation that there'd finally be no point in going.

Her mother did suggest coffee. They took it out on the terrace. Alec and Kathryn stayed standing, drained their cups in less than a minute. But then Kathryn's mother asked Alec for some professional advice about an extension she was hoping to build on the back of the house. She guided him by an elbow to the western part of the garden. Kathryn followed. Her mother was still wearing her tan dirndl skirt but had changed her shirt for a pale blue nylon blouse with a scoop neck. Kathryn could see the back of her white lace-edged slip through it, and when her mother turned to Alec, to point out one of the mouldings on the west side of the house, and then stood hugging herself against the cool of the evening, her breasts were very evident as well—hugged as they were into a high freckled fullness. Kathryn, sensing Alec was making an effort not to stare at her mother's breasts, hung a hand on the back of his shoulder, like a girl supporting herself while hopping on one foot to shake a stone out of the toe of her shoe. Then she started to tell her mother about how Alec was always making the other tellers down at the bank laugh with his wild Cockney talk. She mocked him, in a flirty way; entertained him with an imitation of his own accent. But the fact that she had some success at this and was even able to provoke him into turning to smile into her eyes and say to her, "You're a daft one, you are," only seemed to make her feel more depressed, as if they'd had something together but lost it.

After Alec had helped her with the dishes, Kathryn slipped out into the pantry for her blazer. It was starting to rain. She could hear it drumming on the tin roof of the old shed out in the back. On the panelled east wall, where a pair of deer's antlers had been nailed up for windbreakers and coats, a transparent plastic raincoat was hooked on one of the antler's horned twigs of bone. Next to it, a forgotten sleeveless dress was hanging by an armhole from a porcelain peg. The dress was jade green with a mandarin collar. She had worn it in high school. She remembered standing out in the foggy May mornings in it, waiting for the school bus to come; books pressed tight to her breasts; nipples tightened and stiff from the chilled morning mist; shaved bare legs and bare feet freezing in her high-heeled sandals. She wondered whatever had happened to the green dress's bolero. She could picture it all balled up in a corner, smelling of turpentine or Varsol. Or maybe it had been used as a rag to clean out cupboards and toilets. Above her, she could hear her mother traipsing around in her bedroom. She could hear her creak back and forth between her bed and her dresser. What was she *doing* up there? She could imagine her twisting her hair up so she could spray the nape of her neck with her Tigress cologne, then leaning low toward her mirror and applying her make-up with severe skilful strokes. On her way back into the living-room she didn't even stop off in the bathroom; she was so terrified that her mother, by now dressed in her cream-coloured slacks and black rain poncho, would come running down the stairs calling out, "Darlings! I've decided to come with you!"

"Let's go, let's go," she hissed to Alec when she came back into the living-room in her blazer. She gripped the suede-backed lapels of his grey tweed jacket and, walking backward, tried to pull him after her.

But he batted her down sharply from his lapels. "Will you for Christ's sake stop behaving like a child?"

She obediently dropped her hands and looked away from

him, her eyes gleaming. She could feel a pinprick of tearful resentment in her throat. She thought, all I want is to be alone with him. And what do I get? I get punished for wanting it.

Out in the wallpapered gloom of the high-ceilinged Victorian kitchen the phone started to ring. Kathryn's father went to answer it. "It's for you, Peg!" Kathryn could hear him calling up the stairs. "Can you take it up there?"

Oh God, she thought, it'll be some old crony of Mother's, inviting us over for the evening, and Mother will say we all have to go. In the hallway above her, she could hear her mother pick up the phone and say hello. She could hear her father out in the kitchen, running a long blast of water. She seized Alec by the wrist—*now* he was willing to go, now when no one was looking!—and they slipped out the side door and together pounded their way across the driveway's crescent of gravel to his car. It was raining a battering rain by this time, and as the car took off, it beat its enclosing tattoo on the windshield. Kathryn could picture her mother, stunned by the ripping sound of Alec's tires spitting gravel, racing down the stairs to try to stop them. The front door flung open to the rainy night; the car's dying drone; the scent of tire-gashed earth; the immense post-drone silence.

They seemed to carry the echo of that silence along in the car with them, but then guilt, for Kathryn, began to be guiltily edged out by triumph. They drove past stands of sapling birches and alders and long groves of quaking aspens, whose round leaves were being needled and jiggled by the rain. Kathryn flicked something non-existent off Alec's tweed collar as a pretext for letting her hand rest on his shoulder. His eyes on the rain-attacked road, he ducked to give her a quick kiss on her fingers.

They passed through Wolf River, Bellwood Beach, Bramley. They drove through North Dover, with its shacklike grocery store and romantic graveyard. On the outskirts of North Dover, they caught sight, in the distance, of a long, rain-damp, grey covered bridge. Someone had painted the last third of it blue. They emerged into farming country and passed by a white horse, thoughtfully appraising them over its barn-grey Dutch door. There were daggers of damp in the door's dried grey wood. The half-door made Kathryn think of the bank, and especially of her supervisor, whose office was behind a teak Dutch door. She could often be seen there, a slim, pale eyed woman in a sleeveless blouse and straight black skirt with metallic threads in it, halved and huddled, talking conspiratorially into the phone.

West of Point Keenleyside they drove along a high ridge that looked down into a deep valley whose orchards and grey farms were brooding greenly in the rain. Then straight ahead for long but pleasantly tedious miles into a plain of dark pine trees. When they dipped again into leafy wet woods Kathryn whispered, "Could we stop somewhere soon? I have to go to the bathroom." Right away she hated herself for the childish way she had asked this question, but she couldn't think of how else to put it. In this part of the country there were no gas stations, no human habitations or even shacks for miles and miles. The terrain had changed absolutely; now the road was up and down, up and down, making her feel seasick. Leafy banks of alders crowded it like hedges. Then came a gap; a small field of tall grass. In it sat an abandoned country school house, once white and now peeling, a squat Tudor steeple at its front. It looked unspeakably forlorn—lost in time, lost in the woods. Lupin flowers were overrunning its grounds; their regal-looking pouched spears could blurrily be seen through the fogged runnelly windows—pink on one side, blue on the other, flanking the steps of the decklike front porch. The porch had a raw look, as if a quick-witted carpenter, only a half-hour before, had slipped out of the woods to hammer it into place when no one was looking. The jolt of Alec's stopping the car seemed to bring back a memory of something unpleasant. Getting blamed for something. Kathryn got out, feeling car-sticky, disoriented; started to wade through the high faded grass that never got green, not even in this country that turned into a jungle in the rain; made her way round to the back, then squatted there, in the old school's eerie shelter, the trees crying their creaky tree-cries in the dark woods behind her. She got such an old sad sense of long-ago feuds and secrets here. School! The foolish old word almost thrilled her. She dumped her lipstick and compact out on a flat wet rock behind her. Her lipstick was called Pretty Pink. She drew some of it on and wet her lips. She combed her hair. She pulled out her bottle of Ambush cologne and sprayed some of it between her thighs and behind her knees. Then she aimed the atomizer at each nipple and sprayed her dress with it. Her dress was spotted with rain anyway; you couldn't tell what spots were Ambush and what spots were rain. But then she thought, what have I done? What if he kisses me there? What if he tastes the perfume? What if he wants to suck them? Last night, after her parents were asleep, he had sucked one of her nipples through the nose-cone of her bra and her peach nylon blouse. In the lamplight of her bedroom his eyes had had a sated milky look that had almost repelled her. She wanted him to do it though. She loved it. It made her feel so abundant. And so she unbuttoned her dress and shook herself out of the top part of it and unhooked her bra and pulled it off and stuffed it into her shoulder-bag, bedding it down carefully under sunglasses and Kleenex. Then she buttoned up her dress again, but not quite all the way, and finally started her self-conscious trek back to the car.

As she edged along the side of the school house she gathered her dress into a high bunch at the front to keep it free of the timothy grass that had a pollen of mist on it. She shivered a little too, the grass's wetness making her think of pee, not rain. She passed by the school's side door. A faded red, it was dried-out and hairy with age, but this evening had a haze of mist on it. She shoved it open and cautiously stepped inside, glancing quickly to right and left. The desks looked very small to her, very small and obedient, all facing front. Everything else had been carted away—blackboards, globe, teacher's desk. She had been a good student; the lingering fragrance of pencil shavings reminded her. But she had an unsettling memory of herself back then, having to take her turn standing at the front of the class to recite "The Lord Is My Shepherd" in French. She remembered standing with her head bowed—out of shyness, not piety. She recalled her childish fear of making a mistake.

She walked back to the door, stepped out again into the rainy twilight.

When she climbed back into the car, she smiled up at Alec, her eyes anxious. "I went into the schoolhouse."

Alec said he'd been thinking of going in to have a look too, but had decided not to get himself wet. "You got yourself wet," he said. "Your nose is wet." He kissed the tip of it.

"Nothing left in there now but the desks."

"No beds?" he asked her.

The question made her feel as shy as she had felt as a child when she was the butt of some adult's affectionate teasing.

"No beds," she said.

Alec drew her head to his shoulder and sang with a Cockney accent into her hair:

> All we want is a room somewhere
> Far away from the cold night air . . .

Kathryn, looking up at him with nervous affection, pulled a cigarette out of her package of Player's and asked in a small voice, "Could you give me a light?"

"Sure thing."

He got out a packet of matches and struck a light for her. But he held the flame far from her, down between his slightly parted thighs, so that she had to lean in close against him, and over and down, to get at it. One of her freed breasts squashed itself against him, just above his belt. She rested one hand high up on his closest thigh, breathing life into her cigarette. Then feeling for once in her life totally grown-up, she huskily whispered, "Oh God, I'm afraid I'm starting to spill ashes on you."

And Alec, his voice sounding as if he had just caught an instant bad cold in the rain, answered, "Feel free. Go ahead, spill some more. Just don't set me on fire."

Kathryn sat up and nervously bore down on her cigarette. Alec dived for her left nipple, was starting to suck it through her dress. Remembering the Ambush, Kathryn whispered "Wait," then laid her cigarette down in the aluminum drawer of the ashtray under the dashboard. She whispered "Wait" again; then, like a mother struggling with fastenings in order to feed a ravenous child, unbuttoned her dress, let out a breast.

As they began the little settlings and hitchings of making themselves more comfortable, Kathryn experienced a moment of powerful doubt. But Alec was already starting to suck her exposed nipple and unbutton the rest of her dress. As he sucked and unbuttoned, she could feel her body changing its mind for her. She could feel it making a claim for itself, wanting what it wanted. Alec was trying to work her shoulder free of her perfumed dress. She rubbed her nose back and forth under his jaw. "Let's get into the back," he urged her hoarsely. "We can stretch out better there."

Kathryn gripped his hair in her fists and rhythmically massaged his skull with her thumbs while he dipped down to kiss her—her eyelids, her nose. Trying to decide, she stared up at the top of the gully through the fan of cleared glass being made and re-made by the windshield wipers. She could see how the wind was moving like a whip through the trees up there and how all the trees were nodding their heads as if in agreement.

The Students' Soirée

Thursday is mild and grey, but with such a smell of snow in the air that Bridget, on her way to work, turns up her car radio so she can hear the weatherman when he comes on. Her hair is still damp—she washed it this morning right after breakfast—and its ends are dripping little cold drops of damp on the pale-green silk scarf she's wearing shawled over her old duffel coat. When she hits the last traffic light in front of Parliament Hill she combs her fingers through the hair on the right side of her head and then moves her fingers back and forth between the two frontmost sections, trying to press them dry with the end of her scarf. This last part of the drive usually pleases her—the Parliament Buildings on her left, looking down over their great long lawns of snow. Grim stone government castles where the nation's business is done —or not done, as the case may be. Then the last light turns green and the traffic shoots toward the National Arts Centre, and as Bridget swings into the chaos that everyone here calls Confusion Square, the CBO weatherman predicts a drop in temperature by noon, snow squalls in the early afternoon, freezing rain by nightfall.

Her heart sinks; she's going to be going out tonight—to a party to be held at a community college on the outskirts of Ottawa. By the time she's ready to take off for it, the whole city will be treacherously gilded with sleet. Driving in the winter makes her feel tense at the best of times, and the college is a good forty-five-minute jaunt from her end of town. Still, there's no way she'd want to stay home on this particular night—she's waited too long for it.

Ever since the early fall she's been taking French lessons by telephone—"Francophones teaching Anglophones on telephones" was how the college flyer announcing the course phrased it—and so although she now feels she knows her telephone teacher, Gaétan Framboise, extremely well from their extended and leisurely late-night conversations (she's always his last student for the night) she has no idea what he looks like. Wonderful, she's inclined to imagine, but she's lived long enough in this world to hope she knows something about irony, and so is braced for his not looking wonderful at all.

There's also his possible disappointment with herself to consider. This has been a worry for her almost from the beginning, at least since the point when she started to feel they were becoming very attuned to each other. That he too has begun to get anxious has become very apparent from the remarks he's been making lately—from his saying she will recognize him because he'll be wearing a rose in his lapel, but on second thought he won't be wearing a rose because he won't have a lapel because he won't be wearing a jacket. Finally the only real hints he would give her were a beard (black), black-and-tan cowboy boots, a guitar. And she told him she would be wearing a long, plain, black silk dress and a white-and-silver shawl with a silver fringe. But now she's afraid that a black silk dress sounds like the slinky dress of a slim person, when in reality she's forty-seven pounds overweight. The shock she fears Gaétan's face will register when he is making the connection between familiar voice and black dress and silver-fringed shawl is making her feel very apprehensive.

Her job is a job that has helped to make her fatter. When she first started to work as a theatre seamstress she was a slim young woman of twenty-three, but at thirty-six she thinks of herself as someone who resembles one of the big-voiced Nordic opera contraltos. And no wonder. She spends her days hunched over a sewing machine or else curled up at one end of the Wardrobe Room sofa, stitching away like a medieval tailor. Whenever she has to rise from one of the seamstress's squats she's been down in, having finished pinning up the hem of one of the actress's elegant dresses, her bones creak. Lately she had taken to wearing a roomy striped caftan instead of jeans and a workshirt.

As for the social part, it is true that actors do occasionally ask her out. Almost always just after she's measured them for a costume. This is not something that she likes to admit, to a woman friend, because it makes her feel she would never have got asked out if the actors had seen her on the street, say, or at a party. She supposes it must be some kind of bonding ritual, measuring a man for something. That it must hark back to his childhood memories of having half-knitted sweaters held speculatively up to his thrown-back young shoulders; to memories of having the measuring tape drawn tightly around his hips, just above his tensed, clenched buttocks; to memories of having the tape drawn so tightly around his chest that it pressed in his embarrassed, excited nipples. In the world of the theatre where sex is supposed to be so easy come, easy go, being measured seems to throw the actors back into a time when they were more formal and shy.

Bridget is fairly formal and shy herself. And she often thinks that what men want more than anything is for someone to lay hold of them as if it really matters. The functional touching she must do as a seamstress possibly also brings back memories for the actors of the pretend-functional touching of children playing Doctor and Patient; they have such a dreamy waiting look in their eyes when she loops the tape over their heads and then lets it drop to a stop halfway down their backs. It's as if she's lassoed them. She is sure she can feel them holding in their breaths in that moment before she starts to rein in the tape, bringing its two ends to meet directly over their hearts.

Bridget has fallen for a lot of actors in her time—her ex-husband, David, is an actor, now living in the States—and so she knows, from first-hand experience, how actors can turn themselves off and on at will. At work she has sometimes stood in the wings of the theatre and watched an actor she's waiting to measure for a costume go through his paces out on stage; or strut his stuff for Fight Practice, really getting into jousting around in a pair of tights and an unbuttoned, billowing, sleeves-rolled-up workshirt. And then the director releases him to go and get measured, and as he comes bouncing towards her she can see all the animation drain out of his face. It's as if he's been out in the blaze of the sun and then passes under a cloud, and the cloud is Real Life.

She is sure Gaétan is not the type of man she has come to know so well in the theatre. He's too warm, too good a listener, too human. If she ever gets involved with a man again, she's promised herself, it will be someone like Gaétan. Someone she has already decided she likes very much without being influenced in any way by charm and good looks. She's finished with charm and good looks; she's finished with men who can turn themselves up high for a party and then, five seconds after saying goodbye to the hostess, turn the wick down so low it wouldn't warm even a baby mosquito.

She met David when she was a seamstress at Stratford. He came into the Wardrobe Room in beige tights and a sweaty, faded-red T-shirt, his chest heaving painfully (he had just been at Fight Practice), to be measured for a dark-green velvet cutaway coat. And as Bridget had slowly, methodically circled different parts of his body—his neck, his upper arms, his chest, his hips (feeling all over him the powerful beat of his heart)—she had felt him starting to fall for her, starting to fall for her and embarrassedly wishing he wasn't wearing only his tights. When he came back for his final fitting, his eyes were the eyes of a shy man who has just taken a tense breath of resolve, and she knew he would ask her out. Two months later they got married; eight months after the wedding their daughter, Tania, was born. The marriage lasted nine years, and now David lives and works in Los Angeles. Sometimes late at night when she turns on the TV, Bridget sees him standing insolently in some drab little kitchen, or sunk deep in the sofa of some expensive big-lamped living-room, the knobs of his knees at the level of his pale charged eyes, and these eyes staring moodily out at the female lead over a glass of what is supposed to pass for beer or whiskey. He was moody in real life too, although at times a much kinder, more tender man than any of the men she's ever seen him play on stage or screen. The screen in particular seems to bring out his meanness and sexual magnetism; she sometimes wonders if there isn't something physiological in all of this, if it isn't the effect of working under all those high-powered lights.

Coming out of the theatre and into the world of the city, Bridget feels a little disoriented, as if the snowing world she imagined while she was inside was the romantic, harness-jingling world of Moscow or St Petersburg in the elegant 1800s, but what is really out here is the grey bureaucrats' Moscow of the present day (although any dour northern capital city will do), and she feels a kind of mad pity for all these civil servants and mandarins whose tired, hardy faces, grimacing above their gun-metal parkas and stone-grey over-coats, make her feel they can know nothing at all of life in the theatre—the panic and euphoria of Opening Night, for example, or the intense and sweet, although often false, sense of family.

When she gets home she runs herself a hot bath, and in her bath remembers how kind Gaétan was to her the night she cried on the phone. For over a week she had been working on costumes for two plays at once, *A Midsummer Night's Dream* and Chekhov's *The Wood Demon*—titles that are shortened at the theatre to *Dream* and *Demon*—and then had been asked if she'd be willing to act as wardrobe consultant for a small alternate theatre's production of *Crimes of the Heart*.

Although "wardrobe consultant" was really an overly fine phrase for what she was doing, because in reality all she had to do was read the play and then pay brief visits to the actors and go through all the clothes in their closets with them, picking out things for them to wear on the stage. But what had tired her about the whole enterprise was the way one of the actresses, a slim, haughty-looking girl who was really stunning, had kept stealing peeks at her fat bare arms with darting sidelong looks of fascinated pity. Bridget left out this part when she was letting her frustration and exhaustion tumble out on the phone to Gaétan—in fact she left out the slim actress entirely—but she still recalls the really kind way he refrained from correcting all her errors in grammar.

A fling of sleet hits the bedroom window while she's getting into her dress, making her feel the cautious driver's trickle of fear in the heart: the streets will be slippy now, silver. Being a parent has turned her into a coward. She hikes her chair in under her dressing-table and then swims a hand through the tangle in her jewellery box, feeling for a necklace that might look good with what she's wearing. When David was learning his lines for a new play and wanting his tea he would come to whatever room Bridget was in and poke his head in the doorway and bleat like Lopakhin in *The Cherry Orchard*. There are still two photos of him, pinned up beside Tanny's mirror. In one of them he's in an old shirt and jeans, leaning against one of the handsome restored houses in Upper Canada Village, one knee drawn up so that the sole of his tennis shoe is pressed against the wall of the reclaimed house, a paper cup with beer in it held to his heart; in the other, he's in tights and a T-shirt after a dress rehearsal for *As You Like It*, ghoul-faced in the floodlights and giving a chummy sideways hug to one of his co-stars, a vivacious-looking (but also ghoul-faced) actress, whose green-silked, vase-shaped torso is squeezing her two white apple-breasts out over the top of her bodice.

"Shakespearean actors always look so *gay*," a woman friend of Bridget's—possibly feeling guilty for having gazed too long at the picture of David in his tights—remarked after the split, and then she plucked Bridget by the sleeve and whispered, "Was David?"

Bridget didn't dare to say she wasn't sure. Feeling some old loyalty to David as a lover, to themselves as a couple, she only said, "Isn't everyone? Just a little?" and when she added, "He was on the road a lot, that's all I can tell you," her friend, apparently thinking she must still be in love with him if she was trying to cover for him, moaned, "Lord, it must have been a gas back in Shakespeare's time—all those strumpets and crumpets and all the men running around half-undressed all the time."

But she still must have felt fairly enchanted with David her*self*, because a few minutes later when she and Bridget were down in Bridget's little blue-and-white kitchen making coffee, she was so vehement about him (and Bridget's awful life with him) that Bridget looked out the window and lamely said, "Oh, you know—love is blind."

Still, she does wish David would try to find work closer to home. It scares her, being Tanny's only parent in this country. Besides, Tanny misses him. After he took off for the States, Bridget pinned his phone number, with the Los Angeles area code and a big black 1 printed in front of it, beside the kitchen phone, along with the numbers of some of the more responsible people she works with at the theatre. She also often finds herself telling people at work what she's been up to; behind all this chatter is the hope that if anything should happen to her at least some of the people she's talked to will realize that Tanny will be requiring their attention. But this afternoon when she said to one of the actors she was fitting—an inquisitive little man who smelled of beer and wet wool—"Tonight I'm supposed to go to a soirée that's going to be held in the cafeteria of a community college way out in the suburbs," he smiled down at her with a teasing smile and said, "Your life is extremely decadent, Bridget." Twice she puts on and hauls off a string of black and red African seed beads, thinking yes, then *no*.

She hears Nadine, the babysitter, arrive while she's doing her eyes. Then Tanny's high excited voice telling her things, then the TV being turned to some commercial, then the liquid spooky music of the theme song of a local puppet show called "Bertie Who."

As she comes down the stairway she sees that Tanny, already in her nightgown and with her long fair hair combed out into an electrified blonde fleece, is sitting on the sofa with Nadine and looking down at one of her comic books. Nadine, an athletic, shy girl with light Nordic eyes, glances up at Bridget with a self-conscious smile. But when Tanny looks up and sees Bridget in her long dress, her face blazes white with alarm. "Where are you going, all dressed up like that?"

"I'm going out to meet Monsieur Framboise, my French teacher. You remember, Tan. I already told you."

"I forgot." (Tanny, at ten, has been in a French school ever since the second grade and finds it amazing that her mother, an adult, should still be taking French lessons.) She pokes a nightgowned elbow into Nadine's blue-sweatered arm. "You'll never believe this—my mum's teacher's name is Mr Raspberry."

"Weird," says Nadine, bestowing on Tanny an adolescent version of a mother's amused smile and then glancing quickly up at Bridget with the anxious-eyed smirk of someone young seeking admission into the Club of Adulthood.

Loyal to her little daughter (if she's not, she's afraid Tanny'll grow up to be a whiner), Bridget does not smile back. She only asks Nadine what it's doing out. "Raining? Snowing?"

"Freezing rain. My dad wouldn't even drive me here. He said I'd be safer walking."

"The main streets shouldn't be too terrible, though." But this is only a hope, not an opinion, and to cover her anxiety Bridget says firmly to Tanny, "Now remember, Tan, straight to bed, right after Bertie What's-his-name!"

This is an old joke between them and gives Tanny licence to hurl herself against Bridget's stomach and pound her fists into it. When she was smaller she used to call it her favourite pillow, her favourite marshmallow. "Mummie, you *know* his name is Bertie *Who*!"

"Take care!" Nadine calls out to Bridget as she's shrugging and shaking herself into her coat out in the chilly little front hallway, and Bridget wants to moan back at her, "Oh, don't say that! Please! The world is depressing and dangerous enough as it is." But then everybody says it: cashiers, bus drivers, neighbours, waitresses. Only stage actors, who must live with terrible, foolhardy risks every night of their lives, have the wisdom to yell, "Break a leg!"

It's the actors Bridget is thinking of as she steps out on the path of solid grey ice leading from her housing development down to the corral where the tenants' cars are parked. The sleet and wind have dislodged dozens of ice-splinters from the second-storey window mouldings and poplar branches; they're littering the ice-path like fish bones. Cautious as a cat, Bridget crunches over them on her way to the parking lot. She edges her car onto the street, and after an exquisitely careful crawl across the treacherous city—*breakaleg, breakaleg*—parks on the street side of the college parking lot, then dips the hem of her dress into a small crater of freezing slush when she half kneels to pick up a dropped glove. She makes old foolish wishes on the glove: love, happiness, not too terrible an evening.

The entrance to the administration building is as cathedral-like and gaping as the entrance leading into the main section of the Parliament Buildings and has a steep black roof shingled with shingles that the wind, blowing hard against this side of the edifice, has blown nearly clean of snow. Only the finest traces of gleeming powder remain, making scalloped rick-rack waves of white on the steep black of the roof. There are a lot of lights on, high up, and lights in the stairwells. With her white shawl hauled bridally up over her freshly washed hair, Bridget trudges in fleece-lined boots up the main walk between hedges the college gardeners have tied into shaggy dark cones. Each cone has what looks like a giant ice-cream scoop of old snow on it. And there are other cones too, aluminum ones, mounted on the front of the building; in fact they are double cones—upright ones and inverted ones welded together, and they send cones of light up, cones of light down. Snow falls into the upright cones of light and seems to be falling out of the inverted ones, seems to be falling through hourglasses made out of metal.

As Bridget opens the door to the cafeteria building, she hears party sounds coming down a stairwell from several floors up. They are sounds that rev up her already too-agitated heart. She must find herself a washroom and dry herself out. She wanders around on the dim lower level, peering at ill-lit signs and arrows. The tender, high-up cry of the music and loud volleys of laughter pierce at her.

Finally she locates the women's room logo on a dim, mustard-coloured door; when she shoves it inward the glare of the shining white tiles makes her wince. She checks her face and her hair in the mirror over the sinks, then lifts her water-logged hem to dry at the spout of the hot-air machine. When the hem feels like warm cardboard in her perspiring hands she goes back to the mirror and is just on the point of applying a little more eyeliner when the harsh gasp of a flush from one of the cubicles lets her know she isn't alone in this place. A moment later a tiny, bright-faced person in spike-heeled sandals with thin gold ankle-straps comes carefully out, looking like she wants nothing so much in the whole wide world as to wash her little white hands. While she washes them she also seems to be watching Bridget in the mirror. A faint odour of menstrual blood seems to cling to her ruffled green chiffon dress. "Are you coming to our party?"

"Yes. I'll be up in a minute. Are you one of the instructors?"

"*Oui. Qui est le vôtre?*"

"Gaétan Framboise."

It seems to Bridget that the name Gaétan makes the tiny teacher look up at her with renewed interest (but is there pity in her glance?) and she decides: he'll be fat. This will be the irony of the evening. Fat or disfigured.

The girl in green says, "You're lucky, then. Gaétan is amazing. Gaétan is the best."

Last night Bridget dreamed that when Gaétan was intro-
duced to her he turned away from her, bored. The memory
makes her draw her light-leafed, silkily pale shawl tightly
around herself. "I thought he might be."

On the fourth floor the doors to the cafeteria have been flung
widely open; the party inside looks like a giant cocktail party.
People of Bridget's age (give or take ten years) are standing
about in their evening finery, talking and laughing shrilly
and forcefully; also making more hand-gestures than she
senses they would ordinarily, to help give their French life.
Off to the left are long tables with silver candelabra and long
daffodil-yellow tablecloths on them, and at the far end of the
room a small group of men and boys in jeans and jean jackets
are setting up musical equipment and microphones for the
teachers' concert. Bridget squints to see if any of them are
wearing black-and-tan cowboy boots. In the crush of people
it's impossible to tell. A stunning but cold-eyed girl whose
stockings look as if they've been neatly dipped in metallic
gold sugar, offers Bridget a drink from a tray. She chooses a
Bloody Mary, then starts to make her way around the room,
looking for the ruffled green dress of the girl she met down in
the toilet.

She finally spots it. Its diminutive owner is standing talking to two older, white-haired women who are smiling down
at her with head-cocked, indulgent smiles. Bridget makes her
way over to them. The taller woman, in turtleneck and dark
ski slacks, gazes at Bridget as if she's thinking, "Why don't
you exercise, for Christ's sake?" The other woman, who's
lame, is more wizened and fashionable; something the little
teacher has just said to her has made her give a social gasp
and bring a ruined hand to the patterned silk scarf she's tied
at her throat.

"Can you point Gaétan out to me?".

The girl in green (her name card says Ginette) takes
Bridget's hand. "Tell me your name."

"Bridget."

Ginette leads her out into a clearing about forty feet from the musicians, drawing her along like an out-sized little sister while Bridget marvels at the spitefulness of a fate that's so publicly paired herself, so moth-pale and huge, with this vital little person in emerald chiffon. From the middle of the clearing Ginette calls out, "Gay-tan! I have here another student for you!"

A well-built black-bearded man who's helping one of the boys adjust one of the microphones looks up, and the tiny teacher shouts, "Here is Brigitte!"

Gaétan gazes at them a moment, then turns back for a brief word with the boy. Then he starts walking toward them, picking his way over cords and cables.

He's not fat and he's not disfigured—feature by feature he's extremely handsome, even—but his face is totally expressionless. In point of fact, he's not her type; he looks too impassive and stodgy. Also, he appears to be looking at someone just over her left shoulder rather than at herself, and although she tries to hold a smile of composed welcome on her face she can't help feeling wounded by his apparent lack of interest in her. Maybe he's so shocked by the size of her that he's closed down all his feelings. Or maybe he thinks that this stocky person can't possibly be his Brigitte and that the real Brigitte is whoever is behind her. But when he gets closer, she sees that his eyes have a strangely milky look. "*Bonsoir*, Gaétan," she says in a tremulous voice that draws the odd eyes straight to her face, and it's only at this moment that she understands he's blind.

At the table reserved for Gaétan's students, Bridget sees that the people who for all these weeks Gaétan has known only by voice he can now pick out by fabric and position in the seating arrangement. With a hand on tweed, a hand on polyester, a hand on cashmere, he makes his way around the table, introducing Bridget to the other students: Shirley, Tony, Gail, Douglas, Mandy, Peggy, Mitch. Some of these people are already familiar to Bridget: Gail is the white-haired athlete; Peggy the lame, lively one; Mandy the girl in the sugared gold stockings. At the end of the introductions,

Peggy says, "Gaétan, you're incredible. You didn't make a single mistake."

In reply Gaétan says, *"Nous devons parler Français toute la soirée."* He also says that even compliments to the teacher must be in French.

Right after this, as tuna casserole and scalloped potatoes are being served (and Gaétan is pouring everyone tall glasses of beer without spilling a drop), another student arrives—a tense-looking Scotsman Gaétan introduces as Rory. A moody-eyed man in his late twenties or early thirties. Black hair. Black corduroy jacket. Pale mohair muffler wound round his raw throat. His hair is sleek from the walk across the huge college parking lot in the freezing rain, but Bridget has a sense of an unseasonable night in late summer with him; he gives the impression of being cold and secretly excited, as if he has just come in from swimming underwater in a deep summer river after dark. Not that he's so amazingly handsome—he's too long in the nose, has too jutting a chin (you could shelter under a chin like that, in a heavy summer rainstorm), but telling herself all this is only another way of telling herself that he is her type, the male equivalent of a fatal woman. As if he is aware of all this, Gaétan seats him between Bridget and Mandy.

But Mandy is the one who talks to him, all through the first course. Bridget cuts her potatoes and shells of iceberg lettuce into neat little squares, like little squares of meat, listening in. Mandy is talking about last year, when she was living in Cairo, teaching English as a second language. Egyptian men followed her everywhere in the streets, she says, and she tells Rory how she used to turn on them and grab them by their burnooses (she demonstrates, holding her linen napkin aloft and making a fierce upward grab for its throat). "I used to hiss at them," she says. "I used to yell, 'Get lost, scumbag!' in Arabic."

Rory says he supposes this only inflamed them.

"Damn right." And mimicking a gutteral male Arabic voice, Mandy lifts up her throttled napkin and does a shaking and bowing little dance with it, crowing, "A woman with spirit!"

Rory and Bridget both laugh, but Mandy makes it clear that only Rory's laughter is of any interest to her (she's an egomaniac, surely—she has an egomaniac's eyes, she will do herself in), and then Rory starts to talk about a trip he took four years ago to South America, where he also taught English. In Lima, in Bogotá. He seems, with a slight angling of his body, to be including Bridget in the conversation; now and then she can feel his nearest eye grazing her nearest eye, her breasts, but it isn't till Mandy turns her back to them to accept a slice of lemon meringue pie from one of the waiters that Bridget gets a chance to ask him if it's easy to get jobs like that, teaching English, in Africa and South America.

He turns on her the first full gaze he has given her. "As easy as pie," he tells her, taking her in. "Especially if you have any kind of degree."

"A degree in English?"

"A degree in anything. And do you," he asks her with what seems to her to be either contempt or a careful flirtatiousness, "have a degree in anything?"

"A Bachelor of Fine Arts, years ago."

"With a Bachelor of Fine Arts, you could teach Ugandans how to be brain surgeons."

They both laugh. By the time Mandy rejoins the conversation, Rory is telling Bridget about a mad trip he took through Venezuela with three other Scotsmen and how the three other Scotsmen all got dysentery. "Then we joined up with a political science student from the University of Montreal and he got dysentery too."

They all laugh at this as if it's the funniest thing they've ever heard, but Mandy's laugh, Bridget notices, is the most insistent.

During dessert, while Gaétan is down at the far end of the cafeteria consulting with a group of teacher-musicians, the students at his table all start to talk about him. They are all in awe of him and all seem anxious to make sure everyone else at the table knows it. Especially the women. Maybe they've had telephone crushes on him too and want to compensate for no longer being smitten by expressing a lot of hushed praise.

Bridget wonders if any of them are bothered by his being blind, or if only she is—or if it's really only that she had a different man in mind when she fell for his voice on the phone. She wonders if any of the other women cried on his (telephonic) shoulder and consequently feel ashamed to discover that his life is so much harder than theirs could ever be. She does know one thing: his being blind makes her feel guilty for not feeling the same way about him any more.

People also seem to be anxious to compare notes on exactly when it was that he told them. It turns out that he told some of them about it two weeks into the course but that he didn't tell the others until the beginning of last week. At this point Rory says that he didn't tell him about it till yesterday.

"You're *kidding*!" cries Mandy. She's had more to drink by this time; her egomania, Bridget notes, is starting to make its presence felt. "That's so weird. He told me about it right away. We get along like a house on fire," she adds, and when she says this it seems to Bridget that all the others at the table gaze at her coldly. Rory even turns away from her, to Bridget. Who makes a confession.

"I don't think he told me about it at all." Then she remembers something. "Gaétan's a lawyer, isn't he? Did he tell you that?"

Rory doesn't think so. "I think somebody said he's studying history."

Bridget brings a fist to her forehead. "Oh God, I think he *did* tell me. I think he must have been trying to tell me he was blind and I thought he was telling me he was a lawyer. I knew the word for lawyer was also the word for something else and for some reason when he said what I think now must have been the word for blind, I thought he was saying the word for lawyer. And then I must have decided that *aveugle*— that's the word, isn't it? for blind?—was also the word for avocado because by this time I'd remembered that the word for avocado doubled as the word for lawyer. Oh God—I must have been drunk or self-centred or something. I was even kidding around with him in English about it—referring to him as 'Mr Raspberry, the well-known avocado.'"

Rory and the man on her left both laugh, and then Rory, a little drunk, says, "Don't give it another thought, love— Gaétan's a pretty good-natured wee mannie."

"You think he knew I was speaking out of ignorance, not malice?"

He grins at her. "Sure. You have to bear in mind that his being blind is a big deal to us, but not to him—he's used to it." And as if to prove it, he asks her if she'll be using French much in her work.

"Not in my work. But I want to know it anyway." When she tells him that her ten-year-old daughter is already bilingual, he looks so swiftly down at her hands that out of gratitude she says, "Even my ex-husband is more bilingual than I am. And he doesn't even use it—he lives in Los Angeles."

When she asks him about himself he says there's a good chance he'll be using it in his work; he's a geologist and goes on field trips up north in the summers. This coming summer he's going to be going up to the Ungava district. "Although I guess maybe up above the timber line English would still be the lingua franca."

A sleepy-eyed woman named Shirley, listening in, says, "Well it sure is the lingua franca around my house, buddy," and standing up, she shoves back her chair and pats and sucks in her tartan-skirted abdomen. "*Mesdames et messieurs*, you'll have to *pardonnez-moi*—I'm going to have to go look for *la salle des petites filles*."

Bridget tells her there's one in the basement.

"Thanks, chum, but there better be one a whole lot closer than that!"

Peggy wants to ask Bridget something. She's leaning earnestly across the table toward her. "What sort of work do you do, Bridget?"

"I work at the National Arts Centre. Theatre seamstress."

"That must be interesting work."

"It's just sewing, basically, but it's usually okay."

"Working with actors must be exciting, though."

"Mostly it's just measuring them for things, so I don't get to see them all that much, really." And she thinks of the theatre, far away across the freezing glimmering city, a monolithic stone box up on its podium of terraces and dried gardens, gone dead for the night. "What about you, Peggy? What do you do?"

"Don't ask." But her voice sounds pleased. "Boring work. Up on Parliament Hill. Minion to a mighty man in the cabinet."

Later, there's dancing. A white-faced anorexic girl in a black dress and black nylons and a pale man who has an ill but agile look and is perhaps some sort of radical priest (for he too is all in black—black running shoes, black suit and that most priestly of pullovers, the black turtleneck) dance a parody of a tango—if it's possible to dance a parody of a parody. Their right arms are held down in the stylized forced V, their two ghost faces are clapped together and gazing, horror-struck, at the same dread tango vista. Rory asks Peggy to dance, then Mandy, then Bridget. When Bridget dances with him she can smell how his beer-fevered skin has been permeated by the muggy fragrance of damp mohair, can feel how the imprint of his hand is making a brand on the chilled, rocking oval of her bare back. But they've no sooner got started than they have to stop; one of the teachers, imperiously clapping, pushes her way into the clearing to call out an announcement: "Time for the teachers' concert!"

During the concert Bridget ends up standing next to Gaétan. Ever since she met him she's been feeling she must speak with him about his blindness; she's afraid if she doesn't, everything will be awkward between them for the remaining two weeks of telephone talks. She tries to think what to say. She feels anxious about how her voice will come out; worries that it will come out in a cry-whisper, conspiratorially poignant. Or sappy with pity. The thought of blindness has always filled her with panic. To live with being blind, she's always imagined, you would have to trust the whole world. On these grounds alone—huge grounds, when it comes down to it—she's sure she would fail. And suppose you were struck by it when you were still only a child, at a stage when you were still afraid of the dark? Or, come to that, what did you do if, even as an adult, your mind filled up with dark thoughts and you had no fresh images to edge them out with? Not that dark thoughts would compare, in final horror, to not being able to see, ever again.

She tries to imagine what total blindness would be like. Would it be worse than a dim, frustrating world that let in a little weak light? Or would it be as black as the mass total blindness that briefly afflicts a theatre audience just before the curtain goes up? But that was a wonderful blindness—communal, anticipatory, with a reward at the end of it. Total blindness would be a world in which there was no reward, only black night forever.

"Gaétan!" she whispers—in English, because she's afraid she will sound affected if she whispers in French. "How long have you been blind?"

He does not seem to be taking offence. "Since I was eleven."

"How did it happen?"

"A disease of the retina. Retinitis pigmentosa."

"Is it total?"

He whispers yes.

As people have more to drink, the evening moves from teachers' concert to free-for-all Amateur Night. A middle-aged male student, a benevolent busybody, corpse-pale, even cadaverous-looking, with toffee-coloured hair that's been wet-combed in sculptured wings and layers, jogs around the cafeteria, drumming up volunteers. From Bridget's table Rory and Douglas consent to do a song-and-dance number together. They weave their way over to the musicians' corner, their arms thrown around each other's shoulders in a parody of comradeliness, and then make a big production out of having the microphones adjusted to accommodate their considerable heights. Rory has undone the top two buttons of his long-sleeved cotton shirt and loosened the noose of his dark red tie. He now seems to Bridget to be a generous person, willing to make a fool of himself for the general pleasure. Tony, also a Scotsman, moans, "The daft loons," and Mitch (on is name-card he's printed Meetch) shakes his head and says, "The poor sods. They're totally pissed."

A drunken bit of soft-shoe follows, with a few Rockettes kicks thrown in—a lot of kicking each other in the shins instead of kicking straight out—and then they begin singing a French translation of some ribald old Scottish song. But as the song goes on they get more and more bogged down in faulty syntax and scandalized weeping gasps over boyhood memories of the original words, and so debilitated, so really broken down and sapped by laughter that they can't continue, and end up having to stagger back to the table.

Throughout all of this the young French teachers' faces have a mystified look, a frozen expression of puzzled goodwill. Rory throws himself down into his chair beside Bridget and immediately seems to plunge into a deep gloom. Peggy leans toward him and touches his shirt-cuff and says in a spirited voice, "Now I'd certainly love to hear the original of that!"

"Don't delude yourself, lass. You wouldn't."

Then the musicians start up a Gilles Vigneault song, and one of the teachers spins singing out into the clearing and flings open his arms and starts to tap-dancingly clatter out a Vigneault-style jig.

"The whirling dervish sings again," Rory says out of the side of his mouth to Bridget.

She smiles up at him, and she can tell he knows she's smiling because she can see a muscle start to twitch in the corner of his nearest eye. But he doesn't look down at her, and she finds this—God help her—fascinating.

After the Vigneault song is over, people get up and stretch, mill about. But then there's a cry, a kind of teasing, challenging chant, from the other teachers: "Gaétan *et sa femme!* Gaétan *et sa femme!*"

Bridget, amazed, turns to look for Gaétan.

"Gaétan's wife," says Shirley. "Haven't you met her?"

Bridget shakes her head. "I didn't even know he was married."

"Oh, she's a little doll. A *doll*."

But when Gaétan's wife is pushed out into the clearing she's not so much a little doll as she is an Asian madonna in a schoolgirl's pleated skirt and short-sleeved white blouse.

"She's Vietnamese," Shirley hisses to Bridget. "I think she was one of the Boat People."

Gaétan says he would like to introduce Thuey. "In Vietnamese her name means 'blue water.'" And then he makes his first English joke: "Mr Raspberry marries Ms Blue Water."

There's laughter and applause and even a wolf whistle from the back of the hall. Then Gaétan and Thuey prepare to sing, and it seems to Bridget that there's something unmannered and pure about the way they stand together so simply, arms hanging down, unspotlit, side by side. They sing a quick upbeat version of "A La Clair Fontaine," and then Gaétan announces a solo by one of the other teachers as the last song of the evening. It's to be "Un Canadien Errant," which happens to be a particular favourite of Bridget's. She's extremely partial to its heartbreaking funeral march beat, its keening slow melody that could wring tears from a stone.

The teacher who is to sing it turns out to be the tiny teacher in green. She steps out into the clearing and Gaétan takes her hand, and then they stand, shyly swinging hands, and Bridget has a recollection of the way the little teacher's eyes shone while she was singing Gaétan's praises down in the washroom, and she's able to see what she couldn't see then—that Ginette has a hopeless crush on her blind married colleague. Then Gaétan shouts, *"Je vous présente Ginette!"* There's powerful applause from the teachers, scattered applause from the students. One of the jean-jacketed boys Bridget saw earlier makes his way through the crowd and kneels to lower the microphone for her. The tenderness of his matter-of-fact gallantry makes Bridget feel like weeping. It's been a strange evening anyway: ironies fighting ironies, like fire fighting fire. Mandy, over by the main doors, an Oriental quantity of bangles sliding down a slim bared arm, switches off all the lights so that the cafeteria is sunk in darkness except for the drunken light from the candles on the long tables.

Bridget's eyes hunt for Rory in the privacy of the near-dark, but she's not able to locate him. He's not talking to Mandy, in any case; the priest who danced the tango is the one doing that. Or at least he's the one listening to Mandy talk. She's resting a hand on his sleeve and seems to be whispering some sort of conspiratorial confession.

When Ginette starts to sing, her voice is a surprise. It's a mournful, powerful voice, filled with all the sorrow and dark strength that a song of exile requires. Silence falls on the gathering while she sings, and holds for a fair moment after she's finished. Then there's explosive applause. Full-bodied, insistent. It's a relief, this applause, like the relief that comes with explosive applause in the theatre. Torrential-warm-rain-after-a-dry-spell applause. (After an evening of dry coughs from that great cavern where eyes and rings and earrings glint here and there in the dark.) But now Bridget can see that Rory must have made his way over to Mandy in the darkness, for he is standing talking to her, while Mandy, arms hugged under her breasts, is staring straight ahead. Is he asking her out? Is that it?

And then the soirée is over, because just after the applause peters out, people seem to wake up to the fact that it's late and there's sleet on the streets and they have to get up to go to work in the morning. On the way to fetch her shawl—gleaming over the back of Rory's abandoned chair—Bridget overhears herself being discussed. She hears Shirley's voice first: "I think it belongs to that fat girl"; then Peggy's eager, aging tremolo: "The one who arrived a bit late, Gaétan. The big redheaded girl. She got here just before the Scottish boy came." Stung, Bridget turns back the way she came and on her quick walk away from the table collides with someone who turns out to be Rory. He steadies her by placing his hands on her hips. "Hey!" he says. "Hey, there."

She caps his hands with hers at the same moment that someone turns on the lights. "Hello."

"Fancy meeting *you* here." He's made his speech sound

comically clipped, British. But then he drops both his voice and the accent: "I been lookin' for you, girl."

Her eyes harbouring doubt, she searches out doubt in *his* eyes (so she can doubt more? or so she can doubt less?), and seeming to spot some—at least a little, she begins to think he might be worth the trouble. "I'm glad we found each other, then. I was going to look for you, too. I was going to suggest we meet sometime and have coffee or something."

"That would be great," he tells her, giving her hips a jiggling little shake. "I could give you a ring tomorrow night if you'll tell me when would be a good time to call."

"After ten. That's when my nightly call from Gaétan is over. I'm always his last student for the night." She smiles up at him. "I almost said 'his last patient.'"

He knows what she means. "The father confessor to us all," he says.

Together they go back to the table to reclaim Rory's jacket. And Bridget's shawl. Remembering the sleet, she draws it up over her head as she walks with Rory to join the line of people waiting to say good night to Gaétan. They are five people away from him, then only two, then they are taking their turn shaking hands with him. An onlooker, standing off to one side and watching them, might conclude from their humble, joined look (and from their look of gratitude, gratitude in advance) that they are asking his blessing.

The Age of Unreason

The night staff in the Operating Room would set up odd banquets in the night—rows of scissors, blades, clamps— sterile surgical cutlery laid out on dull green tablecloths. And when they had finished setting up every table, every room, they would make themselves coffee, using the Pyrex pot in the supervisors' kitchen. If they wanted a glass of milk as well, or a glass of orange juice, they could walk down the hall to Blood Bank. There was always a quart of milk and a bottle of orange juice there, in with the bottles of blood. But usually they didn't. Coffee was the drink of hospitals and night. They would carry it into the stretcher room and sit on old office swivel chairs, their feet up on the window sills, and drink cup after cup of it, black. The the sun would rise and they would hear the cooks and orderlies calling out to each other, far below them in the hospital courtyard, in Estonian and Italian and Portuguese.

At the end of her night duty in the Operating Room, Ingrid Hessellund had two days off and so she decided to go home. The morning, just after sunrise, was foggy and balmy with a hot humid day burning behind it—pointless, then, to sleep, when there was sun, when she would be free. People on night duty didn't sleep all that much in the summer anyway; they preferred to snooze up on the sun roof of the nurses' residence, or to charm some boy into driving them out to one of the stony beaches on the rim of the Bay of Fundy. He would be one of a noisy crowd who would tell jokes beginning, "Meanwhile, back at the ranch..." Sometimes the words following these words would be "the little moron..." for there were many Little Moron jokes as well; Ingrid didn't like them, would even feel a little frightened of them, would feel, when some golden boy with golden bristles on his freckled good-natured arms would begin, "Meanwhile, back at the ranch the little moron..." that his next words would pertain, however foolish and far-fetched this fear was, most horribly to herself. And the ranch, too, would seem somehow to suggest her parents' house—*one* of her parents' houses: either the house at Gully Bay, an old farmhouse way out in the country and now used by her parents as a weekend retreat, or the grander house they'd recently bought themselves in Annetteville, although this, too, was an insane comparison, since neither of these houses was in the least ranchlike. And I am not a moron, either, she would think, and yet the words of the joke, whenever she heard them, would plunge her stomach into dread. Such a fear seemed to suggest that she didn't enjoy going home, that she didn't look forward to it, when in fact she did, she did, she adored going home, there was a whole world of young life at home, at least at the house in Annetteville, and hundreds of people coming to call—musician friends of her mother's and men from the local drama guild and reporters from the *Annetteville Record* and officers from the nearby army base and friends of her brother Arnie (when he was at home) and old boyfriends and friends of her sister and cousin.

The senior student she was on duty with in the OR let her off early since it was her last morning on nights. Running down one of the hospital's back service stairways she was met by battalions of day girls on their way up—fresh-faced juniors coming on duty out on the big public wards. They were bright-eyed and noisy from having slept nights. Whereas *I* look haunted, thought Ingrid, running happily down the service stairway, I look like a cadaver—although a tanned cadaver—and she was so eager to be off and on her journey that she paraded very fast past the cafeteria's stainless steel basins and tubs of scrambled eggs and bacon bits and oily omelettes whose edges were fried into rust. And in the end couldn't stomach more than half a cup of tepid institutional coffee. But for some reason she was feeling that something wonderful would happen this trip. Maybe she would fall in love, even. For the act of stepping onto a bus on a hopeful misty summer morning seemed almost enough to put into motion something enchanted and amazing.

But at the main desk of the nurses' residence there was a message for her. She was to go over to Male Surgery to see Miss Killeen. She packed her nightgown and a pullover in a suitcase and got into a skirt and blouse. I can't have done anything wrong, she thought. And besides, Killeen was her friend. (The year before, when Killeen had still been a student, she'd been the senior on a night duty they'd shared on Male Surgery and from working with her then Ingrid liked her a lot. But God, what a madhouse that place was! And of course it wasn't true that she hadn't done wrong. She had. They both had. The only two nurses for forty patients, they had faked graphs on temperature charts, skipped dressings, left comatose patients unwashed.)

Ingrid walked back to the hospital. A glassed-in catwalk joined it to the nurses' residence, but she walked below it, on pavement. She crossed to the ambulance breezeway and entered through the Emergency wing; took the service elevator up to the seventh floor. When the doors parted she saw Killeen, standing with her back to her, over at the medicine cupboard, pouring pills into the kind of tiny paper cups the staff cafeteria served marmalade and jam in. In spite of her fondness for Killeen, in spite of the soft summer morning, she felt a surge of terror. Killeen turned around. "Oh, Hessie," she called out to her. "Did I scare you, ordering you over here like this? I'm sorry, but they said you were coming off nights and I wanted to catch you before you took off." She came back to her desk. "I've got a little problem here and I wondered if you could help me out."

"What is it?"

"They brought in this sailor a couple of nights ago, from a boat docked in the harbour. A Danish boat. He doesn't speak any English. We know what's wrong with him because we've been in contact with the doctor out there. But this morning I suddenly remembered: you come from a Danish family. I wondered if you'd go and talk to him a little."

"I don't speak much Danish," said Ingrid. All she knew were songs and jingles and silly things. Her parents had assimilated completely and spoke perfect English. They even made jokes about the Danish language. Said it was not a language at all, but a disease of the throat. Said it sounded like the baa-ing of sick sheep.

"Don't worry," said Killeen. "All we need is for you to say a few words to him in his native tongue, to cheer him up. And if you could find out if he has any problems or complaints."

Ingrid walked down the hall and into the sailor's room. There were three men in there, sitting cranked up in their beds, eating their breakfasts in the bright morning light.

"The Danish man?"

"Behind the curtain, miss."

She parted the curtains and let herself in. He was about thirty-five, dark and taciturn-looking. She wished him good morning in Danish. The dark face broke into a slight but hopeful smile. You speak Danish, he said to her in Danish. In Danish she answered no. Yes you do, he said. He thought it was some kind of game. So she decided to show him what she knew, to make a joke of it, to show him that all she could do was count to ten, wish him a Merry Christmas, ask him how he felt (but not understand too fulsome an answer), and thank him a thousand times for the lovely evening. She hoped he would laugh but he did not. Then she remembered that the way to say "good luck" in Danish was *til lykke*, but she didn't dare to say it to him; she just put her hand on his shoulder as a way of saying goodbye. But it wasn't to be so simple as that. He gripped her hand hard by the wrist and guided it down from his shoulder. The moment she guessed where they were going, her hand started to resist, so that his hand, feeling the fight in hers, caused the flight down to his genitals to be forced and rapid. Held to holding her hand down there, Ingrid stood motionless and with a bowed head. She silently vowed: I will never tell this to anyone, ever, and right after her silent vow the sailor released her.

Killeen was at her desk. "Were you able to communicate with each other?"

"I think he's just lonely." It made her feel wonderfully grown-up, to reveal only this.

The person Ingrid sat next to on the Wolf River bus was a woman in her sixties. Her hands were covered with liver spots and freckles, and three of her fingers were fitted out with diamond rings. She had a smoker's cough and an American accent. It turned out that she was a nurse too and had been born and raised in Canada, not far from the countryside they were at that moment travelling through. She had trained in Halifax. As a young woman she had moved to the States, had married there, and had ended up in Florida, where she was now the owner of a nursing home. "When I was thirty-eight years old I was left a widow. Thank God for my training. I took a job in Tampa—private nursing—and I started to save up my pennies. Ten years later I bought the establishment I'm running now. I'm very successful. I'm not telling this to boast but only to show how it pays to stick to your training." She pinched Ingrid's sleeve as if she could read her mind. "Oh, honey!" she cried, her shrewd old Florida eyes on Ingrid's. "I can see you have doubts."

Ingrid confessed she'd been considering giving it up.

"Oh no!" the old nurse cried. "Oh, don't do that! Don't ever do that. Remember, it's always something to fall back on."

The odd thing was, the year before, she had been even closer to leaving than she was now. She had sat in her parents' car outside the hospital and cried and said, "I want to leave here, I want to leave here *now*." They had persuaded her to stay until her third year. Then you will have tried everything, they said. You will have been in the Case Room and the Operating Room and Emergency. If you still want to leave then, after you've tried everything, then we won't argue with you.

When Ingrid got out of the bus at Wolf River, her hoarse and freckled Florida friend touched her arm again and said, "Remember what I told you, honey," and Ingrid told her she would. She made a good connection with the bus to Annette-ville, and had plenty of time to think about her life at the hospital on the long trip there. The first birth; the first death; the first post-mortem. The first post-mortem had been easy, coming more than a year after the first death. Six student nurses walked over to the morgue together. On their way there they met three interns. It was a hot afternoon and there was the smell of tar in the ocean air. The morgue sat behind the hospital and looked like a garage; it was made of concrete blocks, painted white, and it had a big garagelike door. The moment they got inside they saw the body, lying on a marble-topped table. It was a woman, past middle-age, with faded orange hair and, even in death, a look of authority about her. Ingrid imagined that she had once been head of something— the purse section of a department store, say, or maybe a business office. Maybe she had even been a nurse. She was glad she wasn't young.

One of the interns stretched. "Cooler in here, anyway," he said, and then the door opened and the chief pathologist came in. He was a Scotsman and very small and quick, in a clean white lab coat. "Good day," he said in his Scots voice, and he strode to the table and at once picked up a scalpel and made a long vertical incision. There was something flamboy-ant about the way he did this, as if he wanted to give them all a bit of theatre. His next move was to lay down the scalpel and pick up a pair of rubber gloves and draw them on in the swift, fastidious manner of a thief about to plunder some-thing small and precious. Then he parted (by strenuous, even violent shoving) the walls of the dead woman's flesh. To Ingrid it was like watching curtains being parted, curtains thick as thick carpets, plush with blood, and in order to keep herself from fainting at both the parted curtains and at what they were revealing she made herself recall the definition of anatomy that they'd been given at the beginning of Anatomy and Physiology:

> Anatomy is the science which deals with the structure of the bodies of men and animals. It is studied by the dissection of the bodies of those who die in hospitals and other institutions, unclaimed by relatives.

This woman had no one who cared for her then.

"Ladies and gentlemen," said the chief pathologist. "Look at the lady's lungs."

They all looked. They were very flecked with black. "A lifetime resident of this city," the chief pathologist said, and they all nervously laughed. Then he started asking people to show him things. The falciform ligament. The seventh costal cartilage. The interns did all the showing, they were good at it. And after a while the pathologist forgot about the nurses entirely and addressed all his remarks to the interns. He exposed a small globe of flesh deep within the abdominal cavity. "Which of you good gentlemen knows what this is?" he asked them. And he allowed his eyes to shine. He was sure, this time, he had them stumped. And in fact they seemed to be. But Ingrid was not. At the time they had studied it she had been infatuated with one of the orderlies on Male Surgery, a dark solid boy named Douglas MacKinnon.

"The pouch of Douglas?" she whispered.

The pathologist gave her a quick, sharp look.

"Dead right," he said.

As for the first birth, when she saw her first birth the first day of her first shift in the Case Room, she had a sense that she'd never had before of the connection between tension and bringing forth, and at the same time a feeling of being in *good hands*; every death she'd witnessed after that first birth was easier to take, except for the deaths of a few children. But then she'd hated the Children's Ward anyway; it had almost done her in. The sunniest place in the whole hospital, skylit with a great dome of frosted glass and walled with glass bricks that gave it the architectural serenity of a giant city igloo, everything else about it was desperate: the noise, the smell, the overcrowding—it was as noisy and smelly as a zoo set up in a greenhouse but without the blessing of green plants. But the crazy thing was, the odd silent wards were no better. Here a great many small children were in a state of shock from having been separated from their parents and sat, hardly moving, in pyjamas sporting pink lambs or pink poodles, their eyes as unseeing as black pools. And in the chronic wards there was a deceptive lightness. Here the children smiled and joked and knew all the routines and all the nurses' names; but they were the worst of all—it was as if the bewitched monstrous children of German fables had been given medical verity. Here were children who had got puffed up into strangers overnight, their eyes turned into slits by the held-in fluid; here were children with enormous circus heads; here were children whose legs and arms had grown to different lengths; there were medical names for all of it. Ingrid got sick on the Children's Ward—diarrhea, bronchitis, high child-style fevers—even though normally, like the others, she was immune to everything. The problem was, courage in very young children was a frightening thing. So pure, so absolute, so detached from the very experience that could give it meaning; she knew they would give up life as easily and naturally as they would take their medicine.

And the Children's Ward wasn't all. There had been other places as well; places where they hadn't just been overworked, they'd been humiliated too—some of the older supervisors, especially, had taken pleasure in humiliating them. On certain night shifts, where the supervisors coming on duty in the morning had made the students stay late doing things they said they'd left undone and threatened to take their free time away from them until it seemed to them, in their exhaustion, that these supervisors held their freedom and self-respect, even their whole lives, in their hands, Ingrid had given up eating almost entirely, preferring to sleep instead. The new wing of the nurses' residence was under construction then, and every morning before she went off duty she'd fill up her pockets with phenobarbitol pills to blot out the sound of the jack-hammers. She couldn't open her window, either. Her best friend, Joan Cosman, would come up to her room at suppertime and snap up the blind and open the window to show a part of the hospital's brick wall going pinkly light from the last of the sun. Or was it the sunrise? Rising out of a drugged sleep, it was scary not to know which. "What time is it?" Ingrid would moan, and she'd scrabble around on her dressing table, looking for her watch. "Six o'clock," Joan would say. But the words "six o'clock" wouldn't have any meaning for Ingrid—not until she could figure out where she was working, where she was supposed to be.

Smelling of the day's smells, Joan would plunk so heavily down on the bed it would bob like a boat on rough waters. She was working in the Case Room then; there was the sweet-sick blend of ether, Dettol, coffee. She'd fish the food she'd brought Ingrid out of a paper bag; peanut butter sandwiches she'd made up herself in the nurses' kitchen; bananas and cookies left over from supper in the cafeteria.

Eat, Hessie, she would say.

I'm not hungry.

You've got to eat.

Maybe they'll notice how thin I'm getting and give me time off to rest up.

Do you think they give a good goddamn?

They make us weigh ourselves every month, don't they?

You're a dreamer. Eat.

Ingrid knew she was slated to go back on duty in the OR after her time off; she knew she'd be put in with Tiny Baxter, the holy terror of the place—she was the only one in her class who hadn't worked with him. Yet maybe I should just leave now, she thought. I've tried everything but Emergency, I've seen it all now, and at that moment the May River delta came

into view, far below them, down to the left of the bus. Elm
trees grew on lush tracts of grass that stretched, in the way she
remembered, out into the river, but in the still August morning it all looked majestically altered; in the hazy pre-noon air
it had turned bridal, sensual, oriental. It made her know what
she wanted: she wanted to have a baby. This was what she
had liked best at the hospital—birth and babies. In fact, the
first birth had marked the beginning of a kind of Golden Age.
She'd moved from the Case Room to the Maternity Ward and
from there to the Nursery and had felt happy all the time,
especially in the Nursery, giving the babies their baths in the
generous big-blocked light of windy sunlit mornings that
seemed always on the promising edge of spring; or sitting
with three or four other students in the little windowless
feeding room at night, feeding the babies their night bottles
in a world so comfortably cut off from the rest of the hospital
that they might have been under the ocean or out in space.

Through the starboard windows of the bus she could see
the far-off green and yellow meadows of the most easterly tip
of Kingsmere Island. She knew the east end of that island
from a camping trip she'd taken there with her parents and
brother and sister years ago. She could even see the old field
they'd pitched their tent in—a wedge of green held in the
long V of what looked like two dark green hedges but which
up close was really a V of majestic old oak and beech trees.
She could recall pulling away from the island at last, in their
overloaded rowboat, and then half turning to glance back—
the morning sun and wind in their eyes like a message of
good health, the cupped cluck and squeak of the oars just
before they were raised up, two dripping white wooden
blades, in the pause to look back.

This was the summer her mother had decided she wanted
her children to call her Klara. At first this had brought out a
lot of bratty behaviour in them, but after a week or two it had
seemed normal. Their father they had decided to call Pup—
short for Papa. It had begun as a joke and Pup had answered
woof woof when they hailed him, and when they were walking through the woods he would now and then hitch a leg up

by a bush or small spruce tree to keep the joke going, but the changed names had carried on after this—they still all called him Pup or Puppie. And Klara they still all called Klara. They'd had their real pup, Digger, along with them too. The whole time they were on the island Digger's hindquarters were matted with dried mud and straw, and bits of straw and pendants of dried mud had swung from the dirty, stained, white wool fleece of his coat.

The mildew in that horrible tent! The mildew in their sodden straw mattresses. It was almost pleasant to look back at it all—it was awful but it was also so far back in the past. Terrible rainstorms the whole two weeks they were there. Sickness too—colds, boils, sore throats, sties. She got a sty. Pup got a boil on the back of his neck. The old man who owned the field they'd pitched their tent in was named. . .what? A name close to the name of the island. Kingsclear? Kingsqueer? No, something more ordinary. Kingston? Yes, Mr Kingston. Mr Kingston, the self-appointed local historian. Klara was crazy about him. She was crazy about the history of this whole area in general. It was only personal family history she didn't want to know about. It's wrong to talk about the past, she would say when one of them would be so foolish as to bring up some old grievance. Mr Kingston would invite Pup and Klara up to his place after dark, and Ingrid and her older brother, Arnie, and their little sister, Tina, would be left to their own devices down in the tent. A lot of giggly talk about sex and trying to scare each other with stories about graves in the woods just behind the grove of poplars where they peed; Arnie flicking the flashlight off and on and pretending to be the Green Hornet. The tent the colour of the pumpkin filling in a pumpkin pie and spotted as an old pear with mildew. Digger's black dog-freckles looking like mildew too. All the tent smells: sardines, straw, Jergen's Lotion, Ozonol. Digger smelling a little skunky and also of Jergen's Lotion because that's what Klara had rubbed his belly with after she'd shampooed his skunky fleece out in the river. A bad thunderstorm and Tina crying because the flashing and fearful cracks across the back of the sky scared her. Pup and Klara still up at Mr Kingston's. Arnie saying that if they started down to the tent and on their way got struck by lightning they would disappear in a blue flash of phosphorescence. The lightning gradually getting weaker, like a giant walking away from them through the woods and lackadaisically swinging his giant's flashlight so that it flicked on and off in the trees. Then the giant changing his mind and lashing back at them again, thrashing through the windy swish and crack of the forest, brighter and fiercer than ever. Then a smaller, more human-sized flashlight, bobbing hurriedly down toward them in the dark. "Robbers!" Arnie hissed and Ingrid and Tina whimpered and hooded their sheets up over their heads and played dead although they knew it was really the drenched Klara and Pup, accompanied by the old drenched historian coming down to tell them it was only a bad storm and they were not to be frightened.

Trying to be friendly, old Mr Kingston squatted beside their straw pallets and told them tales of the storms of his youth. Farmhands struck down and turned into idiots by lightning. Horses turned into galloping mad beasts and even driven insane. Babies born in fierce blizzards, in sleighs, out on the frozen river. Parents skating off to the city to buy Christmas gifts for their little children and never being heard from or seen by human eyes again. The old man looked ghoulish, crouched on the straw-strewn hard dirt floor of the tent in the flashlight's sinister, churchy light. He stank as well—his shoes of manure, his shirt-front of cooked mutton, his pants as if he had peed in them (but years ago), his pockets of raisins but with a cool burning breath in the smell, like peppermints. Also of old damp mattress and raincoat smells that were close to the tent's overpowering aroma of mildewed canvas and straw. "Those were the days," he cackled, and his laughter sounded broken and spooky. Pup and Klara looked a little alarmed—they did not approve of adults telling frightening stories to children. Possibly it was to distract him from more tall tales that Klara crouched down beside Ingrid and smoothed her hair back from her forehead as if she had a fever—Ingrid wanted to twist away and viciously cry out *no*—and said to the old man, "This poor little lady has got herself a bad sty." Old Mr Kingston made a joke about that—pretended he thought Klara meant a sty for the pigs. "So you've got yourself a sty there, have you, young lady? So you're living with the pigs?"

A moment of terrible embarrassment followed. The night before, Klara, singing Mr Kingston's praises while she'd ladled out hot brown beans for their supper around the campfire, had tempered her praise with a judgment. "But it's a crying shame the way he lives. That kitchen is a *sty*! He lets the chickens in there. He probably even lets in the pigs."

With Mr Kingston now crouched down among them, they felt wary and ashamed. Was it possible he'd been lurking nearby, eavesdropping in the poplars? It was possible. But then again, maybe not. Maybe not necessary for him to eavesdrop; it was said he had second sight. It was said that if he had a vision of you riding in a stage-coach and dressed to the hilt in old-fashioned clothes it meant you would die before sundown. They had all watched him divining for water. He had let them all have a try with his divining rod but only Pup was able to do it.

Like a surgeon, Mr Kingston held out his hand for Pup's flashlight and then shone it into Ingrid's swollen pink eye. In the tent-pole mirror before bedtime it had looked like the pink swell of the skin of the nostril of a person with a bad cold. The old man's pale blue eyes were more ancient and watery than ever in the unearthly light. Diagnostic, ruined, afraid of nothing. In his broken voice, but still peering with clinical fierceness into the eye, he said to Klara, "Are you wearing a wedding ring, missus?"

Klara slipped off her gold wedding band and placed it on his palm.

"This is what we recommend for the sty," said the old historian. "We rub the eye with this ring and in the morning the patient will be cured."

But Ingrid flounced away from him, crying, "I don't want a wedding ring rubbed on my eye, I don't, I don't!" and it ended with Mr Kingston going off looking a little bewildered, and Klara telling Ingrid that she was ashamed of her.

"But I don't like him."

"Nonsense, darling, of course you like him. He's a fascinating old local character."

"He *stinks.*"

"No need to be rude, now."

In the deep of the night a whispered argument between Pup and Klara. More about a sty, and pigs too. Pup saying, "But you can't use the child as a guinea pig," and Klara saying the child was spoiled. Pup saying, "I suggest we leave here tomorrow morning. We're all getting sick anyway. If we aren't all sick already."

"I'm not sick."

"No, no, of course not, but the children are. Arnie's got his sore throat, Tina coughs half the night, Ingrid has her sty."

Klara saying she'd told Mr Kingston they'd be staying for the weekend so they could go with him to the Kirkmeyer fair. "If we leave tomorrow we'll hurt his feelings."

Pup saying something about boil. Makes my blood boil? There's also my boil? Whatever it was, he got his way, because in the morning they did break camp, (the sun had come out brilliantly while they were taking down the tent before breakfast and with it a big wind that billowed and thudded at its canvas, making them feel like they were already out on the river) and then, shivering in their thin shorts and dew-dampened sandals, they'd shoved the boat, by now loaded up like an explorer's toboggan, down the sand that was the same cooked pumpkin colour as their tent, until the dory's nose was out in the powerful slow swing of the icy green water.

Klara, giving the boat its final shove from the shore—barefoot, sandals stuck into her raincoat pockets—lost her balance and slipped on the slimy stones near the strand line, dipping a corner of her grey poplin raincoat into the river. Then she lunged aboard, making the boat dip and wallow. As she made her way out to the prow—supporting herself with a brief but heavy plunge on each child's shoulder—Ingrid, with fastidious swiftness, jerked her knees away from the creepy cold greeting of the raincoat's dunked triangle.

On the far shore there was the movement of fleets of small clouds down over Cape Duncrannon. Thumbprints of shadow, thumbprints of light. And then, with a racing speed for its size, an immense dark cloud moving down over the whole massive treed bluff so that all of the Cape and even the coastal part of the river was suddenly steeped in day-dark. And right on the heels of this shadow, the sun. Moving down with cloudspeed, hellbent for the river, bringing its melancholy bounty of light.

Everything had changed so since then. Tina grown from little sister to sophisticated woman (when did this happen?); Klara and Tina thick as thieves; Digger dead. Probably by now even old Mr Kingston was dead.

But although Tina was now the sophisticated lady she was also the one who lived a young life—going to college in the town of Stettler, starring in plays put on by the Stettler Drama Guild, full of stories about her life away from home. One night last winter a gang of her friends from the Drama Guild had come to call on her at her dorm while she was washing her hair in the women's showers. She had come out to greet them wrapped in a short white terry robe, a white towel turbanning her wet hair, and "in no time at all they talked me into driving out to the airport with them, just as I was, to meet a friend of theirs who was flying up from Boston for the weekend," and she smiled at them with a small shrug in her smile, a shrug that seemed to say, but you know me— the compleat teen, the quintessential teen, the teen with a vengeance, that's why they all call me Teen, my darlings, I'm Teen, the teen above being a teen and therefore *damn* good at it, I'm Teen, the undisputed queen of terrible teendom. Out at the airport one of the men in the group had wrapped her up in a car blanket and then carried her, bride-style, across the snow-swept tarmac to the terminal. Inside he had set her down and unwrapped her and she had fished a pair of dark glasses out of her shoulder bag and then proceeded to parade barefoot—"nothing at all under the damn robe, my dears, I swear to God"—up and down the length of the dinky little airport, her phalanx of admirers jostling around her.

Ingrid could not picture this scene without feeling an envy

so intense it made her almost ill. Yet at the same time she was fascinated—by both Klara and Tina—and actually enjoyed thinking of them at home, busy with their exciting, irresponsible non-hospital lives. And now that Ingrid's and Tina's Danish cousin Kamille was visiting the family, the duo of Klara and Tina had become a trio, with Kamille being towed along as the silent partner—to evening meetings of the Ladies' Morning Musical Club in Port Charlotte, to university parties held by the Drama Guild people in Stettler—bringing her shyness and her scrubbed Danish glow to the late-night campus and club suppers of cold cuts and Brie and Algerian wine.

Kamille, who'd been in Canada five months already, was helping out with the housework and the music camp that Klara ran in the early part of the summer. Pup and Klara had invited her out from Copenhagen—they had sponsored her and paid her a small salary—but after she'd been in Canada for a year she planned to leave for the States. She was twenty-two and came from Klara's side of the family. She always dressed in black. Black pants, black T-shirts, black aprons, black umbrella. "Elegant," people said. "You can certainly tell she doesn't come from around *here*." This was a compliment, a supreme one. Kamille was also the most practical person her Canadian relatives had ever seen—she had sewn all her own black clothes, with the exception of the umbrella, she could make men's jackets and coats, she could even upholster chairs and sofas.

When Ingrid got out of the bus on Burton Street and started walking up the hill toward her house, she could see Kamille in the distance, on the front steps in her black clothes, shelling or peeling something. She looked classic, forebodingly right, against the grand white backdrop of Pup and Klara's Greek Revival house. Pup and Klara had bought the Annetteville place after Ingrid had started her training. When they got it, it was a hovel, but a hovel with grandeur— all partitioned and warped and cracked inside, but with a good foundation and a beautifully proportioned shell. They'd spent several thousand dollars fixing it up. They'd asked Ingrid if it would be okay if they took the two thousand dollars they'd kept in a fund for her education and used it for renovations for the house. "Klara figured you wouldn't be needing it since you won't be going to college," Pup said. This was true.

Ingrid approached the point where the driveway split, sweeping up on either side of a great heart of green grass.

"Hello, Ingrid," called Kamille. "We are having a party tonight! Tina has gone off to the liquor store. She has with her two missionaries."

Ingrid sat down on the steps beside her cousin. "Are there still missionaries in these parts?"

"These boys are Mormons," said Kamille. She spoke an emphatic British English. "They come from America." Her voice sounded very tender when she said America.

"You should call it the States, Kamille."

"The States," Kamille said, tender again. "Utah. Wyoming."

"Wyoming," Ingrid said. "I read a book about Wyoming when I was little. *My Friend Flicka*. About a horse." She would have to remember to ask the Wyoming Mormon if he knew Cheyenne.

Tina came back with the boys and the liquor. Getting out of the car she looked very svelte: slim white skirt; sleeveless rayon blouse; her pale hair done up into a chignon and stuck with ivory chopsticks. She brought the two Mormons—two lanky Americans with mouse-coloured crewcuts and attired in formal dark blue suits—over to the front of the house to introduce them to Ingrid. Ingrid hoped she wouldn't introduce her as her little sister, as she sometimes did. The terrible part about this was that whenever she did it people always believed her. But she didn't. She just said, "My sister, the nurse. Ingrid this is Elder Rodale. And this is Elder Clayton."

The lanky elders both shook hands with Ingrid.

"Sometimes also known as Al and Gary," Tina said. "I'm trying to talk them into staying for the party tonight. I've even promised them apple juice instead of punch in their paper cups. And they have to promise not to try to convert people." She smiled. They both smiled back at her although the one called Al looked a little uneasy. But Gary gave Tina a serious look. "We know how to behave," he said.

"Help me take this stuff inside," Tina said to him then, and they went into the house together. Al stood on the porch a moment, looking unhappy, then—devout enough to spy on his friend—followed them in.

"God," said Ingrid, "that Gary guy really seems to like Tina."

"I guess so," said Kamille. "The trouble is, Teen has invited an older man to this party. Someone she really likes. A Norwegian. She met him somewhere at someone's house. He's twenty-seven."

"What's his name?"

"Karl something."

"Oh *him*," Ingrid said, in the despairing voice people will use for someone they covet. "Karl Risvik. I thought that's who it would be." And she told Kamille everything she knew about this Karl. How he had come to Canada right after the war and learned English in no time at all. How he had done so brilliantly in high school and on the junior matriculation exams that the *Port Charlotte Herald* had written a special editorial about him. How his father was a veterinarian and had once saved the life of their late dog Digger. How, the first time Digger was almost dying she and Klara had driven him all the way to the vet's place, and how, while they were there they saw this Karl (a college boy by now) and how, going back home in the car, she'd said to her mother, "That's the man I'm going to marry."

"Tina is very nervous," said Kamille.

At supper that night Tina put all her energy into telling funny stories to Gary. Al continued to look unhappy. Ingrid asked him if he was the one who came from Wyoming. He said he was. She asked him if he'd read *My Friend Flicka* and he said he had. She told him she'd read it when she was young, that she'd thought it was a very beautiful book. Al asked her if she'd read *The Book of Mormon*. She said no. "*The Book of Mormon* is a very beautiful book too," he said. "It's an even more beautiful book than *My Friend Flicka*." They all laughed. Except Kamille. She was banging lids on counters and slapping plates on the table. She said to the Mormons, "These girls! They are not very domestic!"

This was true but it hadn't always been that way. At fourteen, fifteen, sixteen, Ingrid had worked as a cook in her mother's music camp, cooking meals for the campers. She'd made pails of puddings and basins of macaroni salad and jugs of custard sauce to pour over Lemon Snow. In her spare time she read *Fanny Farmer's Boston Cooking School Cookbook*. On Sundays she made Maryland Chicken and in the middle of the week she made something the mother of one of her campers had taught her to do: ham and pineapple slices fried together, then simmered in Coca Cola. In the winters it was the same, but then she would cook in smaller quantities. She would come home from school right after the last class and concoct pies, soufflés, casseroles, layer cakes, cookies. But then she went into training in Port Charlotte and learned what real work was. Real work wasn't anything like cooking for thirty children; real work was something that made you too tired to read, or even eat. They usually did have some time off in the middle of the day though, but only if they weren't too far behind in their work, and even then it was tied in with lunch hour or a class they had to go to. These classes were presided over by the doctors in a classroom in the basement of the nurses' residence. One of these doctors, in a class on obstetrics and gynaecology, had distinguished himself by defining menstruation as "the weeping of the disappointed uterus." They had a lot of fun with that afterward. They would go around saying to each other, "Is your uterus disappointed? Has it wept yet?" Or they would say, "Well, my dears, my *uterus* may be disappointed, but *I* sure as hell am not."

After she'd started her nurses' training though, Ingrid lost all interest in cooking—lost interest, in fact, in any work she did not strictly have to do. She would come home on days off and sit and smoke or stare into space. Sometimes she would go out for walks, interrupted by frequent stops so she could lie down in the grass and rest. Sometimes, even long past the season for it, she would go down to the river and languidly swim. Sometimes she would haul an old mattress out of the shed (this was at their old place, down at Gully Bay) and drag it over to the apple orchard and lie there and watch the yellow leaves delicately detach themselves from the trees to sail to the grass all around her mattress. And she couldn't be on any mattress long—either indoors or out in the orchard—before she would fall asleep.

Tina was describing Ingrid to Gary. "Ingrid is a sweet person," she said. "Always kind to everyone." There was something about this that made Ingrid uneasy but she wasn't sure what it was. Listening for irony, she couldn't quite believe that she wasn't hearing any.

After supper Tina washed the dishes and gave the Mormons matching tea towels so they could help her dry them. Kamille and Ingrid went out into the back garden to pick flowers for the front room and the parlour. They walked single file along the rows of the vegetable and flower garden. The lower leaves' cold spittle trailed itself along their bare ankles. The sun was going down; it was too quickly chilly. Kamille pulled a pair of stork-billed scissors out of the pocket of her black apron and when she cut the flowers' hairy green stems they released a cold milky discharge that made Ingrid recall feeding the babies their night bottles in the hospital nursery and shaking the warm drops of milk onto the pulse part of her wrist.

They hurried into the house and poked the flowers into vases. While Ingrid was lighting the candles, Kamille went into the kitchen and fetched a tray with six tall tumblers of water on it. After she'd come back into the front room, she carried a drink of water to each vase of flowers and, with her bizarre Scandinavian efficiency, poured it in. It was amazing how it altered the place, to light candles, to arrange flowers. Now it looked polished and proper, a house-in-waiting. They linked arms and ran up the dark stairs to change into their dresses.

Ingrid went into the room she shared with Tina. She could feel excitement rising up from the flickering rooms below her; could smell the cold fragrance of the flowers. It was as if the house had become an enemy but a charming enemy. She was feeling the exhilarated dread she always felt just before a party. It seemed to be extremely important to arrange to speak calmly. "What are you wearing tonight?" she asked Tina.

Tina lifted her red taffeta dress out of her closet and laid it down on her bed. A dress Ingrid liked, but it was too tight for her across the breasts.

"Can I wear the green one, then?"

Tina lifted out the green dress and laid it down beside the red one. Ingrid coveted the green dress; it was almost exactly the colour of the gowns they used in the OR, but a little softer, embossed with little flowers that were also green but slightly lighter, almost silver. She held it up to herself in front of the mirror. It was a colour that went well with tanned skin.

"On second thought," said Tina, drawing the green dress away from Ingrid, "I think I'll wear this one myself."

"What'll I wear then?"

"Borrow something from Klara."

"Where *is* Klara, anyway?"

"Off gallivanting with Pup."

Ingrid went into Klara's dressing-room. Everything in there was in zippered bags. Rich formal things, for winter and for Klara's concert recitals. She lifted out a pleated black cocktail dress and pulled it on. Black went well with tanned skin. She searched the shoe bags and found a pair of gold sandals. She strapped them on and went over to her mother's dressing table in them. She unstoppered her perfumes and sniffed them. She dabbed Tigress on her wrists and Fleurs des Rocailles between her breasts. She felt uneasy with Klara, but not with Klara's clothes. Klara never minded lending her daughters things; she had more clothes than either of them; not just clothes for concert tours but young clothes—plaid dresses, square dance skirts. Sometimes she would even *give* Ingrid and Tina clothes, things she'd simply got tired of wearing. There was a certain innocence about their mother— she was in so many ways innocent of the dull and thankless responsibilities of parenthood. When they were little children and she embraced them, her embraces were almost never to celebrate *them*, her children; they were rather entreaties to her children to endorse some fine quality in herself. She used to hug them and say, "Do you know how lucky you are to have a mother who doesn't smell? I never smell, do you realize that? I always smell sweet." They would wriggle away from her as soon as seemed decent. Or at least Ingrid would; she really could not bear it, being caught in a hug and forced to admit things.

Downstairs the doorbell rang and Ingrid ran down to answer it. A lot of people she didn't know were standing there, a shy group, wondering who she was.

"Come in," she urged them. "I'll call Tina."

Tina came down then, and Kamille and the Mormons came down behind her.

Next came Pup and Klara. They had two old friends in tow, Dorie and Kay, two older women who had been friends of the family for years and who worked as photographers in Port Fairweather.

Pup walked through the party like a man who's given himself, on pain of death, orders not to flee. Ingrid felt affection for him—for his fine grey eyes, his Napoleon forehead, his shyness. He was very dark for a Dane—had olive skin and dry dark hair that was mismatched to his moustache, which was stained yellow under the nostrils from years of clearing salty discharge from his sinuses. He made his way awkwardly among the party guests and then beat a retreat to the kitchen, but Klara, looking very pretty in a red dirndl skirt and a white-embroidered white blouse with a white cardigan caped over it, walked about greeting people. And as she greeted she sparkled. But there was something strict and tight in her sparkle. She said to Ingrid, "I met your old friend Ian Carmichael and told him to come join in the fun."

Ingrid stared at her mother. "We don't even see each other any more."

But Klara was already gazing across the room at a group of people she wanted to say hello to. She said, "It doesn't matter.

There'll be plenty of other people for him to talk to."

Knowing that Ian Carmichael was coming, Ingrid thought with alarm of his British shyness. His shyness and her shyness had together added up to two such explosive shynesses that when she was with him she sometimes feared the silent high whine of tension would kill them both. Tina and Kamille had laughed at him, and Tina had said, "How can you go out with someone like that? He's so falsely whimsical. And he has BO." And one of the girls at the nurses' residence had laughed at him too, after she'd seen him coming to fetch Ingrid one rainy green spring evening, wearing a black suit and flapping black raincoat and carrying a high-hoisted black umbrella. "Is your boyfriend a priest or an absent-minded professor or what?" was the question she had pretended to want the answer to. "Anyways, I'll say this much for the two of you—you suit each other."

How like Klara not to listen, thought Ingrid bitterly, and for a few moments she was gripped by her old intense dislike for her mother. When she was a kid Klara used to get her to read aloud to her, was forever calling out to her (from her bath, from her bed), "Darling, come and read to me!" She remembered how she had felt: both honoured and interfered with. But of course as she had got older, less and less honoured, more and more interfered with. Still, it had taken her some time to discover how intensely Klara desired attention. Even when she had been, technically speaking, audience, she had renounced the role; in her bath and as she slept, always and everywhere, she was centre stage. So it must have been only the act that mattered. *Being read to.* The words had been mere background music to the performance of Klara listening. Ingrid was sure her mother hadn't heard more than a key phrase or two a page; the words seemed to wash over her like ocean water, and with that kind of attention span her tastes had naturally been catholic—Gogol, A.J. Cronin, it was all the same to her.

Ian Carmichael arrived then, speak of the devil, but was such a wounded-eyed devil—tonight in a hairy dark brown tweed jacket and with an unhappy hand thrust into the pocket of a pair of new-looking flannels—that Ingrid couldn't bear to look at him, and so the next time the doorbell rang and Tina ran for it, Ingrid, in order to have something to do, ran for it too.

Karl, the Norwegian, was standing on the doorstep. He was Ingrid's height with hair that was a faded kinky orange. His V-shaped smile and light mocking eyes gave the impression of being more in cahoots with each other than most people's eyes and smiles did. He bowed, and there was an air of parody (of Tina? of Ingrid? of himself?) in his bow. Tina, with a surprising tremor in her voice, said, "This is my sister, Ingrid, the nurse, I don't think you've met?" and he stared at Ingrid as if to say, definitely not—I'd remember if we had.

Karl asked Ingrid for the first dance. After this, he went off to look for "my hostess." Then one of the officers from the nearby army camp asked her to join in a Virginia Reel, then the boy who delivered the family's eggs from a farm in Bramley asked her, then Karl again, then the officer from the camp. She was hardly ever *not* dancing. She didn't know how to account for this. She didn't know if it was her mother's sexy low-cut black cocktail dress or if it was the fact that she hadn't slept for a night, a day, plus half of another night and so carried a fast girl's longing for bed in her eyes.

Sometime after midnight, she thought of her classmates back in the OR: pictured them getting ready to drag themselves awake after their midnight nap up on the stretchers in the stretcher room; pictured them staggering into the scrub room to scour their arms and hands with hospital soap and harsh bristle brushes; pictured them scouring and scrubbing until their hands and arms were raw and freezing and tingling to their fingertips, the only parts of their sleepy bodies that were awake, whereas with her it was the exact opposite and her arms, hung around the necks of men she danced with, were feeling limp, drugged—crossed at the wrists behind small-town necks and thick farm-boy necks, drooping as heavy-lidded eyes must droop. And although it was true that she was feeling attracted to Karl—Tina's face, an unhappily bobbing moon in the Virginia Reel, confirmed this—she was feeling even more attracted to the officer from the camp she'd danced with the most. She even, from a distance, was feeling attracted to Ian; he was looking so manly and lonely, huddled by himself into a corner and darkly nursing a drink. In fact, popularity had made her feel grown-up and fond toward the whole world. She even felt tender toward Gary, who she overheard saying seriously, but with quiet missionary triumph, to a girl with too-lipsticked lips, "It's not our *name*, it's a form of address. You see, we are Mormon missionaries. . . ." She thought, So this is what it's like to be in demand. And she was able to understand for the first time how popular girls could get to be so kind, so good-natured. Why not, after all? The world made way for you.

At two o'clock Ingrid said her good-nights to Karl and the soldier and went up the stairs to the room she now thought of as Tina's room, stepped out of her clothes, fell into bed, immediately fell into sleep. But all night she kept dreaming that she had insomnia, that she had to get up early to work a middle-of-the-night shift at the hospital. She had no alarm clock. Her bedroom was in a little alcove off the Emergency wing. At one point, she half-awakened when Tina came in in the dark, heard an angry cry-whisper ("Damn!") heard her hiss at something (a run in a stocking?), then fell through the hiss and web of the moment to a place where Ian Carmichael, wearing a flapping white doctor's coat, came hurrying by her. But not so fast she couldn't see, in the brilliant hospital light bathing both him and her alcove, the betrayed look he cast down upon her. But then he said something odd to someone nearby: "This room smells like magazines."

The next morning while Tina and Ingrid were still in their bedroom, combing out their hair before breakfast, Tina said to Ingrid, "Do you know what Gary said last night about you?"

"You mean Gary the Mormon?"

"You don't have to keep calling him Gary the Mormon like that."

"I'm sorry. What did he say?"

"He said, 'Do you still think Ingrid is a sweet person and a thoughtful person and kind to everyone *now*?'"

Ingrid didn't dare to meet Tina's eyes in the mirror. She

busied herself with sliding her comb and brush away in a drawer and then with rubbing scented cream into the insides of her wrists. Behind her she could hear Tina say in a voice low with knowledge and bitterness, "I knew right away that Risvik was falling for you. Right when you met each other at the door. He had such a dumb, enthralled look."

Everyone was at the table when Tina and Ingrid came down to the kitchen. All the people who'd stayed the night—Karl, Gary and Al, Dorie and Kay. Karl fetched a chair for Ingrid and fitted it in beside his own. A picnic was being planned. They were all supposed to drive down to Booth River Cove in Dorie's car. Kamille had already made the sandwiches.

Gary and Al said they'd have to stay in town, calling on people. Kay said she had a headache. This was the excuse Ingrid had planned to use and so she said, "That's funny, I have a headache too," and everyone laughed.

Karl leaned over and whispered, "But you're coming anyway, aren't you?"

She whispered, "No." A few minutes later Klara excused herself from the table and a moment after this she called down to Ingrid from her room.

When Ingrid got up there Klara was in the little bathroom adjoining her dressing room, running a glass of water. She shook two aspirins out of a bottle and handed them and the drink to Ingrid. "Tina has had lots of boyfriends," she said. The terrible corollary to this hung unspoken between them. "Take these," she said. Ingrid took them. Why not? She wanted to go on the picnic. She wanted to be *ordered to go*.

Tina came into the room then and closed the door tightly behind her. "It's not fair if Ingrid comes," she said.

"Teen, darling," Klara cried tenderly to her. "Don't take this too hard! You've had lots of boyfriends, and you'll have many more." She threw her an imploring look. "But facts are facts, darling. Karl seems to care for Ingrid."

Tina started to cry. And because her little sister had always been their mother's little darling, Ingrid stood rubbing the flat of her hand along the warm window sill, amazed and uneasy.

Tina talked a great deal on the way to the cove. And after they'd found a place to eat and had finished eating and had taken shelter in an old covered bridge to wait out the rain that they'd feared and predicted all the way there she started to sing. Songs from *South Pacific*, *Oklahoma*, *Singin' in the Rain*, *An American in Paris*. She sang well, in a light, sad, chanteusey voice, but Ingrid could tell that Karl didn't care for that kind of thing, and after Tina had been singing for a while Ingrid leaned back against the wall of the bridge and closed her eyes.

The following morning she was back on another planet—in the Ear, Nose and Throat Room, setting up a tray for a tonsillectomy. In the room with her were an intern—an emotional-eyed East Indian, Dr Rupert Advani—and a circulating nurse, Mrs Shirley Jenkins. Jenkins was newly graduated, newly married. She was the whitest person Ingrid had ever seen; she had the whitest face and big greyish-white false teeth. A sour face, a doughy face, out for blood. She was chewing gum—how could she do that, with her clackety teeth?—and picking at a scab on her elbow.

Ingrid was threading little crescent-shaped suture needles —some with catgut, some with black silk. There was also a glass ampoule of a mauve-tinged liquid; she would be needing to have it open. She scanned the tray for a file to file its neck with. There wasn't one. "I'll be needing a file," she said to Jenkins.

Jenkins tied on her mask and came into the sterile area. "For what?"

"This." Holding it up.

"Haven't you got a pair of scissors there?"

"Scissors?"

"That's what I said, lady. Hit it at the neck with the scissors."

Ingrid didn't move; she was finding it difficult to breathe.

"You heard me, lady. Hit it."

"But in class they told us we must never use scissors to break—"

Jenkins had a staff nurse's contempt for anything learned

in class. "That was *in class*," she said. "You're here now, remember?"

Ingrid picked up the scissors and struck the ampoule at the neck. Disaster—as Miss Plowright had warned them in class. Tiny shreds of glass, like a rain of crystal fingernail slivers, lay over everything: the piles of gauze squares, the pyramids of cotton balls, the pristine, once-bare blades of the instruments. "*Now* you've done it," said Jenkins, and the tears in Ingrid's eyes gave her double the number of knife blades.

Then another nurse came in and held the door open for Dr Tiny Baxter, who with his scrubbed hands raised, was coming in to be gloved.

"Mother of God, what's been going on in here?" he howled when he saw the carnage on the tray. Above his white mask, his eyes were burning, enraged.

"Bring a new tray," he barked at Jenkins, and a new tray was brought over and with speed—but also with the proper medical ceremony—unwrapped of its beige linen wrappings. Jenkins (dead-eyed, giving away nothing) tore the gloves off Ingrid, in case they'd been powdered or cut by bits of glass. Being torn off, they made two sucking slaps. Ingrid was sent out to scrub again. A humiliated scrubbing that seemed less connected to hygiene than to transgression. When she came back in she had to be re-gloved and then she had to start threading suture needles again. Advani and Jenkins and Baxter talked a little, about a fishing trip that Baxter had just come back from, but there were terrible tracts of silence, too, when she imagined that they were all just standing there with their eyes riveted on the tray. This time when she looked for a file to file the ampoule with it was there, where it should be, to the right of the ampoule. She filed the neck and it broke off clean.

"There," said Tiny Baxter, in a voice that sounded both patronizing and spookily gentle when he came over to peer at the set-up. "It's always best to do things right in the first place. Saves time."

Advani's East Indian eyes—their whites white, their darks liquid with recognition of the irony of Baxter's words—sent an emotional beam of sympathy to Ingrid. And the next morning, when Tiny Baxter walked in, Ingrid understood that Advani had told him about the ampoule incident—it was the only explanation—because both Advani and Baxter were openly kind to her, and Baxter's voice, when he spoke to Jenkins, had a fine thrilling edge of contempt to it. So after this it was very pleasant, really, working there. Baxter was very patient, if patience was required, and it hardly seemed to be since it was clear that she could do no wrong. And in the middle of that week there was a letter from Karl. He was coming to Port Charlotte two days later and wondered if he could see her. Maybe they could go to a beach, he wrote. He signed the letter Love.

On the beach at Cape Bonner—they had to drive out to it along a shantytown road that had been named, at war's end, the Burma Road—Karl told Ingrid about growing up in Norway during the war and about coming to Canada in 1945, when he was sixteen, and about how people had laughed at him when he went out skating because he wore britches and knee-socks. He told her about going to school in Oslo in '42, '43, and about trying to get in the back end of the soup line so he could get more of the meat that sank to the soup pot's bottom. Ingrid found she liked him even better for the romance and deprivations of his past. He told her that a Norwegian Nazi had been shot by someone from the Underground in the street right in front of his school. He said that at the end of the war the Americans had wanted to make a goodwill gesture to the Norwegians (who had suffered so much) and had hit on the idea of sending over a freighter filled with peanut butter, but that the Norwegians had found it, when it arrived, to be revolting stuff—*they* thought the goodwill boat was filled with. . .excrement. "The Norwegians were hungry," said Karl. "But they were not *that* hungry."

Ingrid smiled. "Speaking of. . .excrement," she said, "I should tell you about my life at the hospital." His turn to smile. But she only told him the funny things; she didn't want him to know she was thinking of leaving there. It was her secret. She would move when she was ready. She saw it happening on a clear fall day. She saw herself decently, adultly concealing her pleasure at getting free. She saw herself walking out of the nurses' residence carrying a small overnight case, her coat folded neatly over her arm; she saw how her eyes would give the impression of being nobly infatuated with a far horizon, like the eyes of a Red Cross nurse in one of the wartime posters of her childhood.

Reclining on an elbow, she told him stories of hospital life. She told him about Crazy Jake, the head orderly in the OR; she told him about the chief anaesthetist in Emergency, Dr Wyse, with his bedroom eyes; she told him about the grim frog-faced supervisor everyone called Napoleon because she patrolled the hallways of the nurses' residence with one hand thrust into the slit of her nurse's cape.

Karl said, "I've been having some trouble with abdominal pain." And he told Ingrid that a surgeon in Hoyt, the city where he was living with his parents for the summer, had booked him for an exploratory abdominal operation in three weeks' time.

"Well, don't worry," she said. "It's a common operation. People come into the OR for it every day." In fact she felt positive there wouldn't be anything terribly wrong with him. She had never had a patient his age with anything terminal or even serious. Chronic appendicitis, she thought, that's all it'll be. She dug up a handful of damp sand and breathed in its dry peaty smell; dug into the hot dry sand behind her and picked up a handful of that, sieved it down on his knuckles.

He was looking extremely depressed. "He says he'll be taking my appendix out, too."

"They usually do do that," she said, smiling and sieving. "Makes sense. While they're in there."

On Ingrid's next day off, Karl couldn't get down to Port Charlotte and so she decided to go out to the Gully Bay house. Pup and Tina and Kamille were supposed to be out there. After she'd finished her three-thirty shift, Ingrid took a bus out to the closest ferry. This was a paddlewheel boat, bigger than either of the cable ferries, and with a longer run. Two miles over the water, among little islands, across a bay. The boat made a wake of beery black water. She sat on the wake-end and gazed at the left-hand side of the sky ahead. It had been washed almost clear by an earlier rain and had produced, with a kind of celestial sportiveness, a whole flock of little clouds, golden gulls, low over Gamblers' Island. But after fifteen minutes the ferry veered south and left the view of Gamblers' behind. All the south-shore islands were much smaller than Gamblers'—small groves of cedar trees riding the darkening water. How strange life was! Three weeks ago she was without hope and now she had a lover. It came to her then that everything had come to her late, and acknowledging this, she believed what she supposed all romantics must need to believe: that the abundance of choices a person would get from promiscuity, say, would rule out the possibility of the right choice. And that lateness guaranteed perfection. As the ferry came flushing and churning up to the Gully Bay dock, she remembered that Tiny Baxter liked to fish. And then the dock's drawbridge came down and they were there, they had crossed it, a two-mile moat of water. She decided not to hitch a ride to the home. She wanted to be by herself a little longer. She wanted to walk and to carry the feeling of being loved, with her into the country night.

The first part of the road ran through a thick wood. Then there was a long grove of birch trees with the occasional summer cottage in it, then the start of the farming country. After the cottages there were no paint jobs at all, only old grey barns and old Victorian farmhouses, all gone grey too; even the porch columns and gingerbread trim were grey; and no flower gardens either, only the most undemanding shrubbery —bushes that carried, in spring, lilacs and cinnamon roses, and all without flowers now, in simple clear-aired September. These farms already stood in shadow. Only the high pastures, still held in the sun, burned green. She felt like someone in a Russian novel. As if many years had passed since she had last seen her village. As if, by the time she got there, everyone would be dead, or moved away, or married to someone else.

As she approached the Hessellund house, also grey except for the west wall, which had long ago been painted a pale yellow, she could smell fish frying. She walked into the kitchen. Kamille was at the stove, carefully laying leaf-shapes of white fish down in flour before she consigned them to the frying pan. She was wearing one of her black skirts and a black cotton T-shirt. There was a thunderhead of white flour-clouds above the horizon of her skirtband.

"Hello, Kamille."

Kamille didn't answer.

"I walked here from the ferry."

Kamille lifted a floury leaf-shape up from the flour plate and laid it down in the pan.

"Smells good."

Kamille turned her back to her and opened a window.

Ingrid walked down the hallway. Kamille and Tina were going to gang up on her, then, because the way they'd see it, she was the flirt who'd stolen Karl from Tina. This made her start to feel fearful of seeing Tina; Tina could be so vicious and witty. Then she did see her, through the parlour window, out on the terrace, standing very erect in a high-necked flowered dress, her ivory chopsticks stuck into her chignon. Pup was off to her right, talking to two solid men who could have been insurance agents. Or more Mormons? No—Tina, a cool-looking hostess, was holding a tray of drinks.

Ingrid took a deep breath and stepped out onto the terrace.

"You're just in time for supper!" Pup called out to her.

Tina made a wide berth around her with the drink tray. "Oh, it's *her*," she remarked in a clear, bored voice.

Ingrid called out to Pup that she had already eaten. Then she walked down to the shed by the barn and got out a pail and shovel and went over to the potato garden to dig up some worms for Tiny Baxter. After this, she went for a walk to the beach and thought about Karl. Also, because it couldn't be helped, about Tina and Kamille. But to hell with *them*, she thought. They can't shame me into giving him up. And they can't shame me into not thinking about him, either. I'll think about him just as much as I damn well please. When she ducked into the woods to make the trip back to the house, she found places where they could lie down together.

When she got back, the kitchen was in darkness, so she went in there and made herself a supper of jam sandwiches and tea and transferred the worms from the pail to a jelly jar. From Kamille's room she could hear dance music on the radio and Tina's and Kamille's bursts and snorts of excluding laughter. She felt stung.

She stepped outside again. The yard was dark. She carried the tea and her cigarettes over to the shed where she'd heard Pup sawing wood earlier, when she'd come back from the beach.

In the old days, while Klara was away on tour giving piano recitals in small towns all over the Maritimes (under the auspices of the Ladies' Morning Musical Club), Pup used to look after the children. In her absence, they were all very peaceful and lazy together. When she came back, to remind them of the sloth they had lived in while she was away, she used to make them clean house. And as they cleaned she would change their jobs around. If a child was in the middle of washing the dinner dishes she would send her off to wash the bathroom floor; if a child was arranging a bouquet of flowers she'd picked—there were always flowers on the table when Klara was at home, she was always sending people out to pick them—she'd tell the child to let her do that and she'd send her off to fold the laundry. She was filled with a violent nervous energy, she was restless, she shifted furniture around —sometimes juggled whole rooms, so that bedrooms would move downstairs and sitting-rooms upstairs; she cooked impulsively and well; made magnificent potluck evening buffets; used her own herbs; founded and ran a summer music camp; gave piano lessons; gave lectures and recitals to the Ladies' Morning Musical Club in Port Charlotte; went to all the local auctions (recklessly driving a pick-up truck); bought carloads of ten-cent chairs and two-dollar chests of drawers; didn't have the patience to sand these pieces down but was so wild to see what they looked like under their chipped cream paint that she would take nine or ten pails of lye-water out to the back of the house and slash them over the chests and chairs. That part of the lawn was always a livid chemical yellow. And sometimes, after having done too much, she would lie on the floor in her bedroom and scream and beat her heels onto the floor. And sometimes, after the heel-beating, she wouldn't speak for days. When she went off again they wouldn't move a thing. Not a picture, not an ornament. They wouldn't even bother to pick flowers. They were all around them anyway, in the fields. Instead of the flowers being the table's centrepiece, the children became the flowers'. They lay out in the fields of them and read—*The Wind in the Willows*, *King of the Wind*, *The Ship that Flew* —their bare legs cross-hatched, engraved by grass.

The next day was Ingrid's last day in the OR. She brought the jelly jar of worms for Tiny Baxter over there in the morning, hidden under her cape, and stowed them above the coffee-cup shelf in the stretcher room. After lunch she transferred them to the doctors' and staff-nurses' room. When they'd finished the last case she went into the doctors' room and stood there a while, looking across the sand flats to the suburbs of Port Fairweather. Port Looneyville, some of the nurses called it, because the Provincial Asylum for the Mentally Ill was over there. She could see bits of its whitewashed back wing, which was here and there partly shielded by tall, dark fir trees, perched grimly above the rooftops of the lower town. She had brought a present to the hospital only once before, to a patient she'd got attached to. A woman who was dying of cancer of the bladder. She had been on her way back to the residence after a day off and had seen some children selling bunches of mayflowers outside the bus depot east of Bucksfield. She saw that someone had moved the jelly jar of worms. Maybe Baxter had. Maybe he'd thought, *Worms! How pathetic.*

The door opened. "So you have brought me some worms," he said.

"Yes."

"Well, I'd like to thank you very much."

"I hope you enjoy them," she said, horribly embarrassed.

"Oh I will, I will. I'll be going up to the cottage this weekend again so I'll be making good use of them then." But he was studying her while pretending not to. He asked her if she would like some coffee.

Really no. But she said yes.

He went over to the coffee urn by the sink and filled up two paper cups, then carried them over to the window and handed one of them to her. They both sipped, looking out the window, until Baxter broke the silence by saying, "You're an intelligent girl—I wonder that you didn't study to be a doctor."

"I never thought of being a doctor. In fact," she said, surprising herself, and for some reason on the edge of tears, "I've been thinking of giving all of this up." He turned and gave her a quick, worried look. "The nursing, I mean," she said. At this he seemed to feel free to look away from her. He gazed out the window. He squinted. He communed with the view of the flats.

After a time (an age, it felt like) he said, "You know, that might not be such a bad idea at that." And then he was paged on the PA, wanted in the Recovery Room. He tossed his cup into the garbage pail and grabbed up his cap from one of the stretchers. "Be good," he said, fitting it on.

After he'd gone she started to cry. It was the attention, she was sure of it; she couldn't bear it when people paid attention to her.

She was transferred to Emergency, days. She liked it there. It was the first place she'd worked where they weren't short staffed. And she liked the people she was working with— Smitty Cooper, Ginny Hilliard, McBride, Becky Fullerton. Her first Wednesday off, Karl was able to get his father's car and drive down from Hoyt. He could stay overnight, so they drove out to the ferry at Point Jerusalem and rode across the water to Gully Bay. Klara was at the Gully Bay house and was expecting them and seemed overjoyed to see them. She was wearing a pink towel hung boxer-style around her neck; she had just washed her hair. When she gave formal parties she always did her hair up into a dignified confection of braids and buns—using her own young braids, kept in a hat box—but now it hung fair and fluffy down to her shoulders. She was barefoot, perfumed. She gave them each a hard, theatrical hug. She had hot drinks already fixed for them and a fire in the fireplace. Ingrid got the impression that Klara thought she'd dreamed them up, that they were her production. She wanted to say to her: listen, this would have happened any-way—he's already told me that my coming on that picnic didn't make any difference, we would have seen each other again, he's crazy about me. And he never was interested in Tina—not seriously; he thinks she likes herself too much.

Klara took Karl on a tour of the house and showed him the paintings and the things from Europe and her "country piano." She said, "Later, if you'd like, I'll play for you." Karl said that would be marvellous. And when Karl and Ingrid went out for a walk after they'd done the dishes Klara came with them. By then there were big clouds—nicotine-stained at their edges, thin as cigarette smoke—racing darkly across the sky. It was the first night that summer seemed conclusively over. Even the river had got more wild and fall-like; they could hear the waves coming in harder against the beach. Karl held hands with Klara. They swung their hands back and forth like two children. Ingrid's hand he lifted into his pocket with his own. He made love to her between all her fingers with his thumb. "Isn't this inspiring?" cried Klara, sniffing the wind, inhaling the view of the sky and the river.

On the way down the pasture hill, making their way back to the house—how unwelcoming it looked! All the windows were dark and only the porch light was on, illuminating the dark mounds of the lilac bushes that stood guard at each side of the door and were now being bowed back and then down by the wind—Ingrid could feel how intensely both she and Karl were conspiring to ditch Klara. She could feel it in her desire for him, and in the reassuringly insistent way his thumb kept rubbing her between her two middle fingers. But they were approaching the house and the deed still had not been done. And looked in danger of not being done, for Karl was still swinging hands with Klara, and Klara was still looking flushed with pleasure, as if she had plans for them (cocoa maybe, or a marshmallow roast on the beach). Ingrid inwardly moaned, oh Lord, we'll never get away from her now, but a few moments later Karl lifted her hand out of his pocket and then drew her to him with his free arm and said firmly to Klara, "Now Ingrid and I will just be going off for a walk by ourselves."

Klara, startled, said, "Oh," but then quickly rallied with a "Fine!"

In the weakening light, Karl and Ingrid walked across a field of tall grass to the cedar grove at the south boundary of the farm. But at the logging-road gateway into the woods they turned to look back. They could tell Klara was out in the kitchen; the only lights on were in the converted shed that was attached to the west (kitchen) wing of the house. Are her feelings hurt? Ingrid wondered. If they are, there'll be hell to pay tomorrow. Don't think about it. She took Karl's hand and they ducked into the scratchy bower of the woods.

Karl said, "She's awfully demanding to be with, isn't she?"

She felt grateful to him; said, "Yes, she is."

"You take more after your father, I think. You have his eyes."

She was pleased, glanced warmly up at him in the dark.

"But why do you call him Pup? It makes him sound like a runty little fox terrier or something."

"I don't know." She leaned back against a birch tree and placed her hands on his shoulders, imagining herself the heroine of a novel set in wartime, saying a heroic farewell to her lover. "I always think of it being short for Papa. I always hear the 'ah.'"

He cupped her breasts, then started to knead them; worked his knee in between her thighs. He could make her feel excited so fast. He said, "I am the doctor, you are the patient —say 'ah.'" They laughed, then quickly stopped; kissed. When they emerged from the kiss, Ingrid, smiling, said *"ah,"* and then they laughed again and quickly stopped laughing again and kissed again.

When they walked deeper into the woods they found a little clearing with tall dark spruce and cedar trees ringed around it. It had a spooky, holy look. "We used to have picnics here sometimes—on Sundays." Were we a happy family in those days? she wondered. She remembered worshipping her mother. She remembered how they used to carry their lunch out to the dandelioned slope at the back of the house. Ingrid always sat in the shade of the crab apple tree with her father because she was his honey and because she didn't like the taste of her milk once the sun had got on it. But it was her mother she dreamed of as she sat beside her father. She dreamed of having a long closet filled with silky and darkly glittery dresses like hers; she dreamed of getting the kind of applause Klara got when she and her students gave their annual violin and piano recital in the auditorium of the May River high school. She dreamed of growing up to have breasts like hers.

The next morning Ingrid woke up to the sound of Vivaldi on the record player, the Double Trumpet Concerto in C Major; also the smells of coffee, breakfast cooking. She ran downstairs in her nightgown. Klara was standing at the stove, frowning. Her hair had been harshly brushed, tied back; she was wearing a sky-blue sundress. She was frying French toast in one pan and scrambling eggs with chives in another. In the big black skillet bacon was spitting. On the counter beside the stove there was a plate of tomato slices waiting to be added to the bacon. She had also made muffins, put peach jam in a blue bowl and strawberry jam (wild) in a clear glass dish. And she had picked fresh field flowers for the table, poured orange juice into wine goblets, made up pots of both coffee and tea.

"My God," Ingrid said. "This is fantastic." In truth she thought it weird, excessive, showing off. Klara didn't even make breakfasts ordinarily, except on Sundays. On weekdays she always took her breakfast in bed, brought in to her by Pup, on a tray. Soft-boiled egg; thin slice of rye bread toast smeared with honey; pot of green tea.

"I suppose I better put all this in the oven to keep it warm," said Klara. She seemed to be feeling bitter about something.

"I'll go wake Karl."

"But fix yourself up *first*," Klara said.

Ingrid went up to her room and pulled off her nightgown. She inspected her tan, then washed and dressed. She rubbed cologne on her arms and neck and hand lotion on her hands and legs. She fastened on a pair of high-heeled sandals and put on two rings and a bracelet. Then she went down the hall to Karl's door and scratched on it with one of her rings so Klara wouldn't hear. Karl called to her to come in. She went in, closing his door behind her with exquisite stealth. The whole house smelled of sleeping breath and sun on rugs and coffee. Karl yawned and stretched, then pulled her down on the bed.

Lying beside him, she posed one leg in its sandal. "My mother's made a big breakfast," she whispered. And then she whispered, "Do you know what I think? I think my mother wants to marry you." And then she felt her face start to glow because she had come so dangerously close to saying, "I think my mother want to marry you her*self*."

But Karl, instead of answering her, started using one of his fingers to trace the outline of her sandaled heel, calf, thigh: a phrase he was writing. When he got to her panties he put a period between her legs. With a low whimper she spread them a little.

"Children!" Klara was musically calling, in the voice she used for company.

Karl slipped his finger out from under Ingrid's dress and slid it up over her belly and then up over her left breast. At the nipple he pressed in another period. Ingrid caught his hand to her, cupped it over her breast. He let it rest there a moment, then worked it free and proceeded up to her throat and around her chin. He outlined her mouth. She parted her lips. He put a period in her mouth. She licked, then bit, his finger.

"Everything's going to get cold!" called Klara. Less music in the voice now.

"Coming!" yelled Karl.

Now the finger was outlining Ingrid's nose. She hated that. Her nose was too big and had a bump in it; she sometimes believed it had ruined her life.

"If we got married. . ." Karl was saying, the finger coming down over her nose again ". . .do you think our children would have big noses?"

She sat up. Her sinuses and eyes felt waterlogged, as if she'd been swimming too long under water. She tucked her hair back behind her ears and swimmily blinked. Her throat hurt her. "We better get down there," she said, "or she's going to start to get angry."

She left him alone to get dressed and walked down the sunlit carpeted stairs that looked as if they ought to be the stairs of a happier household. Her arms were aching, along with her throat and eyes.

In the kitchen she asked Klara if there was anything she could help her with but Klara wasn't speaking. She looked at the table to see if there was anything missing. Maple syrup for the French toast. She got a bottle of it out of the pantry and poured it into a small silver jug.

This drove Klara to speech. "That jug's for the *cream*."

"What do you want me to do then? Pour the syrup back in the bottle and wash this out and put cream in it?"

Klara didn't answer.

"Or what?"

"Oh, it doesn't matter," said Klara—not in an exasperated voice but in a voice as dead as dammed-up water. Ingrid tried to help her ladle the food onto serving dishes but Klara wouldn't let her; with a face tight with hurt she elbowed her out of her way.

Two days before Karl was to be operated on he phoned Ingrid from Hoyt. She was on night duty and so was asleep; the switchboard had to page her in her room. It was lunchtime. "It's the middle of the night for me," she told him. But two days later he phoned her at lunchtime again. This time she couldn't get back to sleep. She moaned and twisted in her bed and when the intercom buzzed again she flounced up in a fury. It was Klara this time, offering to drive her up to Hoyt to see Karl the morning she came off night duty. She said, "I don't know if I can. When would I sleep?"

"Don't worry about sleeping. You can sleep in the car."

The night of Karl's operation, Ingrid, putting her own patients to bed down in Port Charlotte, imagined Karl lying on the operating table. She saw the masked surgeon receiving the scalpel from a masked nurse and making a careful incision. But when they opened Karl up they found a woman inside. I must be either perverted or insane to be thinking like this, she thought. And yet she couldn't cast the fantasy out of her mind.

Two nights after the surgery he phoned her. The operation was a success; they hadn't found anything and so they'd just taken his appendix out. He was feeling rotten.

Ingrid said, "Klara is driving me up to see you tomorrow. She's going to pick me up at ten-thirty tomorrow morning."

But when she came off duty the next morning the thought that she would have only two hours to sleep before she would have to get up again was so enraging to her that she couldn't get to sleep at all. After half an hour of tossing around in her bed she hauled the top blanket off it and dragged it down to the second-floor west wing and found herself an empty room down there. Hide-and-go-sleep, she said to herself as she climbed in between the new bed's coarse cool sheets. Old chants from childhood came back to her:

> Back, back, wherever you're at
> Don't show the peak of your great big hat

She was awakened a little over two hours later by someone from the downstairs office. "We've been looking high and low for you. Your mother's been waiting for over half an hour down in the parlour—fit to be tied."

The trip was not an enjoyable one, but Ingrid knew that she could hardly have expected it to be. She couldn't argue with Klara either—not after trying to hide from her. But to

feel so scornful and at the same time so frightened! There was
something humiliating about that.

Klara was saying that Ingrid did not amuse her. She liked
to be amused. Tina is amusing, she said. You're young, she
said, You're in love, I do everything for you, I've made all this
possible, why don't you act happy? A wonderful young man
like that, she said. Ingrid looked out at the landscape as if she
believed it could help her. Her stomach winced and it seemed
to her the light in the fields did, too. She stared out at grey
houses, at white houses, at clotheslines strung with faded
plaid laundry and white sheets, at everything flapping and
beating in the wind—laundry, shed doors, faded flags (Union
Jack country); at all the harsh fresh colours—royal-blue hills,
orange and flag-red leaves. She thought, But does anyone ever
get away from here? I wish I could sleep.

The Fowler Memorial Hospital in Hoyt was a smaller
hospital than the General in Port Charlotte, and the nurses
looked more sloppy and tolerant. On Karl's floor the superintendent and her sleepy deputy were both wearing cardigans
over their uniforms and they were both, wonder of wonders,
smoking. The sleepy one looked up Karl's room number on a
chart, then gave Ingrid a heavy-eyed once over.

It was a heady feeling, walking along the halls of an
unknown hospital, knowing no one could make any claims
on her. She found his room, the last one on corridor B. He
was sitting up in a chair with a blanket tucked around him,
reading. He was even whiter than the bloodless Mrs Jenkins.
And the other patient, a lanky man who had his radio on,
had a disease that was turning him yellow. Cancer or hepati-
tis. Cancer, surely, because there was, along with the oriental
colouring, a falling away of hardy, drink-pocked flesh from
the coarse-featured occidental face.

But what shocked her was her own nurselike lack of sympathy for Karl. He was looking so woebegone. She wanted to
hiss at him, *Buck up, man, for God's sake!* When she bent to
kiss him he signaled with his eyes in the direction of the radio
of the dying yellow man. "He plays it all the time," he
whispered, and he looked sadder than ever.

She thought, oh God, now he's going to start to whine as well, and to stave it off she whispered, "What are you reading?"

It was a book on economics. He knew so much more than she did. She hadn't read a book in more than two years. Would she understand this one?

That night Ingrid and Klara stayed with some family friends—music festival organizers. They shared a bed that belonged to a daughter who was away at college. It was a three-quarter-sized bed and was covered with a pale blue spread that had a pattern of grey and white ferns on it. Ingrid surprised herself by not being able to sleep. She lay there all night thinking, is it the coffee? Am I going crazy? What's the matter with me?

The next afternoon she went back to the Fowler to visit Karl. He looked even sadder than he had the day before. She asked him if anything was wrong. He said it was the state of the world. The world made him sad. He did not see much hope for it, he said. He mentioned Eisenhower, Suez. Ingrid sat on his bed and absently stroked his hand; again she was shocked at the depth of her lack of feeling for him. And again she felt a nurselike disapproval of his whiny voice, his self-pity. But after a time she started to feel very sad herself. Or simply to allow an old sadness to acknowledge itself inside her. It didn't seem to be because the world couldn't come up to her standards but rather the opposite: she saw no hope of herself measuring up to the world's.

Three weeks after Karl's operation he was ready to leave for Toronto where he'd had a job waiting for him since the beginning of September. He stretched the time out a little longer to coincide with Ingrid's coming off day duty in Emergency so they could spend a day together in Annetteville.

His bus came in two hours after Ingrid's, and when he arrived at the Annetteville house, pale as a dying prince, they all went into the living-room for cakes and tea. Kamille had left for the States by this time, but Arnie, thin and sunburnt from having worked up north in a logging camp, and Tina, all in black and with a small gold scarf tied cowboy-style at her throat, were both at home. It was a cold, cloudy fall day and the house seemed very draughty and polished. Klara told Karl that the family cleaning woman, Vi, had asked her if Karl was a doctor and when she had said, no, Vi, why?, Vi had said, because he is so pale. They all laughed at this, and then Karl talked in a very informed way about the Royal Danish Ballet and Tina asked him a lot of questions.

After they'd brought the tea things out to the kitchen Arnie took Ingrid aside and said, "Are you going to marry this Karl, with his *clipped English*?"

She said "Maybe I will. I don't know yet."

When Arnie had gone back to the living-room, Tina said, "Everything Karl said about the ballet was very interesting, I thought."

Ingrid said she thought so, too.

After a silence that seemed to indicate a short battle with doubt, Tina said in a low, light voice, "He got it all out of *Time* magazine. All of it. I read the whole review when I came down here on the bus. Not a single one of those opinions was his own."

"That can't be true. He doesn't even read *Time*. He's a socialist."

"I have it in my suitcase; I can show it to you."

"I have better things to do," said Ingrid, but her heart had whipped up into a pounding rhythm at what she was sure was the truth.

Karl left for Toronto and Ingrid went back to Port Charlotte. She was transferred to Male Surgery, and with the fair-minded Killeen in charge she didn't mind it too much there. A whole month went by. She was now into the third month of her third year. "What a pity you're leaving," she imagined people saying, "when you've only nine months left to go." And then she imagined the way their eyes would drop, quite understandably, down to her belly.

The first snow came. Karl wrote to her every day. His letters made her ache, they were so sweet, full of quotes from Andrew Marvell, full of missing her body. More snow came. The supervisors got out boxes of Christmas decorations and for part of one peaceful hospital afternoon they all unrolled bandage-sized rolls of red and green crepe paper and decorated the nursing stations. People started talking about Christmas and New Year's, and on some wards they started making trades. The patients' radios played Christmas carols. Then suddenly (and inexplicably, since she'd already worked a long stretch there before) Ingrid was transferred to 6E, the worst ward in the whole hospital, run by a supervisor who was considered, even by the other supervisors, to be a sadist. Her name was M.J. Howard. There was a rumour the M stood for Mary. Sometimes, in fact, she was called the Virgin Mary. ("Hear you're spending Christmas with the Virgin Mary, you poor bastard," a girl named Connors said to Ingrid one day in the cafeteria.) At the end of a week with Howard, Ingrid felt she was in hell. And in the middle of hell she got a letter from Karl. He had been at a party where he had met a lot of new people. He had dropped ice-cubes down a girl's back. She was an amusing girl, he wrote, very dark and lively. You would like her, he wrote. He said he thought it would be a good idea if they occasionally went out with other people.

After this Ingrid started having trouble sleeping. Her skin itched; she lay awake parts of every night, scratching, panicked. What if the lack of sleep made her make a mistake with the medicines? What if she gave someone someone else's injection? And during the days she felt herself in the grip of a secret rage. The patients' radios played the same carols over and over—bouncy barbershop renditions of songs about roasting chestnuts and Christmastime in the city.

Trying not to hear, Ingrid dreamed of Christmastime in the country—up in the woods that looked down on the fields north of the May River delta. She wanted to be out in that countryside, walking up the miles of white fields toward the spruce wood that came into its own at Christmas, with balsam like candle drippings hardened on the cold bark of the trees and the strange high creak of the old branches in the wind. (Even the wind in those old branches seemed ancient, living up there from winter to winter.) And she wanted to hear the carols of her childhood—"Bring a Torch, Jeanette Isabella" and "Oh Come Oh Come Emmanuel/That mourns in lonely exile here..." And the carols that came from England and France, the ones Tina had learned when she'd gone to the boarding school she'd begged Klara to send her to when she was fourteen. Glenwood. Arnie had called it Shitwood. Tina pierced her ears there (using a darning needle and a cake of Camay soap—and then had to have penicillin for the ensuing infection)—and plucked her eyebrows and painted her nails with a clear polish and learned to sing the sweet foreign carols. And went out with rich boys from the neighbouring boys' school. But *that* was the one Arnie called Shitwood; *Titwood* was his name for Tina's school.

Ingrid didn't hear from Karl again and she didn't write to him, but sometimes, in the middle of passing out pills or giving injections, her eyes would fill up with tears. Four nights after his letter came she didn't sleep at all, but she made up her mind to leave the hospital for good. She would phone home in the morning and tell them that she had broken up with Karl and that she was sick and wanted to come home. She knew her mother would be alarmed enough to come and get her; her mother wouldn't want Karl to escape.

When she came off duty the night of her last day Ingrid found her room filled up with people. People from her own class; people from other years, other classes. They were everywhere: on her bed, on her desk, on chairs, on suitcases. It wasn't a popular move, leaving; it inspired envy. And it left yet another ward short staffed. The traditional way to leave was to tell one or two friends, swear them to secrecy, leave when the night and day staffs were safely at work or at supper in the hospital cafeteria. And pregnancy was the traditional reason.

Someone asked her if she was pregnant. She said no. "As a matter of fact, I'm menstruating."

"The weeping of the disappointed uterus," someone said, and there was a patch of uneasy laughter.

Connors said, "Let's undress her and see if she's lying," and Ingrid felt really scared then because technically, at least, she *was* lying. She had had cramps all day but nothing had happened yet.

"Ingrid's been wanting to leave here for more than a year," said Joan Cosman, her friend. And no move was made against her.

She started to pack. She gave away her cape, caps, textbooks, uniforms. Also her late-leave card, to be forged later.

A delegation came with her to the elevator. Smitty and Becky Fullerton kissed her goodbye. Jackson and Devine told her to write. Connors punched her lightly in the shoulder and said, "No hard feelings, I hope."

She said no.

Joan and Devine loaded her bags into the elevator.

The delegation wanted to know: "Are you really going to go down and say goodbye to old Fatface?"

Yes, she was.

The delegation marvelled. And more people gathered around.

"Tell old Fatface I wanna go home for Christmas," someone said.

"Tell her I've been on night duty for six weeks," said Devine.

"Tell her I've had it," said Connors. "Enough, enough, enough, enough."

The doors closed and the elevator started to sink. As it sank Ingrid could hear a voice—it sounded like Joan Cosman's—wistfully call out, "Give her shit for me, Hessie."

She had never been down on the supervisors' floor before; none of them had. The doors were twice as far apart as on the other floors. There was Persian carpet in the hallway. She knocked on the superintendent's door.

"Come in," called a distant voice.

She went in. Two steps into the room. More Persian carpets

and two tall, glass-faced cabinets. She told one of the glass-faced cabinets that she was leaving, that she wasn't suited to nursing.

The superintendent stayed at her end of the room too, an elephantine figure in a white nylon uniform. Deeper in the apartment Ingrid could smell pork chops discreetly cooking.

The superintendent said that if ever she should change her mind and want to come back she would be welcome. Ingrid thanked her and walked (it seemed to her later that she had walked backwards) out of the room. That was all.

Outside, it was snowing again, and Klara's coat was turned into a fat fur bell by the wind. Ingrid hurried behind it down the wide concrete steps. She never expected Klara to refuse to speak to her and yet it often happened; it was happening now. In silence they fitted the suitcases into the back seat of Fritz, the family Chrysler, and in silence climbed into the front and closed themselves in. In silence they drove down Dearborn Street and then Beeker Street, and in silence they left the lights of Port Charlotte and Port Fairweather and the ocean behind. At Glooscap Point the river had frozen and been snowed on, but a channel had been cut open for the ferry. They drove in silence onto it, bumping hard over its wooden flap, and in silence watched the snow falling onto its road of dark water. On the far side of the river, after swinging right, away from the road to Gully Bay, they drove up and down hills that with the new snow on them seemed a little steeper. But by then the snow had stopped; east of Bucksfield there was even some fog. Cedar trees stood in fog on white fields. Country schools and country churches appeared, ghostly close to the highway. Klara drove slowly after this, through settlements and small towns named to hold the wilderness at bay—Richmond, Cambridge, Port Oxford, Sutherland—and as they took the turn-off to Wolf River she even spoke.

"I think you should know what Jack Kincaid said when he heard you were giving up," she said. (Jack Kincaid owned the menswear store in East Annetteville. When he was trying to persuade someone to buy from his range of fur-lined suede gloves he would say, "Feel that. Softer than a mouse's titty.")

"What did he say?" asked Ingrid. For some mad reason she found herself expecting good news.

"He said, 'What that girl needs is a good whipping.'"

Ingrid laughed a harsh, light laugh. "Oh, I would not put great stock in anything Jack Kincaid might say," she said. "I would not greatly respect any opinion Jack Kincaid might have."

"Someone who's done what you've done is hardly entitled to sit in judgment on other people," Klara said. "You turned your back on the sick," she said.

Ingrid turned and looked out the window and would not condescend to reply. But what was Klara getting at *now*? When she thought she knew she turned to her. "If you're trying to imply I'm pregnant, I would just like you to know that I am most definitely not."

"If people think you *are*, then you might as well *be*."

Why, in the name of God, can't you have more character? Ingrid wanted to shriek at her. But what would have been the point? She shrieked nothing.

White highway posts marking the approach to Skelton Canyon started to come at them in a curve to their right. Next came the primeval boom of the water down in the boulder-bed of the canyon's distant bottom. Then five minutes past the canyon, like the response of a mountain trickle to the far-off boom of the sea, a warm stickiness between Ingrid's thighs. Pleased, but very wary of letting any relief seep into her voice she said, "I'll have to pick up some sanitary napkins at the pharmacy in Wolf River."

But if keeping relief out of the voice was a strategy for herself, putting it into the voice was a strategy for Klara. For she responded in a tone of grimmest parental reverence, "Thank God for *that*."

At mealtimes Pup seemed exhausted, a man marmalading his bread in a dream. But Klara seemed not to notice; there were jaunts to go on, she said. Grim jaunts, as it turned out; Klara and Ingrid couldn't go anywhere in the car without trying to freeze each other out. They drove down to Bramley for eggs, and then on to Duncrannon for a Christmas tree. The tree was a Scotch pine; they stood it on the back seat so that its top rested between them on the front seat, seemed to peer between their shoulders like an eavesdropping child. But there was nothing to eavesdrop *on*—only frosty silence.

After she'd been home for ten days Ingrid got a letter from Karl. "Why haven't you written?" he wrote. That night she sat up in bed with a notebook pressed to her knees. She briefly considered writing "How's your new friend? Is she still very dark? Is she still very lively?", but decided not to, being in dire need of a friend herself. And so instead wrote, "Are you coming down for Christmas?," following this with what she told herself was a necessary lie: "We are busy making dozens of cheerful preparations."

"I can't come down till the spring," Karl wrote in his reply. He added that he was missing her, though. "I'm sorry you left the hospital," he also wrote, "when you were so close to graduation."

At night she was back in the hospital; was wrong or had been wronged; had made, or had been accused of making a mistake with pills or injections, had forgotten (with the never-to-be-remedied dream's forgetting) to perform the simple but vital task that would have saved someone's (a young girl's?) life. Even in her waking life the hospital was with her more than she would have guessed it could ever be back in the days when she'd been obsessively plotting to leave it: when she went to sign up for courses in typing and shorthand at the Annetteville High School on a cold December day just after sundown, a hot turkey sandwich she was served in the diner across the highway from the school brought back the chemical taste of the midnight meals that an orderly used to carry down to her through the windy, cold moonlit nights and along the precarious ramps on stilts and down the rickety stairs to the Contagious Diseases Annex when she was serving out her solitary night duty there.

During Christmas, Pup got the flu. It stretched on into the new year. Day after day went by with his being in bed—white pillow, white bedspread, white snow outside the window. An invalid smell in the room, medicated grease—Vaseline, Ozonol, Vicks. Also Johnson's Baby Powder, a light sprinkling over the smeared ointments that gave dimension to his pain—sore chest, cramps in the legs, and what Ingrid suspected was inflamed groin. A light snow over the ice of country roads in winter.

He's been crying, Klara told Ingrid and Tina. Crying in the night. During the day he didn't cry. He lay in bed and gazed out the window as if waiting for someone. Should we be frightened? the three Hessellund women now seemed to be asking each other with their eyes as they sat down to lunch, to supper. But their eyes also seemed to carry the commentary that the fact they should ask the question at all—and so nonverbally, so imploringly—surely meant that they already *were*. One day Pup got up, dressed, wandered through the house. It must have been on a weekend, because Tina was home from her classes in Stettler. It was very cold and clear, and now and then the wind would drive cold clouds of snow-smoke from the hills around the house.

Ingrid was out in the kitchen; she was having menstrual cramps and trying to distract herself from them by reading a novel; she was under the spell of a bewitched inertia. She was also cutting up pieces of meat for a stew. The raw blood smell of the meat masked her own blood smell, also partly hidden by a recent generous dredging of Red Roses talcum powder. As for the book, it was a lascivious story dressed up as a historical novel and was propped up against a stack of Royal Copenhagen dinner plates. And she had an opened cookbook she could use as a cover for the eighteenth-century Danish queen and her lover if her mother should come down the stairs. It was opened at Lemon Meringue Pie. She planned to say she was reading up on how to make pies while she was making the stew.

But on this particular afternoon Klara, as she came down

the stairs, was talking to Tina. He got up out of bed, Ingrid heard her say. And then Klara came into the kitchen, where Ingrid had so recently and so energetically begun to chop meat. Anxiety had made her look more human. Tina came in behind her, looking pale and a little offended, as if she had just been fed a spoonful of some vile tonic. "Maybe he went up to the attic," Tina said. And then they all must have thought the same thing: the place of rope and rafters. "Go after him, Ingrid," Tina said then. "Otherwise maybe he'll try something."

And Klara quickly added, "Yes, darling. Go after him and bring him back down here."

Ingrid, feeling frightened but also nobly competent, started to climb the narrow stairway to the attic. Even before she'd reached the level of the attic floor she could tell that someone had left a window open. And then she could begin to see the effects of that open window: snow, fine as sifted flour, had been sieved by the window screen. It lay on the tops of dark blue metal trunks; it lay in the reed bowls of baskets. As for the attic itself, it was piled high with tables and old chairs. The tables had white paint in their scars. Ingrid's heart started to pound. She couldn't see Pup. The window? Frightened, she stared at it, but it hadn't been shoved up more than two inches. She peered far into the dusty gloom of the cold winter attic. There was old paint too—salmon-coloured, slate-blue—on the spokes of the chairs and on their inverted bibs of wood. Was he *hanging* somewhere up here? She was afraid to look. "Daddy?" she called in a voice that came out in such an anxious bleat that it sounded, even to her own ears, frail with terror, and then she saw him, standing desperately still, out of the range of the light of one of the windows at the far end of the long room. With his back to her, as if he had hoped not to be seen. She went cold with fear. When he turned around would he have the face of a madman or the face of her father? He turned around. He didn't look crazy to her, only sad. As he always had. She made her way down to him, among tables and chairs, took his hand; said, "Come down into the house." And then, feeling like the greatest liar who'd ever lived: "Come down to where it's warm."

His fate must have been decided between Klara and some of her Port Charlotte friends that night on the phone, because the next day an old family friend named Louise Buchanan came and got him and drove him down to stay with her in Port Charlotte. Then contact must have been made with some doctors at the mental hospital over in Port Fairweather, because that same night he was committed. The next morning at breakfast Klara told Ingrid and Tina that if anyone asked them anything about where he was or what he was sick with they were to say he was in the General Hospital in Port Charlotte because of trouble with his heart.

In the asylum in Port Fairweather he was given shock treatments. After he had been there for three weeks the family was to be allowed to drive down to see him. They were to drive down on a Friday so Tina could come with them. On Thursday night Tina phoned and said she would take the bus from Stettler right after her history class the next morning. She arrived in Annetteville on Friday at lunchtime. It was a mild, snow-muffled day in the second week of February. She brought a whiff of the twentieth century into the house with her. Also a whiff of Ma Griffe—the grey paisley shawl wound round her head reeked with it. She undid the shawl and shook out her fragrant hair, but before she'd pulled off her coat she said to Klara, "For you, sweetie, a wee giftie," and she ceremoniously presented Klara with the *Vogue* magazine she'd bought for herself, to read on the bus. But while Klara was up in her room, getting ready for the trip to Port Fairweather, Tina also spoke with sympathy to Ingrid: "Has it been awful, sweetie? Has it been one great melodramatic scene after another?" So she was the same as ever: duplicitous something-for-everyone Tina.

  Still, Ingrid felt grateful to her—she was human at least; she was young; she was someone her own age; she might be two-faced but her two faces were human faces. On a wave of gratitude she said to her, "Last night when she was brushing her hair before she went to bed she said to me, 'It's your fault he had this breakdown. You're a failure and he was ashamed of you. When you left the hospital he was ashamed of you. You made him sad.'"

Tina didn't seem surprised. She had shucked off her coat by this time and was standing peeling long dry ribbons of white meat from the half-eaten roast chicken on the kitchen table. She wiped off her lipstick with the back of her hand and then shoved a wide ribbon of chicken into her mouth. After she'd finished chewing it—"Too dry," she croaked, and she scooped a greasy handful of Danish stuffing (moist ballooned prunes and sweet wet grey slivers of cooked apple) from deep inside the bird's bone-cage—she told Ingrid that Klara had said the same thing on the phone to Arnie. "Because he didn't do all that wonderfully on his finals. He got drunk after her phone call. You remember Mike? Mike Hiltz from the Drama Guild? Here's what happened. Mike and I decided to go out for a nightcap one night after rehearsal and we were too tired to drive out to the Harvest Moon Grille, so we went to this place all the engineering and pre-med students go to—it's called the Lincoln Club, which sounds sort of posh but it's a real dive—and I was sitting at a table near the door while Mike went to the john, and when he came back he said to me, 'I've just seen your big brother and he's feeling no pain, so maybe we better give him a lift home.' So Mike had to lug poor old Arn out to the car and stuff him in. And we'd no sooner got the door closed on him than he threw up all over the back seat of Mike's car. He kept saying, 'Holy Jesus, Mike, I'm sorry, I'm sorry,' and then it came out about the phone call. The problem is, you and Arnie talk back to her and she doesn't like it. You should flatter her—that's what she wants. Don't talk back. I remember the summer you were sixteen and you were always having these great screaming fights. You were such a spitfire. But it doesn't pay, you should know that by now. Because ever since then she's acted like she hates you. I believe she really does hate you." Tina's voice was almost complacent, almost amused. "The thing you have to understand is that all she cares about is praise. That's why she likes *me*, kiddo—I feed her a steady diet of praise."

She really is on my side, thought Ingrid, she must be, because look how she's putting her hand on my arm, as if to warn me *Here she comes*, although there hadn't been any sound from above that she could hear. But then there was: Klara's high heels starting to hit their way down the stairs.

The moment she stepped into the kitchen, Tina greeted her with a "Hello, gorgeous!"

Klara's face lit up. The look she threw Tina was the imploring, on-the-edge-of-happiness look a woman might throw a lover. "Is it really okay, darling?"

"Stupendous," said Tina. "Really. Fantabulous. I kid you not."

"And the skirt—is it subtle enough? Subdued?"

"Perfect," said Tina. "The perfect thing."

Klara brought her splayed fingers to the string of pearls at her throat, like a hostess who's just harvested a compliment on her cooking. She did a slow pirouette so they could see the way her gored grey skirt opened out when she twirled. "And the pearls? Are they the right touch, do you think?"

This wasn't for Pup, Ingrid understood, and she knew Tina did, too. All this concern was for the doctors, the nurses. What Pup thought wouldn't matter. What *would* matter was that whatever he'd told them down there was proved wrong. All this talk about how terrible it is to speak of the past, she thought. But it isn't the *past* Klara objects to, she thought; it's the fact that other people should presume (should dare!) to have their own versions of it.

Tina sat between Ingrid and Klara on the trip down to the coast. The coast—how romantic that sounded! But in a way it was—wild Bay of Fundy winter breakers washing the snow from the rocks. Tina was clearly putting herself out to be diverting; she regaled them with stories of college life. Wedged between the two of them, she must have felt transfusions of gratitude pouring into both her sweater-clad arms. She was wearing her small gold cowboy scarf tied around her throat, and her breath still smelled of chicken and prunes. She brought a spirit of ease, of entertainment, into the car, but while she talked, Ingrid was sure she could feel her storing up impressions of mother and sister for her friends back in Stettler. ("I have this big-little sister who lives this terribly bleak medieval existence.") Ingrid's stomach was feeling swoopy with anxiety. She wanted to see Pup but was afraid to see him, too. She felt pity for him but also some detachment—the slightly disdainful aloofness pity brings. Also, she was wishing that they wouldn't have to drive through Port Charlotte to get to Port Fairweather, and wishing especially that the highway that became one of the main streets of Port Charlotte didn't run by her old hospital. But the city could hardly be expected to rearrange itself just to oblige *her*, and soon enough—too soon—they got their first sight of the town, dominated like a Middle Ages town by its imposing castle up on the hill. Or more like a mosque, really —a yellow, brick medical mosque with its great dome of frosted glass and its glass-bricked top storey walling in all the shrieking sick children. That it should look so remote, so silent! The cold Bay of Fundy fog was doing its fine winter job of protecting the frost; even now, in the early afternoon, the cars whose tops could be seen above the yellow brick battlements of the doctors' parking lot were furred with it. And below the parking lot the steep little hospital park—so sooty in spring and summer—was also whitened, embalmed by frost. The hospital seemed to have gained back some of the austere power it had had when Ingrid was a child. That people she knew—people her own age—should be moving about behind those walls—dashing, cussing, gasping, fetching—now seemed almost incomprehensible to her. Klara had to stop for a traffic light just in front of the Dearborn Street entrance of the nurses' residence, and Ingrid experienced a moment of awful terror that someone she knew would come running down the steps and so happen to glimpse her. She hunched her back up to the window so as not to be seen. Her heart pounded. Tina was telling a story about a tantrum the director had thrown at one of the rehearsals for *A View from the Bridge*. She made Klara laugh. Ingrid's feet urged the car on against the red light. At last the light changed and they shot forward. They flew past the Golden Ball garage and then swung hard right to take the exit for the bridge to Port Fairweather.

The main red brick building of the asylum had the grim appearance of a correctional facility, but its two new pink-brick wings, stretching to east and west, had a ranch-style suburban look. Klara parked the car in the west parking lot. When they disembarked they could see that the west wing had a solarium at its far end and that outside it there was a small brick-floored courtyard, swept clean of snow, with a stone fountain in its middle. Snow-caked low cedar hedges fenced it in. "Really quite attractive," said Klara, and Ingrid and Tina agreed with her and then, almost with reluctance, the three women turned away from it, to the right, to walk up the hilly bricked path to the old part of the building.

Three nurses came out of the main building's front entrance as Klara and Ingrid and Tina were climbing the hill; they were laughing and hugging themselves against the cold as they came running down the shallow stone steps. One of them cast a quick glance in the Hessellund women's direction. How do we look to her? Ingrid wondered. She imagined the nurse would take them for three sisters, with their tense Nordic faces and their tow hair—making their way single file up the brick pathway in their well-cut, dark winter coats, trying to look like they knew where they were going.

At the top of the stairway there was a sign saying Visitors' Bell. Klara pressed it in. The hefty middle-aged orderly who opened the door to them greeted them with an "Aha! Three pretty ladies!" Only Klara gave him a smile. He was not unkind-looking, but Ingrid was sure his eyes were alcoholic's eyes. A big ring of keys bobbed and jingled from a hook on his brown leather belt. Each tall, dark green door they came to he had to unlock.

Pup rose from his chair the moment they stepped into the visitors' foyer. His face bore a tender, shocked expression, was the temporarily stricken face of a priest or a doctor whose job it is to break the news of a calamity to the unfortunate family. To their nervous chatter he had little to contribute, although he was clearly following what they were saying. He looked like he was hoping not to depress them but was no longer sure he remembered how not to.

Ingrid stared obsessively at Klara's hands as Klara talked to Pup—imagined them chilled to the bone in their short grey leather driving gloves that gave the appearance of being a slippery, cold grey second skin, and when she glanced furtively up at Pup she tried to read from his expression if there was any truth in what Klara had said about her making him sad. She decided there wasn't, but the accusation, once having been given voice, made some doubt linger. It was partly pride, along with the pain of guilt, that made her partly believe it: she knew she was his favourite.

Ingrid didn't feel safe in the house with Pup gone. She had trouble sleeping. She was sleeping in the back wing. Klara was out at the front. What Ingrid knew about the hardness of nurses and the coldness of doctors made her feel frightened for her father. He was incarcerated—incarcerated in an asylum. The word "incarcerated" had unpleasant associations with carcasses, incinerators. Institutional incinerators—burning bloody bandages, carcasses. Human ones. She recalled the definition of anatomy she'd learned at the beginning of Anatomy and Physiology—that anatomy was the science which dealt with the structures of the bodies of men and animals; that it was studied by the dissection of those who had died in hospitals and other institutions, unclaimed by relatives. But when she'd learned this definition she'd never considered the possibility of its having any direct application to anyone she was close to. And how spooky that other phrase was now— that "other institutions." She had a nightmare vision of Pup being destroyed there. Weakened, ill, drugged, dead. Swung away on a morgue stretcher bound for one of the asylum incinerators and a high-speed institutional cremation. There wasn't a Psychiatry wing at the General in Port Charlotte and so she didn't know what shock treatments were like. But from bits and pieces she'd overheard she could imagine them—the body stripped and strapped to a table; the head jammed into some sort of padded vise; the temples smeared with a Vaseline-coloured medical jelly. Whatever was someone like her father, who'd never hurt anyone, doing in a place like that? But maybe in a place like that the nurses were kinder than at other hospitals. A lot of people liked Pup anyway. People (even nurses—even nurses at an overworked, understaffed provincial facility) might want to be kind to him. Unless they were actually worse there. Unless they were sadists. There would be electrodes too. She imagined the electrodes as a black belt of bullets taped around the skull. And for thrusting between the teeth, a tongue depressor—bandaged in gauze like a newly cut finger. Everything would be brutal, calibrated, scientific, exact. The nurses she had seen running down the stairs had looked decent, though. Not that that proved anything. The most corrupt people in the world could look decent. She prayed for Pup to come back and not have all his memories wiped out. The problem with interns and nurses and resident doctors was that they didn't get enough sleep. Every second night at the General, the interns were on call all night long. If there was a rash of accidents and emergencies they would go forty hours without sleep. Even the most attractive ones soon lost their appeal. They were young but they were zombies. She had a moment of feeling a little hardhearted toward Pup. Why had he allowed himself to fall into the hands of such people? But he had seemed at ease there. Maybe he was happier there than he'd ever been here. It's wrong to talk about the past, Klara was always saying—she especially said this if any of them brought up a grievance. Had *Pup* brought up a grievance? Now he would not. But what if he came back a zombie?

The hallway outside her bedroom started making her nervous. There was a row of prints and paintings hanging out there. A landscape of a white winter field pricked by stubble beneath a cold mauve winter sky, a birdcage of wind-bowed bare trees in the distance. A painting of Pup's mother in a long white dress, in her shiny-leafed, dark green summer

garden in Copenhagen, at the turn of the century. Before Pup
was born, even, this must have been. The first woman in
Denmark to get a divorce. This meant she came from a rich
iconoclastic family. A sadly smiling pretty woman in her
garden. Her thoughtful dark eyes were bright, as if she had
been on the point of crying but then had switched directions
and allowed herself to be teased into smiling. Her husband
took off with a young cousin of hers who was a guest in their
house. She was left alone with her little boy—Pup. But this
painting must have been commissioned years before that.
Next to her was a print of a naked woman, seen from behind,
standing up to her knees in an inky black lake and using her
long white Nordic hair as a sling for her big white buttocks.
Then a painting Ingrid had done herself, years ago, of herself
and Tina in blue shorty coats, the foggy wind blowing their
hair into their eyes, their mouths. Their hands, which she
recalled having trouble with, she'd finally been obliged to
paint into their pockets. Next there was a watercolour of a
dead bird, some kind of storky bird, a kind of crane—an
Audubonlike dead white crane hung by its tied-together feet
from heavy red twine and in whose expressive belly Pup had
once seen the torso of a woman in a white dress, her face a
beseeching smudge in the tail feathers, her raised arms tied
over her head, swinging pitifully from a red rope. And last
there was a daguerreotype of the old mother-in-law of the
man who'd built the house, a grim Victorian frog in black
bombazine. Or a toad. Like Toad of Toad Hall in *The Wind
in the Willows*, got up in the bribed washerwoman's print
dress and rusty black bonnet to make his escape from the
terrible dungeon.

People in Annetteville believed that the old woman had
put a curse on her extravagant son-in-law; when the house
was finally finished and he was plunged deep in debt he
hanged himself in one of the back bedrooms. No one knew
which bedroom. Ingrid prayed it wasn't hers. Sometimes she
was positive it was. At night she would lie awake for hours,
listening to the house (or the old bombazined lady) creaking
about. The weather turned bitterly cold and sometimes at

night the house, settling, would boom like a cannon in the cold snap. Ingrid was using the one article of clothing she'd brought home with her from Port Charlotte—a stolen, washed-out, green surgeon's suit—as pyjamas. At night she would twist and turn in her stolen surgeon's suit, trying to make herself comfortable. And although she would try not to, she would often think about Dr Wyse of the bedroom eyes. He'd been on nights in Emergency the first stint she'd worked there. He even left there at the same time she did, but she was only moved on to another ward; he moved on to another hospital, another town. One night not long after he took off, his name came up in a conversation in the nurses' kitchen up on the top floor of the dormitory. Several of Ingrid's classmates confessed to having been smitten by him. Now it can be told, they said. Someone mentioned his notorious eyes and someone else said, "A guy like that would insult a woman right out of bed." For her part, Ingrid had offered up a little poem in tribute to him:

> Dr Wyse
> Has bedroom eyes
> Orgasmic cries
> Thrill Dr Wyse

This was very well received, and a few months later was even quoted back to her by someone who told her that one of the seniors working down in the Annex had written it.

In the best fantasy she had about him, they were working together late at night in Emergency, just as they had worked there late at night in real life. When they'd finished their last case Dr Wyse said to her, "Step into my office a moment when you've finished cleaning up here, Miss Hessellund." It was in the summer, so she was conveniently tanned and was attired in the sexy white dress the students wore when they worked on Emergency or in the OR. A slim white cotton shift with a V-neck, it was belted with a white tie-belt. She put herself in her black stockings because she was still a junior in this fantasy, then sat up and pulled off her OR pyjama top and shunted herself out of the washed-out green surgical trousers. Naked, she felt too warm and big-breasted in the cold bed—too soft, too—her body waiting to be brought to a tingling and tightening. Maybe Wyse had worn this very pair of doctor's pyjamas when he was working as a replacement anaesthetist in the OR. What an irony that would be, what a thrill really, and she rolled the pyjama pants up tight as a rolling-pin and wedged the roll snug between the clench of her thighs. Now she was walking down the hall to his office. As she closed his door behind her he came quickly to her. No words were spoken between them. They pressed and rubbed against each other, moving hard. Then they moved slightly apart and he plunged a hand downward; drew it, with a swift little draw, between her thighs. This made her thrust herself toward his hand, nosing after it. But when they embraced again, although she could feel how hard he was, she wasn't really all that aware of touching *him*; she was really only aware of all the urgent desiring things he was doing to *her*. The only part of him she was really conscious of was his breathing—all those hushed, harsh breaths. Which were also her own. Joined, anguished, she could feel how strenuously they were both labouring toward their ultimate bearing-down pleasure; she could feel them achieving, in unison, the perfect hardhearted sweetness that precedes utter happy weakness and lassitude.

In this way she was able, night after night, to forget the old bombazined lady. As for the intense winter cold, it seemed to approve absolutely; on more than one night, at the very moment of her coming hotly over the top—into bliss, into the forbidden glow of good health—the cold in the upstairs halls saluted her with the powerful royal boom of one of its cannons.

In the daytime, she helped out in the house. Washed the floors with a little vinegar in the floor-water to bring up the shine in the wood. Also added vinegar to the purple cabbage she cooked with caraway seeds and cloves. She also ironed— pillowslips, nightgowns, blouses. One of Klara's peignoirs was a cream-coloured silk with a pattern or rosebuds on it.

The rosebuds were linked by a thread of red, like a thread of blood. There were maps of perspiration in the armpits.

She loved cooking and ironing, hated washing floors or any kind of cleaning. Hated to organize things. Klara loved to. Or loved to order other people to. Loved to link arms with Ingrid and say, "Let's organize the office. Then when we're finished with that we should organize the kitchen." Now and then Ingrid went to her typing classes at the Annetteville High School, but not often. She started falling behind. Klara said, "You can learn as much typing here at home anyway, typing up letters for me in my office. But first we should organize the files, the correspondence." She had let her cleaning woman, Vi, go and work for a friend of hers. "I bequeathed her to Mitzi," she told Ingrid with a smile. As if this was good news.

In the afternoons, while Klara was taking her nap, Ingrid would either write to Karl or do the ironing. Usually the ironing; she preferred to write to Karl in the privacy of the night, after Klara had turned out her light. In the daytime, just before Klara dropped off to sleep, she would sometimes call down to Ingrid to come up to her room to cover her with an extra blanket. After this, the house would be wonderfully, almost frighteningly peaceful. Ingrid—ordinarily so exhausted these days that she felt she could barely lift an arm, a hand—would snap into action. Set up the ironing board, sprinkle the laundry, set out the book to be read. The first half-hour would be spent reading at top speed, her heart pounding. In the last week of February she finished *A Farewell to Arms*. She made little notes from it in a spiral notebook. One of the quotes had made her nearly weep for Pup: "Doctors did things to you and then it wasn't your body anymore." Klara was a bibliophile; she revered books. At auctions and sales she bought old books by the carton, but she didn't bother to read them herself and she didn't like to see anyone else reading either (unless she was in need of someone to read her to sleep). But if she saw any of them reading for their own pleasure she would give them a chore. She was like the nursing supervisors down in Port Charlotte.

They couldn't bear to see a student stop and exchange a few words with another student, or gaze out a window, or even glance at a chart. If they spotted you engaged in any of these clandestine activities they would present you with a cannister of liquid ether—surely the coldest liquid in all of Christendom—and tell you to go swab down the stainless steel shelves in the Utility Room with it. Fingers numbed from the cold, brain numbed and woozy from the ether fumes—that's what you got for being caught looking unobsessed or thoughtful. Ingrid read fast, wholesale, like a person ravenous with hunger, pawing words into her eyes. In early March—though it was still winter, with cold glaring days of cold sun on ice and snow—she started reading an ancient-looking copy of *The House of the Seven Gables*. Its spine was bleached with age, its pages dusty with old, old dust; she breathed in the fragrance of age from the opened book. It was mouse-eaten too; there were little mouse-eaten half-moon caves stepping down the pages when the book was closed, like the indentations for the letters of the alphabet in *The Oxford English Dictionary*. Because the book was so old she didn't expect to be much affected by it, but on a Friday afternoon in early March, close to finishing the book, she came upon a passage that shook her: "'I want my happiness!' at last he murmured, hoarsely and indistinctly, hardly shaping the words. 'Many, many years have I waited for it! It is late! It is late! I want my happiness!'"

It was so modern! So close to her own feelings! And if a man in a book that was written more than a hundred years ago (and an old man at that) could feel this, then maybe almost anybody could. Maybe even Klara could. Maybe half the horrible things Klara did only came from wanting happiness. She could even remember when Klara had actually seemed happy. When she was a young wife, during the war. One Christmas during the war Klara had made a last-minute dash across the river to buy everyone presents. As if in sympathy with the dangerous heaving black seas of the torpedoed Atlantic, the river hadn't frozen and so the ferry was still running. Klara came home loaded down with gifts and seemed blissful. The perfumed collar of her fur coat had snowflakes caught in it. Ingrid had thought her mother terribly beautiful and had fawned at the fur collar of her coat. Later that Christmas (or maybe it was another Christmas) Klara had made up a mock marzipan out of Pablum and almond flavouring and used cornstarch to stiffen it with. But then, thought Ingrid (thinking of Klara) she's always been ingenious with her mocking: turning Pablum into marzipan; making unhappiness look like happiness; making *fear* look like happiness; making hatred and disunity and chaos look like united family love. She changed—that was the thing. She got older, but not wiser. It was dangerous, the charmed life she lived in the public eye. She even seemed to like the phrase, its menacing singular—possibly liked the way it sounded magic, like the evil eye. She would say, but dreamily, as if it conferred power rather than taking power away, "When one lives, as I do, in the public eye..." She seemed to feel its insatiable demands as pleasurable. It was cannibalistic but it could dispense grace. And although Pup was a shy man, he must have got to long for it too; in public he could pretend (with Klara) to be part of the happy couple and in this way gain a few hours' peace. But Klara (thought Ingrid) has the kind of scornful mad integrity tyrants have; she despises her victim for telling the lies she makes him tell. Each time she solicits a Devoted Look and he brings it up, he passes the test. And each time he passes the test, he fails it.

The ironing. The iron steaming upstream, up cloth, nosing into pockets, up pleats. The marvellous smell of it. Peppery silk, peppery cotton, sending their essences up with the steam. A fragrant summery mist in the brilliant glare of the winter afternoon. The salt of perspiration alchemized (by soap and water and steam) into pepper.

Then the peacefulness over. Sound of Klara getting up. A cough. Sound of flush. Creaking back and forth. Report of one of the shallow scarf drawers being slammed shut. Ingrid's blood not so much freezing as leaping back. What now, dear God? Klara starting to come down the stairs. Ingrid quickly standing the iron back on its heel so that whatever was coming wouldn't shock her to the point where she would forget to shove the iron back and forth and so leave a Gothic window burn on the seat of her mother's stone-grey denim skirt.

But even prepared for Klara's appearance she was shocked by it. An iron-burn in Klara's skirt would have made the perfect window for her to stare out of. She looked remote, ruined—a dead-eyed ruined queen. Except that she was not dressed for the part—the part being historic, her clothes being modern. She had tied her hair back with a pale blue silk scarf that had a border of white sailboats on it. She had tucked a fresh white shirt into her tan slacks. "You made me dream I was dead," she said, standing with a terrible queenly pallor in the kitchen doorway in her tan slacks, her sporty tan Oxfords. "You covered me with that heavy, heavy blanket and made me dream I was dead."

That night Ingrid had trouble sleeping. She didn't want to think about Klara—she felt almost as if she'd be willing to sell her *soul* not to think of Klara—and yet Klara (the image of Klara, insane and blaming) edged out all other thoughts. Think of Karl, she ordered herself. Think of the spring when he will be here, think of the future, think of getting away, think of the day Pup will come home; but everything seemed pale and insubstantial compared with the thought of Klara. Think of the letter you got today from Karl, she told herself. Repeat it to yourself, line by line. She tried to—it was like doing a memory exercise for school—but she couldn't make it past the first five lines. The second paragraph had begun with his talking about missing her body. A part of a line came to her: ". . .the sweet weight of your breasts. . ."

She sat up in the dark, drew her jeans to her. But then remembered that she'd left the letter in the pocket of her blazer, hanging in Klara's dressing-room. She could get it, by going in through the little bathroom at the back of the dressing-room. Klara, a deep sleeper, would never hear her. She wouldn't even need to turn on the light.

Barefoot, she walked down the cold, back upstairs hallway,

let herself into the little bathroom. As she stepped into the dressing-room, she could hear that Klara was still awake, listening to her radio. Music, from the classical music station in New Carlisle. She went over to her blazer and felt in its top pocket for the letter. Not there. She went over to the doorway leading to Klara's bedroom and opened it without knocking. Klara was sitting up in bed in her faded-pink nightgown reading the letter Karl had written to Ingrid.

It was frightening to see Klara so frightened. She had been creaming her face; it was still shiny from the cream. Klara, whose eyes could burn holes in the people she accused, couldn't meet Ingrid's gaze. "I have been so terribly lonely," she whispered. "Nobody can ever know how lonely I've been." It was horrible. It was like listening to the whisper of a petrified old woman.

Just let me out of here, let me *breathe*, prayed Ingrid. Just let her give me my letter and let me leave, for Christ's sake. She went and stood at the end of Klara's bed. She didn't want to get too close. She felt herself to be too close already, too near to some terrible and pathetic contagion. Did Klara feel it too? Her arm rigid, her face painfully averted, she handed down the letter.

In March, after the first thaw had made Klara start to worry about the fate of the cartons of books stored in the River Room of the old Gully Bay house ("Who knows how high the floods will get if the weather decides to turn tropical too fast?"), Ingrid and Tina took off one Saturday morning for Gully Bay to rescue the books and carry them up to the upstairs den—years ago named by the children the Lion's Den. (All the rooms in that house had names back then: the Womb Room was the little cubbyhole toilet on the first floor; the Tomb Room the downstairs library; the Equator Room the dining-room with its tawny maps of Central America and Africa on its pale lemon walls; the Moon Room the sun-room.)

The fine bright morning they set out in Fritz, there was frost on the long pastures that separated the small country towns, and when they took the turn-off after Bucksfield their childhood seemed to come lightly over the spring hills to meet them. And the house, when they got to it, seemed not to have breathed a breath since their childhood, either; the sun still lay in pale rectangles on the pale green linoleum floors of the Moon Room and the Tomb Room ("Hello, Moon Room," "Hello, Tomb Room"); there was still the smell of apples and wood shavings in the old porch out at the back.

Clouds came and went during the morning as they were carrying the books up to the Lion's Den, and the river that the River Room looked down on kept changing colour; bright blue to slate, slate to green, green to a dark, dark blue that made the whole sweep of it, in the current below the bluff, appear majestic, lethal, morbidly welcoming. Ingrid remembered Pup singing "Good night, Irene" while they were rowing down to the looming bluff in the hazy twilight. On the other side of the bluff they'd found a dead moose, laid out on a small crescent of grey shale beach—the mild evening waves lapping at its hooves, a ravine of bugs and flies in its groin. Soft dim summer evening, years ago. From up in the Lion's Den there was also another view of the bluff, a land view, out over the sloping roof where at the end of the war Pup had built a little sun-pen for Klara so that she could get started in on a tan while there was still snow on the ground. The farmers, coming down the old lumber road from the high bluff with their jingling horses dragging along the final chained logs of the winter must have got a nearly aerial view of her—a naked, penned woman getting her tan to the jostling high chime of sleigh bells. But who had she been tanning herself *for*? Pup? It seemed unlikely. The sex between them wasn't real sex, in their oldest daughter's opinion. We'll do better, she told herself, thinking of herself and Karl, though the thought of living the rest of her life with Karl worried her; there were so many ways she didn't trust him. Which wasn't to say that she didn't feel sensually very lovely in his presence, walking up a path in the woods or climbing a flight of stairs with the sound of his breath mounting right behind her. And yet it drained her, too, this sexual feeling; it seemed to empower her and to sap all her strength away from her at the same moment so that she felt she could sleep a thousand years dreaming sexual dreams so languorous they could tug her out into a calm sea of the most blissful paralysis, and from up in the Lion's Den she stood gazing down at the river, now blown a shallow green close to the shore, cupping her breasts, missing him. If he could be here *now*. From below her in the River Room she could hear Tina singing "La Vie en Rose," moving from hamming it up to what sounded like true feeling, the raw ache of the cabaret in her voice.

They ate their lunch at twelve-thirty, sitting on the sun-warmed floor of the Equator Room. Everything had a fishy taste—the paper-thin slices of ham, the hard-boiled eggs, the sulphured, crown-topped silver teaspoons they'd unpacked to eat their rice pudding with, the oatmeal cookies that had been packed, sardine-style, next to the open-faced sardine-and-cucumber sandwiches in their hamper. Even their tea tasted of fishy seashore, although being a *lapsang souchong*, it tasted less of fish than of tar and the caulking of boats.

Boxes of books that had made it only as far as the Equator Room ringed their hamper, and as they were drinking their tea Ingrid pulled *Out of Africa* out of one of the boxes and said she remembered reading it to Pup just after the war. "He was in bed with the flu for a week and I read it to him every day when I got home from school."

"Just after the war you were still only a little kid."

"Okay, so it was later then. I was eleven—eleven or twelve." In the evenings she had read *My Friend Flicka* and *Thunderhead* and, reading, had imagined lions and horses grazing in a dream country that was a verdant but arid blend of Wyoming and Kenya. Its mountains the Neversummer Range and the Ngong Hills. Its cities Cheyenne and Nairobi.

"Remember when Klara used to make us those little blue books so we could write our own little stories? Stitch them up out of pale blue construction paper and red yarn?"

"But the stories always had to be sweet stories, don't forget."

"True," said Tina, and taking a series of quick plucks at her sweater to make the cookie crumbs pop off it (and without looking up), she asked in a low voice, "Do you think Pup will ever get better?"

Feeling a rare solemn pleasure in being the older one, Ingrid said, "He will, hon."

"If he doesn't, I wish to God they'd just take him away to some hospital far away—Montreal, say, or Toronto—somewhere we wouldn't have to think about him any more."

Ingrid stared at her. *Don't you love him at all?* she wanted to cry out at her, but instead she drew away from her and then, to mask her withdrawal, went over to the window and sat up on the window sill with her legs hanging down like a child's and said in an aloof voice (aloof and sad), "Don't you know they got the wrong parent?"

Tina looked up at her, considering it. "I know what you mean, but no, sweetie, no. After all, Klara can still *function.*"

Maybe it all had to do with which parent you were the favourite of. I'm Pup's; Tina's Klara's. Only poor Arn is left out in the cold. And walking her fingers like a crab's legs down the sill in the sunlight, Ingrid said in a singsong voice, "Poor Arn, nobody's favourite. . ."

"Don't kid yourself, kid. Maybe he's lucky. . . ."

After lunch the sky went dark and they put on their old tooshort raincoats and set out for the long road that curved within the afternoon shadow of the great buffalo hump of the bluff. But there was no shadow today. The ghostly summer applause and clatter of the round leaves of the poplars that used to seem to be the poplars' imitation of the rustling of programs and applause from one of Klara's concert recitals was now only a memory too; now it was the landscape's colour, or lack of it, that seemed ghostly. The countryside—at least the countryside on the way to the beach—seemed to have been whitened, bleached, cracked open by early March frost. The ghostly regiments of spindly trees guarding the swamp were as shattered and bleached as if they had been forcemarched through an explosion.

On the beach, where they paced the tide-line talking of Klara, Ingrid kept wanting to hug Tina and walk tightly arm in arm with her as if they were still schoolgirls. "Do you think she's ever had an orgasm?" was the question they took off with. It led, naturally enough, to an analysis of Klara's personality. They spoke—for they felt a compulsion to be generous, to make way for the times when they wouldn't care to be kind—of how extraordinarily intelligent and really lovely she had looked in her childhood photographs, asked each other what could have happened to change her so, told each other what they knew about narcissism and false pride and the false personality; said, "At some point she decided to walk away from the truth..." "That was when she started going around saying, 'To thine own self be true,' I bet...." "Probably, hon. It's a defence, saying that, it *has* to be...."

At which point Ingrid, staring out at the water, said in a voice that sounded as if it had been dropped to the bottom of a well, "She tried to kill herself once, with me in the car."

Tina turned quickly to look at her, her eyes dark with belief. "But the road was straight as a die, I bet."

And they both laughed. Or half laughed.

"We were on our way to Jimmy Carlson's wedding. And she started yelling at me. 'You turn people on and off like a tap! You don't love anyone!'"

"It was herself she was speaking of...."

"You'd never convince *her* of that."

"True."

"And then she said she might as well kill herself if she wasn't loved. And then she closed her eyes and stepped on the gas and Fritz charged off and I thought maybe we really *would* die." But she didn't want to tell Tina the worst part. The worst part was when she'd finally shouted, "Of course I love you!" to Klara, just to get her to open her eyes and shut up. She could tell this to Tina; she was feeling close enough to her to tell her anything. In fact almost too close; it was a closeness that was an intense physical cosiness so sweetly disturbing it almost felt like sexual desire. Two summers ago when Ingrid had come down here with Teen one cloudy afternoon in late June to feel how cold the water was (they'd been trying to decide what this was the Age *of*—the Age of Antibiotics? the Atomic Age? the Age of Unreason?) Teen had leaned back against the trunk of one of the poplars and, speaking of Klara, had said—grimly, sincerely—"I love her; she's my best friend." Ingrid had distrusted Tina then. She'd felt awe too, though, making her way behind her down to the beach; awe at the way Tina had majestically walked, her long, pale raincoat caped over her shoulders, and even awe at the way the raincoat had seemed to draw the wild flowers lining the path along with it, as if the flowers, those open-faced wild roses of June, were actually sticky and so could cling to her coat's hem and lining (although at the last minute they would spring free of it and go back to being open-faced roses again.) A lot of water under the bridge since then. But then there always was a lot of water under the bridge, in a family. It didn't ever do to dwell on it, how much things had changed or were changing. (For one thing, the moment you did, you discovered how much things didn't change at all.) She remembered playing Husband and Wife with Tina when they were kids. They'd taken turns being Husband, turns being Wife. She had liked being Husband best in the game with Tina, although when she'd played it with Arnie all the excitement she'd felt had come from playing Wife. She wondered if Tina remembered any of this. She hoped to God not. Thinking about it made her feel hot with shame. And nervous too, as if at any moment the shame might turn sexual. But most of all she felt guilt. Teen was only a little kid then—well, they both were, but Teen was the littlest—and she wondered at men and how they could live with the guilt of lying on top of women, hitching themselves hard up and down over someone who was smaller than they were. Maybe that's why men in the other areas of their lives were more decent than women—for she did believe that, that she could trust Pup and Arnie a thousand times more than she could trust Tina and Klara; maybe that's why they were more reliable and tender. None of this could be spoken of to

Teen, though; to speak of this to Teen would be more forbidden even than what they'd done, but at the same moment the pretence on this particular afternoon seemed to be that they could say anything in the world to each other (at least for an hour or two), and she had the feeling that they both were determined to guard and protect this pretence as if it were the one true truth.

It started to rain before they left the beach. Beneath their too-short raincoats their blouses were protected, but their pants, in the race for the house, got drenched. They charged into the kitchen, laughing, their chests heaving painfully but healthily, for what they'd been given on this early spring day was the panting, invigorating feeling of having been swimming in a cold summer river.

First thing, they made a fire in the fireplace in the Tomb Room. Then started in on the huffing-and-puffing business of pulling off wet-legged pants and boots. While Ingrid was arranging her black corduroy trousers to steam over the rungs of a ladder-backed chair, Tina, sitting behind her on one of the old Danish brass-buckled chests (an ankle on a jeaned knee and one hand grasping the ankle-front of a boot, the other hand the heel) called out in a respectful low voice, "My God, you have a beautiful body."

Ingrid's face glowed, and again the feeling was an embarrassed feeling that seemed too close for comfort to sexual arousal. Or maybe it only *felt* queer; maybe a mixture of shame and pride was only natural, under the circumstances. She tossed her hair back over a shoulder (she was remembering the time Klara and Tina had laughed at her because they said she had a bum like a boy's) and asked archly, shyly, distrustfully, "Do you really think so? I *hate* my bum."

"No, no," said Tina. "Everything is in perfect proportion."

But her praise acted like a damper on the rest of the day. Silence fell on it. To cover it, Tina put Bach's Suite no. 3 in D Major on the record player while they were packing up. And when Ingrid said, "God, I love that—I want to be buried to it, married to it," and Tina asked "In that order?" they both loudly laughed. But apart from this, they were subdued with each other and seemed anxious to pretend to be too preoccupied to have time for anything much in the way of conversation.

On the way home in the storm Fritz turned himself into a motorized metronome, his windshield blind with rain, the wipers making their persistent ticking fans in the hammering avalanches of water (a thousand *and* one *and* a thousand *and* two *and* a thousand *and* three...). Ingrid's feet were feeling cold and her throat feverish, although possibly this sick feeling owed more to all the intense talking and cosy confessional arousal than it did to the damp, but there was also the numb-kneed need to go pee and the landscape leap-frogging at them out of the rain—they kept getting rushed glimpses of it, every sweep of the windshield wipers giving them a brief tableau of pure gloom—and the one who wasn't driving was either sleeping or pretending to sleep (in Fritz's awful enclosed leather stink) until they at last came out on the other side of the frenzy to drive through a baleful countryside whose morning-white pastures had been so darkened by rain that a little white country church they'd barely noticed coming down, just east of Bucksfield and set up against its frosty bluff on the crown of a white hill, now stood out against the damp hump of the bluff and the oncoming dark. How *boring* it must be to live way out here in the country, they said to each other, even worse than living in one of the boring little country towns, and then they were coming into their own country town with its car dealers' offices and bleak-windowed canteens looking blank after the rain, and then they were sweeping up the road to their own house and past the great heart of sodden khaki lawn where the driveway split. As Tina was parking Fritz on the plot of gravel on the west side of the house, Klara came out onto the back porch in the cold, after-rain light with a red cardigan caped over her shoulders and greeted them with all the warmth and affection that she normally reserved for guests and acquaintances, and the guilt they felt for having talked about her seemed, in the last brief moment before they stiffly got out of Fritz, to join them in an old sorrow and to say, no matter how much you feel you are right to feel what you feel, you are wrong, you are wrong, you are wrong, and Klara was looking so pretty really, and so eager to be loved (by anyone, even by them) that they were swamped by shame.

Pup was scheduled to come home from Port Fairweather in early April. Tina was still up in Stettler, writing her finals, so Klara and Ingrid drove down to Port Charlotte on their own, planning to combine errands in the one city with the quick trip across to the other to fetch Pup.

Port Charlotte, as they entered its industrial suburbs, was full of fog and bustle. The pavements of Clam Hill were wet from an early morning rain. A tall man in a black suit with a black raincoat caped over his head was walking down the middle of Gilford Street. There was the smell of soot in the mist. Klara was waiting for the light to change at the intersection of Dearborn and Digby Boulevard, and for an alerted moment Ingrid was sure the hooded man was making straight for them. Not only that—it was Ian Carmichael in his flapping black coat. But it wasn't; it was an older man— eyes set deep in their sockets; skin blue from drink and the cold. His black jacket was really a black sports windbreaker with a curler's emblem of crossed brooms and sweep's stone sewn on its front. An old sportsman's skull-and-crossbones in yolk-yellow felt. Now that she could see him up close, Ingrid was sure she knew the blue man—he was one of the Emergency regulars.

Now they were on Dearborn Street, approaching the General. Ingrid's stomach contracted. She knew they'd hit a red light just before they got to the intersection in front of the nurses' residence; they always did. And they did. Two girls came tripping down the main steps and crossed in front of the car while Klara was waiting for the light to turn. They were in new opened raincoats and wearing slim dark skirts and blouses with machine embroidery on them. They were so young, so fresh-faced. So scornful but still so soft. She didn't know them, thank God. They were from the new wave that had come up behind the students who'd been probationers at the time she took off. These two were by now probably already juniors. The one on the left was talking a mile a minute and holding the flat of her hand out in front of her as if testing for rain. Ingrid could guess the sort of cheerful lament she must be making: "And here's *me*, going in*sane*, with all the pre-op enemas still to do, and the trays still not out yet, and the dressings still not done. . ."

Klara said, "Let's go eat at Van Houtte's—the view's so lovely from up there." She seemed tense, white at the gills; she was wearing a new perfume that smelled powerfully of lilacs. Still, it did not quite mask the sour anxious scent of her perspiration.

The sun tried to come out while they were eating their strawberry junket. While she was waiting for Klara to finish her dessert, Ingrid composed an imaginary diary entry (or letter—but who to?) that described Klara eating:

K was eating with her usual bizarre decorum, as if she believed the waiters were only pretending to write down the orders of the other diners and were in reality awarding her marks on how she picked up her fork, how she laid down her spoon.

By the time they came back out into the bracing Fundy air, the day had turned colder. It was sunnier, though—brilliant —but with such a bullying wind they had to tie on their kerchiefs.

They took in the grand view of the harbour, coming down into the port. Klara turned down Besshugh Street and then swung onto Museum Boulevard with its grim fieldstone villas—their big windows looking out on the briney cold sheen of the Bay. A Russian freighter was anchored at the east end of the harbour, its looming hull painted the oil-based yellow of gas stations (did they have gas stations in Russia?), its long Russian name—all those backward R's and N's—reminding them it was foreign. The foghorn at Cape Hood seemed to be presiding over the Russian boat with its mournful-cheerful magnified moo. Suppose she had stayed here? Suppose she had become an R.N.? Maybe now she'd be working in some doctor's office. Have her own little place.

Pup seemed different. He seemed more cheerful, but at the same time not quite someone they knew. When they were all sitting at the table the first Friday night, having supper, he started to talk about the hospital like a little boy talking about summer camp. "Now it's six-thirty," he said. "It's the time we would put on our workclothes and go down to Occupational Therapy. And then when we were finished down there we would fold up our smocks and have a sing-song." Klara's face stayed smooth, expressionless. Having seen this, Ingrid and Tina sat with their eyes riveted miserably on their plates. Pup said no more about it.

Years ago, when Klara was away on tour, Pup had held sway at the supper table, had shoved his dishes to one side, piling them into a precarious pagoda of flowered china; had opened out *The New World Atlas* and taught them things: where Madagascar was, and the Khyber Pass. Had read aloud to them about Corsica, about how seaweed was added to the wine there, giving it the taste of violets. And after supper had let them help feed and groom the horses, Wolfie and Legs (real names Wolfgang and Allegro); had let them try to milk the oldest and calmest of the old cows, squirting the fine pings of milk into one of the big granite-ware pails. They had crouched tensely on the milking stool, trying, like milk-maids, to hold the pail steady between the pinch of their knees (Pup already back in the house by this time, playing Mahler—*Des Knaben Wunderhorn*).

A few weeks after Easter, Karl flew down for a three-day visit. Klara decided she would drive him and Ingrid down to the Gully Bay house—air it out, light up the fires. She invited a group of friends from Port Charlotte out there too, to make up a party.

The first night at supper, Klara, in new ribbed red sweater and with her hands in quilted grey oven mitts, rushed a white china soup tureen out to the table in the Equator Room, crying out, "Make way! Make way!" The guests shoved aside crockery and glassware. Karl, hiding his irritation from Klara, rose and located a ceramic tile on the old oak commode shoved against the map of Mexico. The setting sun was shining through the trellised breezeway out in the garden, beaming a latticed basket of light to Mexico's right as Klara set the tureen down on the tile on the table and then made a big production out of shaking the heat out of her oven mitts. Next came the ceremonious lifting of the lid. But no steam came wafting up; no sweet savoury smells of bay leaf and onion. The guests craned their necks; was this just another of Klara's little pranks? And then Klara, dipping the silver sugar-tongs deep down into the tureen, fished out a letter. It was a stamped, postmarked letter, addressed to Ingrid, in Karl's European-looking handwriting. Klara must have picked it up at the post office in Annetteville before they left home. Now she handed it to the guest next to her and it passed hands down to Ingrid. With a tender smile for Karl, Klara said, "You flew down here faster than your letter did." A flushed Ingrid slid the letter into her pants pocket. Even with her head bowed with embarrassment she could feel how all the guests were eyeing her smilingly, as if it were only a matter of time till the announcement of a wedding would be made.

When Klara and the guests had at last gone to bed, Ingrid and Karl spread out a blanket in front of the fireplace in the Tomb Room and listened to a radio station in Port Charlotte play love songs—"Malaguena," "The Song from Moulin Rouge," "I Only Have Eyes for You," "Don't be Cruel." How sad the love songs of our time are! thought Ingrid. She couldn't believe the love songs of the future would have this tormented melodious ache in them. There probably wouldn't even *be* any love songs in the future. Probably there wouldn't even be any love. There will be no deep feeling *then*, she thought. Deep feeling will go the way of the dodo.

"How's your father? Is he better?"

"He is, I guess, but he doesn't talk that much any more." Talking about Pup depressed her. Who knew what he was really feeling? Who, when it came right down to it, really wanted to know? They were all scared to hear.

They talked about Karl's mother who was away on a trip to Norway. Ingrid recalled, but did not mention, a postcard she had seen in Karl's hospital room. "Mother's dearest boy," it had begun in Norwegian.

"Are you close to your mother?"

He said he was. "Too close, in some people's opinion."

That he should be aware of it reassured her.

He worked an old snapshot out of his wallet. A pretty, laughing woman in the clothing and skates of the 1920s was standing on a blade-scarred frozen pond. She was wearing a longish tweed skirt and a low-belted tweed jacket. Her arms were hanging down at her sides, weak, rag-dolled by laughter. I can't skate, for heaven's sake! she seemed to be crying at the camera. Her speed skates were limp-necked; she was knock-kneed at the ankles.

Ingrid said with some anxiety, "She looks like she has a good sense of humour."

"She likes a good laugh," said Karl and something about the way he said this made Ingrid uneasy. But then, as if the subject of his own mother was making him uncomfortable, he started talking about Klara; how she'd acted at suppertime. "Always trying to focus attention on her*self*," he said. "But do you know what really irritates me about her more than anything else?"

"What?" said Ingrid dreamily. Whatever it was, she was sure she would love to hear it.

"The way she comes up to me and looks at me with those big innocent blue eyes of hers and says, 'Do you love little Ingrid? Do you love her *very* much?'"

Ingrid snorted, appreciative.

"The way she calls you *little Ingrid*," he said.

She laughed. "Little Orphan Ingrid," she said.

"Do you know what I feel like answering her?" he asked her. "When she asks me if I love you?"

Ingrid felt delicious. Her whole belly was jelly, ready to laugh. She felt weakened and lulled by the coming laughter, by that and the uneven heat—half of her face and half of one thigh were all hot from the fire. "What?"

"I feel like saying, "No, I don't love her.""

She sat up at once and, stroking a lock of hair back behind an ear, drew herself a little away from him. "Whatever would you want to say that for?"

"To shut her up," he said.

She didn't respond to this, but after a moment she stood up. "I'm going to go get myself a drink of water."

When she came into the kitchen she didn't need to turn on the light—the field leading up to the bluff was so bright with moonlight and frost. She found herself a wineglass on a tray on the table by the window and started over to the tap with it to run herself a glass of water. But changed her mind midstream and went back to the table and poured herself some wine in the dark. She could see the cedar tree her father had planted in her honour the day she was born—it stood black as a cyprus on the moonlit white field. The tree he had planted for Tina was at the front of the house and the tree for Arnie was at the head of the grove of poplars that led down to the river. When she and Arnie had walked across the river ice in the winter, coming home from school for the weekend, they had sometimes been caught in blizzards. They'd had to huddle in a cave in the rock face of the western end of Kingsmere Island. From their rock enclosure they'd watched the stinging cold veils of snow coming toward them from a great distance across the frozen white plain of the river. A waving, wafting battalion of ghosts and their outriders. Once she had sat down on the ice, too cold and tired to go on, and Arnie had harangued her and nagged her until he had forced her to her feet.

She could hear Karl's feet come walking toward the dark kitchen. She could hear them stop in the doorway. After a moment she could hear his uncertain voice say, "I'm sorry— apparently I've hurt your feelings."

He came up behind her and pressed himself close up against her. She could feel his warm, wine breath on her skin. He cupped her breasts, kissed the bent back of her neck.

She tried to pry his fingers out from under her breasts.

"Don't be cruel," he whispered into her hair.

She didn't want to answer him, she didn't want to speak; she wanted to freeze him out so he'd know, beyond a shadow of a doubt, how much he'd hurt her. But then this deep-freeze treatment made her think of Klara, and in a rush of fear that if she wasn't careful she would turn into her mother, she turned to him and flung her arms around his neck and kissed his eyes and then his mouth—a long, deep kiss during which he got her backed up against the sink. Ordinarily she loved this, being backed up against something; even now, in her confusion, she could feel a dark rose of sweat and desire budding between the thighs of her black velvet toreador pants, and she slid her hands up inside the sleeves of his shirt —it made her feel calm and womanly to do this—but at the same time something was ticking, the kiss was a bomb, there was going to be an explosion, she was still so angry with him. But for some reason she didn't want him to know; she wanted to keep her anger a secret from him; she wanted to observe him in his naive belief he'd been forgiven. And so she said in a normal voice, "Hey! Maybe what we need is something to eat," which allowed them to break away from each other and start to pull bowls of leftovers out of the ice-box—a plate of cold cuts; a cold fogged bowl of black olives; a bowl of mayonnaise with dill in it; a Norwegian loaf of pale cheese embedded with cloves and caraway seeds and coated with a wax red as royal sealing wax; a bottle of red wine; a shallow bowl of pork tenderloin medallions in their cold, sweet, congealed sauce of onion rings and basil and mushrooms and brandy. And all this assembling of food was done in a spirit of greatest friendliness, or so it seemed. Because really it was not; she was, after all, still cunningly watching him, to see how he would behave when he imagined he was putting something over on her. She would never marry him. It was a pity he was looking so attractive, so appealing, had rolled up the sleeves of his blue-striped white shirt and loosened his tie. He took up the tray and carried it into the Tomb Room and they both squatted to it and spread the bowls of food and the wine out on the cold flagstones in front of the fire. She liked to look at him, she did, she loved it, but it was a pleasure she would have to give up. She could give it up. She could, if she had to.

Not that much dark was left before sunrise. The long snout of wood that had been burning all through the night was being transformed, by a burning zigzag of flame, into a long wolfish grey jaw. And when a fiery hinge in this jaw gave way, Karl walked on his knees over to the fire and broke open the fallen part of it with the poker, sending up a startled flock of sparks. "It is better to marry than to burn," he said, and Ingrid felt an awful dread in her abdomen because she knew he was going to ask her to marry him; he was going to ask her now, this minute; it was exactly like him to disarm her by leading into it with a joke, and she wondered how she could ever bring herself to say no (although she knew she must), and when he turned to her she thought, Oh God, *help* me! but what he said instead was "What are your plans for the summer?"

"Working for Klara. In the music camp."

"Do your parents pay you for that?"

"No."

"And then what?"

She didn't know but was ashamed to admit it. She said, "Oh, there are various possibilities."

He wanted to know what these possibilities might be.

"I might go to school."

"And study what?"

Her voice broke a little. "Painting," she said.

"Painting!" It was as if she had said she planned to do her degree in Murder. But then he quickly rallied with a "Sorry— I know you draw well," and she was struck by how much the words "draw well" seemed to leech the power out of her gift for drawing. Such as it was.

"And what about the typing?" he asked in a more reasonable voice. "What happened there?"

"Gave it up."

"Like you gave up the nursing," he said, and his voice had changed again, had become spiteful with disappointment.

She said nothing.

"Do you regret giving up the nursing?"

"No, Your Honour, I do not."

He laughed, a little self-consciously. "I know I must sound like the Grand Inquisitor," he said. And there, wonder of wonders, he seemed willing to let the matter of her failure, her future, lie.

About an hour before sunrise they went for a walk on the beach. They walked to the point where the bluff met the water in a prow of high black rock. A wind-deformed fir tree was mounted on top of the rock, a tattered flag of drooping, low-winged black branches. They walked into what looked like a cave in the leaves, found the old lumber road and started to make their way along its soft mane of grass that was scattered with pale pebbles, as if the beach had tried to migrate up into the woods. There was the smell of resin and decay but also of mist and the river. It was unearthly still. Ingrid shivered from the cold. She had not even taken time to fetch a sweater to pull on over her blouse, and the section of exposed leg between the end of her toreador pants and the tops of her old rubber boots ached from the cold. When Karl felt her trembling, he pulled off his tweed jacket and caped it over her shoulders. She was grateful to him; they stood and kissed awkwardly, formally, beneath the scratchy dark trees. Karl was warmly dressed, even without his jacket; he had on one of his Norwegian sweaters, and as he and Ingrid embraced, Ingrid could smell mothballs, fogged wool. She thought, if I don't go with him, what will become of me? She felt the whole world was closed off to her now. I have failed at everything, she thought.

They came out of the cathedral-like dark of the conifer woods and into leafier country. More and more rattling; more and more light. Slender birch trees, so white and motionless in their trunks, were all hustle and rustle high up in their leaves.

Karl was saying, "If we got married, could you work as a typist?"

Ingrid looked up at him, feeling the doomed cunning of a woman about to be proposed to. "I could, but I'd need to practice a bit first."

"Could you start to practice soon?"

Flattered but feeling it was only wisdom to also be doubtful, she asked, "But *should* we marry, do you think? We disagree on so many things."

He said that if she wanted to know the truth, he had mixed feelings about it himself.

On this they were agreed, then. But knowing that he had doubts, too, hurt her feelings a little. Which was childish, of course. Also, his doubt seemed to make her more keen. Which was mad, really. She tried to imagine herself married. She pictured Toronto looking as modern Moscow or stony Chicago must look—all windy and glaring and grey and concrete; all flattened by windy glaring grey light. She saw herself working as a typist there. Far from home and glad of it. She saw herself wearing a trim little dove-grey suit. But would there be woods like this wood anywhere in Ontario? Or a river as lovely as the May River? It seemed to her it was unlikely there would be. Her whole childhood seemed to have been spent in this wood, on this river. In the early spring she and Arnie and Tina had played on the river when it was no longer safe, finally fleeing home, pursued by treacherous maps of cracks in the ice. And in winter they had played at the foot of the Elf Temple, deep in the woods, building forts and caves in the snowbanks. The Elf Temple was a frozen bluff of water with curdled pale yellow braids of ice in the white—as if a bird, flying above it in the frozen air, had urinated on it while it was freezing. They had come home from the woods with their fingers freezing inside their ice-beaded mittens, their toes paining like bullets in their boots, the need to go pee sharply seeded in each of them, a Pavlovian reflex at the first sight of their house lights. And although sometimes they had found their parents not speaking to each other, at other times they had found them strangely peaceful together (a post-coital peace? but they wouldn't have considered such a possibility *then*)—Klara playing the piano, slowly, thoughtfully, the notes seeming liquidly to stalk reserves of memory, feeling; Pup sitting in the kitchen mending a section of harness or bridle. Ingrid could not imagine such a warm scene taking place between them now. But maybe we'll do better than they did, she thought, picturing herself as Karl's wife. She was lying on the floor in front of a fire, reading a book. Their children were playing near her, three small fair children in corduroy overalls, talking and singing to themselves and making motorboat noises with the toy trucks they were driving along the slope of one of her thighs, along the hill of a hip. It thrilled her, the way they trusted her. They trusted her so much they didn't even see her. She was just part of the landscape to them, and the thought of being so trusted made her feel happy almost beyond belief, so that when she, their future mother, came with their future father out into a morning whose mist was obscuring the hills that ran behind the Gully Bay house and Karl said, "Do you think we should marry, then?" she said yes, she thought they had a chance to be happy.

The house, at the end of its long foggy field, was looking blank—even dead—with sleep. It was hard to believe that the people who were sleeping in it would ever open their eyes, yawn, sit up. Just before seven, the two who were to marry came in among them like thieves, leaving wet mist-tracks on the kitchen linoleum. Then they kissed each other quickly good-night and at once climbed the stairs, not wanting to be obliged to answer any questions put to them by those who would soon enough be stumbling out of their beds to splash their faces with cold water to wake themselves up.

The Teller's Cage

Alec and Kathryn pull open the wet car-handles, slam themselves in. The car stinks of new vinyl and of their own perspired-in raincoats. Also of rubber things belonging to their children: Timmie's rubber duck, the rubber boots Deborah kicked off onto the back seat last night after they got home from a spin up on the mountain. After supper they'd all decided to drive up there together, to one of the lookouts; all tumbled out of the car to gaze down on Montreal's glimmering fields of lights in the mist. From up there they could look down on the towers of the Montreal General Hospital, and could even see below the hospital to the Family Service Clinic. They have just left this clinic now, after their first session with their marriage counsellor, and are on an even lower level of the mountain and dropping lower still. Alec swings the car right, onto Sherbrooke Street. The streetlights have come on early, because of the rain. Some of the tall, narrow shop windows have yellow canvas or yellow-painted metal awnings like one-half a hoop skirt belled over them. In their lighted interiors the mannequins, holding out their hands, seem to be breathily whispering, "Is it still raining out?"

"I think he must have some sort of deficiency," Kathryn now says to Alec.

His voice guarded, he asks her who.

"Mr Chisholm."

"*Dr* Chisholm," he says. But then, more reasonably, "What do you mean, deficiency?"

"Didn't you notice his skin?"

"No, I can't say that I did." And then, fiercely, "I'm not like you! I don't have to notice everything all the time! I don't have to control the world!"

"Those little patches of white all across one cheek?"

"No."

"Lack of pigment," she says.

He asks her what lack of pigment means, and again his voice sounds more human, kinder, as if he has reined it in from some unbridledness.

"I don't know. Like I said, some kind of deficiency." She smiles to herself and sees to it that her smiling to herself gets into her voice. "Maybe a moral one."

"So you hated him."

"Baby, he was *crazy* about *you*, why shouldn't I hate him?"

"That's childish."

Kathryn draws her bare legs up onto the car seat, knees them under her chin. Her feet are freezing in her thin sandals. She caps them with the two bottom corners of her raincoat, tries to press them into warmth. Chisholm! she thinks. And recalling the way he turned to her with a lazy, tricky calm and then lazily, venomously inquired, "Do you always attack him like this?" she parts her raincoat and, pulling back a toe at a time, chants with despairing pleasure:

> This little pigment went to market
> This little pigment stayed home
> This little pigment had *all* Dr Chisholm's love and
> approval
> And this little pigment had none

Alec does not find her rhyme amusing. "I hate it when you act like this."

"I know. But remember, you were the one who wanted us to go see this pious little twit."

"Yes!" he cries tightly. "And why? You know why. So he could help us bring an end to it all."

He really does want it to be over, then. But after he's parked the car in their driveway he sits slumped at the wheel a moment, printing something indecipherable in the mist of his side of the windshield with the leather disk chained to the car keys. But then he rubs his hieroglyphics viciously out, making a porthole in the cold mist with the end of his fist. Through it, he peers gloomily at his wife's future. "I'll tell you one thing, my darling. If we do split up, you'll have to go back to work. Because there's no way we're ever going to be able to swing this on just one salary."

Fear flares up in her as she asks him what sort of work he thinks she'll be able to get. She has a terror of not being able to find anything. Of the word "failure" being stamped in each of her panicked, pale blue eyes. Of being turned down by everyone, everywhere: landladies, bosses.

"You'll probably have to go back to work at the bank."

She says she doesn't like the idea of putting Timmie into day care. "He's too young for that."

"Sooner or later he's going to have to learn he wasn't born with a silver spoon in his mouth." And his sorrowful eyes say, and so will you too, my lovely.

But it isn't just putting the kids into day care that worries her; if she goes to work in a bank she's afraid she might start to steal. She didn't steal when she worked in a bank before, but lately she has found herself wanting things. A rug she saw in a store called Folklore—a worn subtle carpet in sand and dried-blood colours. And in a store only a few paces beyond Folklore, a slippery silver-grey nightgown with insets of beige lace.

They don't stay with Dr Chisholm long. Four sessions in which they see him together; a fifth session alone. By this time the hateful little man has given up all hope for their marriage but has retained his fondness for Alec. Comparing notes the night of the last day, at supper, they compare the goodbyes. To Alec: he hopes they'll meet at tennis club one of these days. To Kathryn: well . . . he will say *this* much—it has been . . . interesting. Meeting her.

Kathryn tells Alec she considers her goodbye to be the finer one, if you take into account the fact that there are people whose perceptions are so utterly inverted that their insults become, automatically, the highest praise.

"Oh?" says Alec, "Well, if you want to know the truth, Dr Chisholm told me I *had* to get out of this marriage. He said you were too destructive. He gave me the names of two lawyers. I told him you were too indecisive to make any kind of concrete move and he said it would be up to me to do it, then. He said, 'Maybe instead of making decisions, she eats.' And then he laughed."

Kathryn jumps up from the table and grabs up her plate and fork and slaps them into the dishpan, where, maddeningly, they bouncily float, like children's boats, on the foam-veined, cold water. She turns on the hot tap full force. "That was very unethical of him!" she yells, over the blast of hot water. She feels constriction and nausea in her stomach. In her heart too, if it is possible to feel nausea in the heart. She punches open a can of Diet Pepsi and casts it into a glass. Cold steam billows up from it, stinging her cheek and one eye with a chilled Pepsi mist. She turns off the tap. "Unethical and superficial," she says in a more controlled voice. "And it proves that my original assessment of the little prick was correct. He's a jerk. A jerk and a moral simpleton." She stares out the window at nothing, darkly nursing her Pepsi. After a minute or two, and with a wounded burning in her throat, she asks, "Don't you have to play tennis?" And she thinks, we always refer to his pleasures this way, as if they are obligations.

"Yes. I have to go. I'm just leaving."

But first he has to finish reading the paper. Then he helps her clear the table. He puts the butter in the refrigerator; he fits the beer bottles into a box under the sink; he wets a dishcloth and rubs at the jammy spots on the children's end of the table.

Kathryn stands at the sink, washing the beer glasses, praying stern prayers. You've cleared your conscience, *go*.

He leaves.

But by now the tears, which have been forming like painful sweat all up and down her throat, won't come. Somebody could write a song about it, she thinks, country and western, something about standin' in the kitchen and tryin' to cry your leftover tears. But it's probably already been done.

Two months after they finish with the marriage counsellor Alec moves out. He takes a six-month lease on a studio in a tall, liverish-brown brick building on Côte des Neiges. Very urban, gold curtains in all the windows. There's a restaurant on the ground floor with greenery hung in it. In the spring Alec will move out of there and into an apartment. And Kathryn and the children will have to find themselves an apartment too.

But before spring comes, there is Christmas to be got through. Alec comes over to the Vendôme Street house to spend it with Kathryn and the children—comes stamping into the kitchen, his voice pitched too high and hearty out of nervousness. Or maybe it only seems this way because for almost an hour it has been blissfully quiet here, with only the lovely clear horn and harp music of Christmas playing low. Debbie and Timmie are in the living room, lying on the floor in front of the fireplace, in nightgown and sleep-jumper, and they are playing low too—some whispering game in the last of the sunlight, the first of the candlelight. Kathryn remembers this Christmas excitement of candlelight-in-sunlight from her own childhood.

In response to Alec's stamping, the goose in the oven spits and hisses. Alec sets his armload of gifts down on the pale green linoleum floor that always looks as if it's been freshly mopped with milk. There are two soft-looking parcels— sweaters?—wrapped in red tissue paper to which he has painstakingly stuck many small gold stars of the sort teachers award to children for Effort and Good Deportment, and there are two handsome cubes big enough to house soccer balls done up in gleaming silver foil and metallic blue ribbon. Holding a finger to the side of his nose, he says in a low voice, "For later." Then he begins to pull off his stitched pigskin gloves, finger by leather finger, beats the snow off the sleeves of his coat with them. Coat and dark grey plaid scarf are then hung up on a porcelain hook in the children's low closet. Heeling off an overshoe, he half turns toward Kathryn. "Your mother sent me a letter. About us breaking up." He seems, over his shoulder and so with only one eye, to be studying her with extraordinary watchfulness. "And I think you ought to know that she's on my side, my love."

"I want to see it," says Kathryn, quick and frightened.

"Didn't bring it with me." Standing guard in front of the low closet, he plunges his hands into the pockets of his almost bell-shaped grey tweed jacket. "Anyway, I'm not sure you *should* see it. Not to put too fine a point on it, the lady viciously attacked you." Still holding her in his watchful gaze, he seats himself in his old chair at the end of the table. He's flushed from the cold, or possibly from a drink on the way over. He looks plumper, although curiously haggard, lost looking around the eyes—at least until some old mischievous sympathy for Kathryn starts to flower in them. "That's some mother you picked for yourself, my darling." And now he seems nearly restored, smiles his old fetching smile. "The lady is a killer."

"Please don't call me 'my darling.' Please don't call me 'my love.'"

He pretends to look offended. Or possibly he really is offended. "What should I call you, then?"

"Don't call me anything. Just tell me what she said."

"No!"

She says maybe he shouldn't have told her about it in the first place, then. "Because this way it's just a tease." But how could Mother *do* that? she thinks. After all, we are still husband and wife. We still have a whole family history together.

And for some reason this thought of their having a whole history together makes her feel like weeping.

Deborah, her thumb stuck in her mouth, comes into the kitchen towing the small red-wheeled wooden horse she got from Kathryn's sister, Melanie, for Christmas. The little horse's nostrils look blue, cyanosed, in the weakening light. Alec signals with his eyes to Kathryn to watch her tongue with Deborah present. But Kathryn, serving the mashed turnips and potatoes in unhappy dollops onto a large oval serving dish, is in no mood to be quelled. "Just who, exactly, does my mother think she is, anyway? Maybe she figures that because she's rich, and in good health, and has always been lucky, she must be the darling of the gods. When, for all we know, she's made a pact with the Devil."

Deborah's laugh shocks her parents in the stillness of the tense, snow-lit kitchen. "Who?" she cries up at her mother, and when Kathryn hesitates, she turns herself into a little nightgowned pilgrim in a storm at midnight, her small face raised up to the second-storey window of Kathryn's face, her small hand knocking on Kathryn's thigh with an urgent fist. "*Who* is the Devil?"

"Your grandmother," says Kathryn.

Alec looks aghast, almost terrified. "I forbid you to discuss your mother in this manner in front of the children."

Kathryn lowers her voice to force some calm into it. "Remember that birthday present she brought to Debbie last spring? That awful big sack of mildewed old peanuts all gift-wrapped with sparkly paper and tied up with rosettes made of gold ribbon?"

His eyes tell her that he remembers but that he considers it would be the height of melodrama to discuss it. He says that the peanuts may have been old but to say that they were mildewed is pure hysteria.

Kathryn says either way it was sick. "Why should a child be tricked into respecting a person who would do something like that to her?" She slaps a plate with a quivering log of cranberry jelly on it down on the table, whereupon the red log promptly waddles off the plate and onto the embroidered tablecloth.

Alec seizes the opportunity to order Kathryn to get a hold on herself. "And you go wash your hands." he tells Deborah. "And get Timmie to wash his hands, too." He lights the candles like a man who believes he's the last sane man on earth.

They get through the first course with only a brief commentary by Kathryn on the nature of her difficulty with her mother. "She was so happy when I got married, to get me out of the house. She always considered me her rival."

"But, sweetheart," Alec says, beginning to carve the goose. "Your father has been dead for years."

"But aren't we talking about the unconscious here? Isn't that just a small point, the person's being dead?" And it is, she's sure of it. The fact that her father has been dead for nearly six years and that her mother, for five of those years, has been married to a real estate tycoon named Jimmie Henderson is not the point really. The unconscious is too wily for points. Kathryn also believes that Alec married her out of pity, because she was living at home with her mother after her father died, working as a teller in the Bank of Nova Scotia in Point Castile and having no real life to speak of.

While Kathryn is serving the dessert—their traditional Christmas dessert of raisin gingerbread and whipped cream—the phone rings. Kathryn goes white. "That'll be mother now, calling to wish us a merry Christmas."

Alec, also pale, rises to his feet. "Do you want me to take it?"

"No, it's okay, I'll get it." And she walks down the hallway of the long, narrow Victorian house, feeling that in its length, and in its faded red bricks, it is like an old, weathered-pink freight car stuck on a siding in the snowbound-still Christmas night. And yet, outside it isn't quite dark. The sky is the fiercely pure blue of the last of the light, and so far—Kathryn can see this through the octagonal window directly above the telephone table—has only the evening star in it. But out in

Victoria, where her mother will be calling from, it will still be sunny lunchtime. No snow, except in the mountains. A big cross, fashioned from holly, on the elegant, brass-knockered black door. The red and gold Christmas teacups. Her mother's traditional Christmas cookies, snowmen and reindeer with sparkle-harnesses of red and pink sugar.

Kathryn picks up the phone as if afraid it will bite her. Her mother's hello always seems to "halloo" to her, far across the great windswept white wastes of the continent, as if she expects not to have a conversation with her daughter but only to hear her own echo.

"Hello-o, darling Kathryn!" she halloos to her now, across the still-sunlit but darkening West, and Kathryn can picture her, her poised, immaculate little mother, perched on the arm of one of the armchairs in her Victoria living-room—her silver-fair hair cut in the windblown style favoured by the Princess of Wales. "Jimmie and I just wanted to call and wish you a wonderful Christmas! And Debbie and Tiny Timmie too!" Her voice has been forced up into a high thin joviality. "And all the very best for the New Year too!"

When Kathryn doesn't respond, her mother asks sharply, "Kathryn? Are you there?" At which point Kathryn, pushing her voice down low, says, "I hear you wrote Alec a letter about me."

After an entrenched silence, although not a pure silence, for choral music can be faintly heard in the Victoria background—a massed, mixed choir singing one of the maddeningly sprightly songs of the season—Kathryn's mother says Alec had no right to show Kathryn that letter.

"No *right*?" cries Kathryn.

Her cry brings Alec urgently down the hallway to loom over her, his eyes wild, his checked linen napkin clutched in a fist at his heart. With his free hand he signals frantically for her to cool it.

Kathryn darts her blouse deeply into the waistband of her long skirt. She looks through him. "He hasn't shown it to me yet," she says into the phone. "He's only told me about it."

Her mother says he had no right to tell her about it.

"He said it was savage. He said you viciously attacked me."

Alec, staring at Kathryn, looks nearly apoplectic with terror.

"You have often done things to hurt *me*, Kathryn," her mother, out in sunny Victoria, is saying into the phone.

"What things?" asks Kathryn, now staring at Alec. Her heart is beating like mad and she can feel great wet crescents of sweat starting to form in her bloused armpits. "What have I ever done to you?"

"Melanie said that when she visited you last summer you sat out on the beach and talked about me the whole afternoon. She said you made her sick to her stomach with your talking. She said she finally had to say to you, 'If you don't stop talking about Mother like this, I'm going to leave.'"

Alec, giving up, starts back down the hall to the kitchen.

"That isn't true!" cries Kathryn. "I wasn't the only one who talked about you!" Five or six paces down the hallway she can hear Alec's feet stop. She can feel his fear, a visceral flash of it behind her own ribs; he's fearful he's about to hear his own name spoken. Into the phone she cries in a high voice, "Melanie and I *both* talked about you!" and now she can sense him, just beyond the range of her sight, starting to breathe again. She makes her voice swing low. "We both always *have* talked about you. It was the only way we could deal with you."

"*Some*one is not telling the truth," comes the voice from out in sunny Victoria and it sounds, for the first time, pleased.

"I got her to say you can show me the letter."

But Alec says he isn't showing the letter to anyone. "You and your whole family are insane. You're sick." He says that right after he's finished dessert he's going to go back to his place and tear the letter up.

"She said I used to be such a sweet girl. But now, according to her, I've turned into a monster."

"I can't disagree with her on that," says Alec, regarding Kathryn with sorrow.

"Why would Mel do a thing like that, though? Why would she tell a lie about me?"

"I've said it before and I'll say it again: when you and Mel get together and get started cutting up your mother, it's like listening to a couple of harpies."

In one of the magazines she bought to help get her through Christmas, Kathryn spots the advertisement of a New York handwriting analyst named Anna Czerwinski. She has always wanted to have her handwriting analysed, and ever since she was told she used to be sweet but now she is hard she's more keen than ever. She decides she'll send a sample of Alec's off, too. *Then* we will see, she thinks; *then* we will see just who's who and what's what here. And so she gathers together some letters to send to New York—a letter she wrote Alec earlier this year; a page from a letter she wrote him the summer they got married; a page from a letter Alec wrote her five years ago. She also roots around in a drawer among old Christmas cards and bits of ribbon and wool for a postcard Alec sent her from a trip to Scandinavia with a documentary crew from the Film Board last September. She recalls that on the front of this card there was a photo of a weathered old Norwegian church that looked more like a giant witch's hut than a house of Christian worship. Brown shingled eaves and, projecting from them, what looked like creepily supplicating dark wood hands with switches for fingers. But when she finally locates it she sees that the projections look more like long dark wooden rollerskates, aimed toward heaven and appearing to be trying to turn themselves into something festively organic —snails, perhaps.

She labels the specimen of her handwriting "K," Alec's "A," then sends them off to New York.

One mild morning early in March when the last of the snow is dripping like rain from the shingled eaves of the front porch, and the earth smells of the earth-rotten but clear-aired aroma of decay and thaw, Kathryn receives a reply from Anna Czerwinski. She breathes in the thaw smell, taking in the mail. She doesn't want to open the letter yet; she props it against the toaster and now and then sneaks an anxious peek at it while she's fixing the children their lunch. She's sure it will tell the truth. She likes (but also fears) the idea of the truth being located in the cellular structure of the words people can tell lies with—in the loops, the knots, the slant, the rhythm, the pressure. But suppose Ms Czerwinski likes Alec's script and doesn't much care for hers? Suppose she is exposed as a manipulator, suppose her script reveals a bent for revenge? She decides she won't open the letter until she's put the children down for their naps. And then she delays even this by deciding she'll give them their bedtime baths now, instead of after supper.

Spring sunlight falls on the bathwater as the children play in it, making bright boats of light bob back and forth across the water-stained ceiling. The children get rosy from the warm water and from the excitement of a bath in the middle of the day. Kathryn catches them shyly spy her pleasure in watching them gaspingly slip and slide over each other in the water. She and Melanie used to take baths together when they were little. They used to play a game they called Tummy Touch. They would tear off their clothes and race toward the bathroom. Just before they sank into the tub's lukewarm lake they would shriek, "Tummy Touch!" and after a quick brushing together of their bellies they would swoon back in the water as if electrocuted by glee. Melanie was always their mother's favourite. That's why she tattled about our talk on the beach, thinks Kathryn. She got rattled; she got scared I'd tell Mother and so she decided to beat me to it.

When she's got the kids settled down for their naps, she comes back down to the kitchen. She feels like a woman on a high diving board. Don't think, just do it. She makes straight for the letter and tears it open, but her desire to know every-thing at once is so great that it's a few moments before she can begin to take any of it in. When she is able to, she reads:

Dear Mrs Blakelock,

Following are my analyses of the two specimens of handwriting you sent.

SPECIMEN K

The handwriting of your early adulthood shows the presence of a highly developed mentality and imagination. And yet you do have a tendency to procrastinate. Inner anxieties grip you to some extent; self-estimate is not as high as you might make it appear, and decisions may be difficult for you to make, in certain areas at least. Confidence wavers at times, and feelings of inadequacy lead you to some emotional isolation from your environment. While your qualities of mind would set you apart naturally, you tend to regress to narcissistic levels that could give you trouble in coping with present and future considerations. Not entirely rooted in yourself, despite self-centered propensities, you may take refuge in past experiences without realizing it. Here you might run into conflict with your desire to break away from the past, possibly becoming caught in a bind.

Amiable by nature, you do not like to fight, and to lessen your conflict with present surroundings you may adjust in a dissimulating way. Ulterior motives may be at stake: You may wish to be protected, looked after—taken along for the ride, so to speak. Certainly the material is important to you, and the good things of life have great appeal; penuriousness is alien to your nature in any circumstance. On the more positive side, you are generous and quick-witted; friends doubtless find you a stimulating companion. Aggression is not likely to come out unless you are antagonized—and even then you might turn it more on yourself than you would on others. Nevertheless, it might prove a source of conflict that could make you unhappy. Possibly it is another reason for the emotional isolation you experience.

In your present sample, you have let down the bars of defence to quite a degree. Not so centered in your own private world, you are notably more receptive to the world outside. Greater self-assurance has released you from some of the inhibitory traits displayed earlier. It looks as if you are finding life more agreeable; at least you go out to meet it with lifted spirit.

SPECIMEN A

A great deal of emotional disturbance shows up in this writing. Possessed of a harsh, uncompromising nature that conflicts sharply with softer but nonetheless compelling impulses, he attempts to suppress both. Severity of mind clashes violently with the vivid imagery of his instincts. Inner tension assails him, stifling impulses and constricting emotions, probably to the detriment of full personality development. His strong individuality poses special problems on that score. Anything contrary to it arouses combative defenses, which might take the form of aggression, obstinacy, tyrannical or domineering tendencies. While they may be cloaked in pretentious gestures or eloquence of one kind or another, the complexities of his true nature are ill-concealed. But he goes to great lengths to conceal, from himself as well as others, the inner conflicts that beset him.

To display superiority (which he does not feel) is essential to him, but this imposes a strain and, needless to say, it plays hob with his adaptability. He finds it extremely difficult to fit in, to follow the thinking and viewpoints of others. Sympathy is difficult for him to experience. Without realizing it perhaps, he opposes rather than adjusts, seeking to impose his will on those around him or upon his environment in general—and what he reveals in close quarters may be paradoxically a weak will that undermines self-mastery.

All this sounds overwhelmingly negative, but it is what goes on within him. He may display a facade that enables him to function successfully within his milieu. Certainly, he has work capacity, plus marked esthetic sense, possibly an artistic one as well. Although distracted by his inner disturbances, he perseveres, enduring the resentments and rancor his emotions inflict.

Relationships with him could not possibly be easy, and the contrasts of character and personality that you reveal seem to speak for themselves. Two more opposite dispositions would be hard to come by. They may attract, but they pull apart, inevitably.

Anna Czerwinski

Kathryn has never felt such triumph. Or a triumph so contaminated by dread. It's like having made a terrible wish against someone and having it miraculously granted. She has prayed for *years* for someone to see through Alec and now someone has. *This is true*, she thinks. *This is uncanny*. At the same time she's filled with a terrible unease. Didn't I marry him? Didn't I love him? And she's flooded with memories of Alec tenderly soaping the children in their baths; of Alec, crouched down to console Deborah in her grief at having torn the jacket of one of her dolls on a nail beside the garage door. He is a charmer, after all, and where is there any mention of his charm? But then she decides his charm is sick, a sick cover for private cruelties; he *deserves* to have his markings commented on and explained. I was young when I married him is what she decides. But she has no sooner thought this than thoughts of being young arouse a vicious clannishness in her; he is her husband, after all, and so what right does anyone

have to speak a word against him—even someone she's paid
to do it? It's like being a child again and feeling outraged
because one of her playmates has been mocking her mother.
But this is surely only guilt—guilt masking extreme pleasure.
In reality she feels nothing but gratitude to Anna Czerwinski
for going straight to the heart of the matter. "They may
attract," she rereads from her letter, "but they pull apart,
inevitably." This is the best line of all. Or maybe it's only
second-best, the best being, "Relationships with him could
not possibly be easy." For a long time she sits in the kitchen
rocker with the sun on her, basking in dreams of watching
his face while he gets an eyeful of *that*.

   At two o'clock, when she hears the first creaks and sighs
from upstairs, she goes up. Into Timmie's room first, to find
him lying on his back in his soaked corduroy overalls, one
ankle sock yanked off, wide-eyed, watching a webbed square
of light shining through the streaky window and hitting the
far blue wall. When he sees her he makes a happy little caw
sound and pulls himself up by his cot's spooled bars. She
goes over to him, stands with his railing fenced against her
belly. Poor baby—yo' Daddy's disturbed an' yo' Ma is a baby
herself. But he's a sturdy, powerful child, built like his sturdy,
powerful father; he doesn't look like a candidate for any kind
of pity. He throws his sleep-warm arms around her bent neck
and laughs when she rubs her nose in the hollow of his
shoulder. There's an abacus built into the arched opening at
the head of his bed. She likes it even better than he does—its
wooden beads in their worn reds and blues and greens.
Sometimes, when they're in the mood, they play with it a
little. She shoves two or three beads to one end and holds
them hidden in a fist, and then he peels at her fingers until
she's forced to let the beads go. She plans to teach him to
count this way. But today when she tries to play the bead
game with him he yanks down hard on a lock of her hair.
"Walk!" he orders her.

   She lifts him up. "But we have to change you first."

   "Change you," he says.

   "We're going for a walk, Deb," she calls, carrying Tim into
the toilet.

Out in the park, with Tim lying in his sled, mummied in blankets and looking sated with the fresh air and with the way the shadows are moving on the snow, and with Deborah playing some delicate but demanding game in a snowbank with a stick, Kathryn sits on a park bench reading her letter, as absorbed as a woman who's just heard from her lover. She goes from Specimen A to Specimen K and from Specimen K back to Specimen A again. *Is* she a narcissist? She must be— even reading about her own narcissism seems to give her pleasure. (Although not quite as much pleasure as reading Specimen A.)

"Mummy! Mummy! I have a letter too," chants Deborah, patting one of Kathryn's jeaned thighs with a snow-beaded mitten. And proudly, shyly, she prints in the snow with her stick: DRER DEBROAH.

A year and a half ago, when Alec came back from the trip to Norway with the Film Board, they must still have had some hope for themselves as a couple. His first night back, he was so worn-out after his plane flight that they lay down on their bed in the dark with their clothes on. Alec curled himself against her back and slid his hands up under her sweater. "Fuck, it was cold there," he whispered into her hair. "Even colder than here, if you can believe it." While he was unhooking her, he told her that the Norwegian word for wonderful was *bra*, and cupping her warm breasts in his cold traveller's hands—she had imagined she could smell Norwegian smells emanating from his sweater (smoked salmon, smoked wood) —he told her a joke one of the Norwegian crew members had told him: when the Queen of England beat the King of Norway at chess, the King, peering insolently down the cleavage of the droopy-breasted Queen, said *"Bra, Your Majesty!"* Kathryn recalls how sleepily affectionate she felt, how she half-turned to rub her head against his chin so that some of the strands of her hair got snagged in the short bristly beard he'd started to grow while he was in Oslo.

Every Thursday, Jean Wilcox, a friend of Kathryn's, drives the nursery school children from Kathryn's neighbourhood home for lunch. She keeps Deborah as her last passenger, along with her own daughter, Suzy, so that she can stay at the Blakelocks' to eat and visit. On the day following the arrival of the letter from Anna Czerwinski she comes stamping into Kathryn's kitchen, bringing some of the freshness of the early spring morning in with her. And she too seems to shine. Her straight brown hair shines, and her long caramel leather coat. Also her eyes, which have a coolly entertained glint in them, almost cruel. The two little girls come staggering in behind her, parkas unzipped, boot buckles undone, strands of silky fair hair caught in the chewed-looking orlon fur of their parka hoods. They make Kathryn think of turning to Alec in the dark. They look drunk with exhaustion. They look as if they would gladly be noisy and troublesome if they could, but at the moment they don't have the energy for it. Pushing her worn-out fair little daughter forward, Jean says, "Suze has a present for you, Kath. Show Kath your present, Suze."

Suzy starts to pull apart the two sides of a stuck-together newsprint painting of a cheerful blue whale riding the waves of a choppy black sea. The newsprint is heavily wet with new paint and Kathryn, watching Jean help Suzy pull the paint-ing open, wonders why Jean makes Suzy do these awful polite things that force adults to be gushy and Suzy to be anxious. And Deborah to be jealous; for she is standing off to one side, pretending to play a game with the salt and pepper shakers, moving them around on the kitchen table and talk-ing to them, but something about the way she is archly speaking (now to the salt) and the stiff way she is standing— very straight and correct in her long-sleeved flowered shirt, her grey cotton overalls jutting puffily out from the elasti-cized back of her waistband—tells Kathryn that her little daughter is hyperaware of every word of praise being spoken over her friend's damp work of art.

Kathryn tacks the whale up on the wall by the fridge. There are several other drawings and paintings here, by Deborah and Timmie, and, presiding over them, an oil pastel of a big-breasted nude done by Alec in a night-school painting class back in November. Kathryn often finds herself pausing to glance up at it. The nude is an older woman, with mammoth hips, tired eyes, grey-streaked coarse black hair falling in pronounced waves to her shoulders. Only the arm whose hand is cupping her chin is slightly out of scale—almost puny-looking. Deborah, who by now has abandoned the pepper and salt, comes over to stand beside Kathryn to formally inspect Suzy's picture up on the wall. Kathryn, drawing her little daughter's head to her hip, starts to stroke her fine hair consolingly behind her right ear, but Deborah ducks out from under her caress, and stepping away from her, plucks at the back of Suzy's plaid blouse. "See that big picture way up at the top? My father made that." And although Kathryn knows that she should rejoice in her little daughter's admiration for her father, she feels a wince of jealousy, like an injection of something ice-cold and lethal, doing its mean work in her heart.

"*Wow*," Suzy is moaning, loading a visitor's exaggerated awe into a voice she has made abnormally loud. "Is that *ever* a big picture."

When the two little girls have gone off to join Timmie in the living-room to watch the lunchtime cartoons, Kathryn and Jean sit down at the kitchen table and Jean says, "So. How are things?"

"Okay. I got something interesting in the mail yesterday."

"From?"

"A handwriting expert."

"A handwriting expert. How come?"

"I sent off some handwriting samples to a graphologist in New York. Mine and Alec's. Also mine from when I was younger, to see if there's been any improvement. Wait, I'll get it."

"Improvement," says Jean, her light eyes looking briefly, dourly amused. "You mean we can hope to improve our sad lot in this crummy vale of tears?"

Running back down the stairs, Kathryn can barely contain her excitement. She has always felt that Jean, although she is in many ways her best friend, has never really grasped the depth of her difficulties with Alec. Feeling flushed (and flush too—the letter held to her heart) she comes hurrying back to the kitchen.

When Jean gets to the part that says, "Inner anxieties grip you to some extent," she shrieks.

Kathryn, clearing the clutter off the table, smiles.

When Jean has finished the Kathryn part of the letter she says, "Well, I don't know how they do this sort of thing but, by God, this is *you*."

"You think it's perceptive?"

"It's so right on it's scary. What does she have to say about old Alec?"

Kathryn hands over the Alec part.

Jean reads it in silence and when she's finished it she sighs. "Specimen A and Specimen K." And then she says, "The gospel according to New York." Then, after another (longer) silence: "Are you going to show this to him?"

"I don't know. I'm tempted to."

"Should you, though?" She massages her elbow and looks out the window. She looks unhappily vague, the way people do when they disapprove of something but don't like to say so. "I can't imagine having Ray's handwriting analysed behind his back like that. I mean, would that be right? And having someone make pronouncements on our relationship would really scare me. Knowing how things really are— what's the point? Having my palm read, for instance; I've never had that done. And I wouldn't. Ever."

"You don't agree with her this time, do you?"

"Oh, I don't know," she unhappily says. "It does all seem somewhat extreme, doesn't it? I'm not saying I think Alec is great, or anything like that, God no, far from it. I'm only saying this sounds a little . . ." She looks out the window for a word, finds it in the elements. Or in the memory of them— the late Canadian winter. "Harsh," she says.

"I think it's so right on it's scary," says Kathryn, and they both briefly laugh. "And besides, things do have to get told sometimes, don't you agree? It can't be good to keep things all hidden and bottled up. In general, I mean—not even talking any more about this particular case. What about people's mental health? What about art?"

"Art," says Jean in the voice that, in another mood, she might have used to say, "Men."

"Do you know what I like best about the woman in New York? That she's *in* New York. And so she can't make judgments on the basis of my being ... overweight ... or Alec's being such a smashing-looking bloke."

"But how much overweight are you?" Jean asks her, and her voice sounds odd—both loyal and cold. "Not that much, surely."

"Not that much if you admire big blousey blondes." But then because she can see from Jean's eyes that she's preparing to hazard a guess, and out of tact is already revising this guess downward—to spare her that, to spare both of them that—she quickly says, "Twenty-five pounds."

Jean looks out at the garden, and after a few moments of seeming to debate something (with the window again) she says, "Do you know what I think about Alec? I think he's a little dull. I mean, he's obviously intelligent but I just happen to find him a little bit boring. I always thought the Brits were supposed to have these savage *wits*." But then she says quickly, her light eyes suddenly nervous, "Very well-meaning though."

Kathryn is grateful to Jean, but at the same time she can't bear to have anyone say Alec is dull. He isn't, she thinks; he only pretends to be, in social situations. It's a trick; it's a trick to get people's pity. "You never saw his tantrums. He was a completely different person in private. Completely. The graphologist caught on to that. Look. Where is it? *Here.* Where she talks about his domineering tendencies. You see! He doesn't even know he's a phoney. That makes the whole thing even more tragic."

"It makes him less of a hypocrite though, you have to admit that."

Kathryn doesn't admit anything. She lifts the cast-iron frying pan down from its hook and turns the heat on under it. She can feel Jean's eyes on her back—a shrewd but doubtful look—and after she's shaken the butter bits around in the pan she turns to her friend with dread. A friend's dread. She admires Jean, and her admiration makes her feel fearful. "You look like you're incubating something," she says to her.

Jean lights up, sighs, looks out the window. The window seems to have great appeal for her today. "What I was thinking is that we are all mysteries, really, in the end." She massages her elbow and turning back toward Kathryn frowns at the frying pan. "Unknowable," she adds. "Don't you feel that, Kath? I know that Ray is a mystery to me. Still. And I am a mystery to myself."

"Oh sure. We are all mysteries and everything is relative and maybe now you'd like to talk about the weather." Kathryn deals the plates out fast—coral melmac for the children, dark brown pottery for themselves. "No, I *don't* feel that. I feel we are all accountable. Every day and in every way."

"You can't be too much of a purist in life," says Jean. Her voice has risen a little too. "I'm right. He's wrong. If you were interested in some other man you wouldn't be bothering with any of this anyway. You wouldn't care what some handwriting expert had to say about poor old Alec, you wouldn't give a—" Here she makes a condensed "shih," like a lampooned librarian, but then only says, " ... damn. Really. You wouldn't."

Kathryn can feel her face trying to manufacture an expression of blankness, and after a short silence Jean, who seems to be watching her while pretending not to, says that there might conceivably be something to handwriting analysis, though. "I did read a book about it once and this book said that people who leave openings at the bottom of their a's and o's have criminal natures."

"How could a person do that?"

"Well, that's just it; it would be hard to do. In the middle of what should be a fluid motion you'd have to lift the pen right up off the paper. The thing is, there's a teller at the bank where Ray and I keep our money and *she* does it." Her eyes

brimming with anxious amusement, she looks up at
Kathryn. "Do you think I should report her to the man-
ager?"

"I used to work as a teller in a bank," says Kathryn, and for
a moment she finds herself on the edge of saying, "I wouldn't
want to work in a bank now, though—I'd be afraid I might
help myself to the cash." What would Jean say, if she confessed this? Probably something reassuring. "We all have
these moments." But she might be secretly shocked by it and
so be careful not to leave her hoop-handled bag lying around
unattended when she's at Kathryn's place in the future.
"That's how I met Alec," says Kathryn. "He used to stand in
line for my cage." And she thinks that maybe she could show
Alec the letter but make a joke of it; say something like,
"Vengeance is mine, saith the Wife."

"In the line for your cage," says Jean, smiling at her with,
after all, affection. "You make it sound like he used to come
to court you at the zoo, for God's sake."

The following night, Alec comes over for supper. Kathryn
can feel the presence of the letter behind her right shoulder, in
the top drawer of the cabinet next to the stove. While they're
eating their roast lamb, the letter seems be beaming a bright
light at her shoulderblade and crying out to her in a tiny but
shrilly insistent voice, "Show him!"

She does not. But while he's lacing up his boots, after his
pecan pie and coffee, she finds herself hoping he'll look up at
her and catch the way she's watching him with an expression
of startled pity. She imagines him saying to her, "What's the
matter with you, for Christ's sake?" She imagines herself
replying, "I sent our handwritings away to be analysed. I
wonder if you'd like to see the graphologist's report?" But he
doesn't look up while he's lacing up his boots. In fact, when
he's finished, he stays hunkered down, trying to catch the
attention of Deborah, who's wearing the heather-mix cardigan he gave her for Christmas and who's pinching the skirt of
her dress up into an apron and skipping around him in a
back-and-forth circle. Kathryn, watching them, is unnerved

by Alec's unkempt English charm, by the boyish way his
black hair is lankly falling over one eye, and when he reaches
out and catches Deborah by a corner of her cardigan while
she, almost at the same moment, flicks it so swiftly out of his
grasp that he nearly loses his balance, Kathryn, embarrassed
at having caught him out in a vulnerable moment, looks
quickly away.

The following weekend when he comes over again, Alec is
carrying a sack of dirty laundry. He presents it to Kathryn,
then goes into the living-room to see the children and read
the paper. He doesn't subscribe to a paper himself. He prac-
tices flamboyant economies. He's looking much better than
he looked on his last visit. He's washed his hair. He's also
bought himself a new jacket, a brown houndstooth check.
He's been out with someone, she's sure of it. Something
about the quick glance he gave her when he came in the door.
A shy dart of a glance, and in back of it the real look: a look
gauging how much she has noted the change in him and
wanting her to see him gauging it. Something in his eyes
discreetly crowing, *a woman, a woman*. He's the one who's
going to make a success of all this, she thinks. And I'm the
one who's going to get left behind.

   After the children have been fed and she has switched Alec's
wash over to the dryer, Kathryn goes and sits at the kitchen
table. She is feeling at loose ends. She can hear, from the
living-room, the occasional shaking out of a new section of
the paper. She can feel the presence of the letter behind her
shoulder again. She imagines Alec coming out to the kitchen
to run himself a glass of water. She imagines him coming
over to peek at what she is reading. But this will never
happen.

   She gets up and goes to the cabinet and noiselessly slides
open the drawer and lifts the letter out. She spreads it out on
the kitchen table and reads it again. She almost knows it by
heart by now and yet it has an odd capacity for seeming
startling and fresh to her. She tells herself it would be childish
to go and show it to him, but the desire to do so is extraordinarily powerful. She feels certain that with almost no effort at

all she would be able to convince herself that it's cowardly *not* to show it to him. Still, she can't decide what to do. She stares out the window for a while and then looks down at the part headed Specimen A. She recalls Jean looking out the window for a word to describe it and finally coming up with "harsh." She hears Alec clear his throat. She recalls a line from a novel she read years ago: "You don't learn anything by hurting others; you only learn by being hurt." Okay, so she won't show it to him. But then she wonders if this doesn't leave her with an unfair advantage over him—knowing something he doesn't. She recalls how he told her about her mother's letter, how he said it was vicious. He was right to tell her about it. He would have been right to show it to her, as well. She recalls a line from Anna Czerwinski's letter: ". . . decisions may be difficult for you to make, in certain areas at least"; she recalls Alec, quoting Dr Chisholm, saying, "Maybe, instead of making decisions, she eats." And then Alec saying, "And then he laughed."

He doesn't look up when she comes into the living-room with the letter. He looks older than she has seen him look for quite a long time. She goes and stands beside his chair. Because he doesn't acknowledge her presence she feels a little foolish and formal. After a moment's hesitation she says, "I sent our handwritings away to be analysed. I thought you might be interested to see what the graphologist had to say about them."

He looks up from the paper. His glance is the glance a man might give a drab and rather bothersome secretary. "Not right now. I have to finish the paper. Just put it down there on the coffee table."

How *innocent* he is, in his own imperious fashion. She lays down the letter. She returns to the kitchen. She has an image of herself as a little girl, skipping away down the garden after having been up to some mischief. But her heart is beating slowly, heavily, like marching feet: right, wrong, right, wrong.

After a while she hears him fold up the paper. A short time passes, then a longer time. A horrible thought occurs to her: what if he reads Anna Czerwinski's letter but then never alludes to it? What if he simply ignores it? Forever? He is capable of it. She pictures him as he amiably sat in Dr Chisholm's office, the way he spoke, in diplomatic generalities, about their marriage: "fault on both sides . . . sharing the blame . . . God knows . . . neither of us perfect." At one point he even placed a hand over his heart like a third-rate actor taking an oath to tell the whole truth. He made the most shameless play for Chisholm—the way he smiled, the way he shook hands with him. And that pompous little twit was taken in. But then she supposes she made a play, as well—for Czerwinski. The extra money, for instance, for the analysis of her earlier handwriting, as if to suggest that the earlier K and the later K were two totally different people, and of course the money for the analysis of A as well, and then money too for the analysis of A's and K's chances together. She supposes that A, if he should start to dwell on all this, might conclude that K has been overly generous with his moola. Still no sound from in there. What if he's had a heart attack? What if she's killed him with Czerwinski's letter? Then you will have to live with this guilt for the rest of your life. A virtuously malevolant voice intones this, inside her head, speaking soft and low. It sounds like her mother's voice. She looks out the window awhile, then aims her gaze at different parts of the kitchen. She has just gone over to blankly study a drawing of Deborah's when she hears Alec get up from his chair. He is starting to come out to the kitchen.

As he rounds the corner by the refrigerator he is looking taken aback but not crushed. He's carrying the letter with him. He hands it to her. "Well, that's just one person's opinion," he says to her. But his eyes look betrayed. "Although maybe there were a few true things in it. But on the whole I didn't find it very accurate. It seemed more accurate about you than it did about me, if you want my honest opinion."

She feels frightened for him to the point of offering him a cup of coffee. Between sips from it, he tells her about a recent flight he took, out to the west coast, in connection with a research trip he was sent on by the Film Board. He tells her what it was like flying over the prairies and then the Rockies and how cold it was in Calgary and how warm it was in Vancouver. And she recalls a man she met once, a long time ago—a German, a good German (she is of the generation just old enough to feel obliged to still make this particular distinction), a German-Canadian who still had a very slight German accent—and how he was describing a trip he'd taken to northern Scandinavia; they were sitting together in someone's summer house at Lake of Two Mountains with people talking in loud voices all around them; it was a Sunday afternoon, they were sitting on a couch by a big window, drinking beer and looking out the window at the beach going dark in the rain, and he was telling her about landing on a small airstrip in Lapland and how there were hundreds of little rolling hills covered with small round yellow leaves, and the sky was all dark ahead of him but the sun was shining behind him, shining on all the little round yellow leaves, and he moved his hand in a lovely shallow motion over the remembered hills while the beer in his other hand somehow supplied the feeling of hilly golden light.

"The roses," Alec is saying. "The roses were really lovely. So unbelievable at this time of year. I kept thinking of how Montreal was still under four feet of snow while people out in Victoria were out in their gardens. . . ."

A small silence takes root in the room.

"But of course this doesn't interest you," he says.

"Well, it's something I more or less knew already. About there being roses out there at this time of year, I mean. . . ."

"You always act so bloody superior," he says. "You think you're so special. I could tell you about flying into the sunrise on the way back," he adds. "But of course you wouldn't want to hear."

He sounds like Deborah in a moment of pique. But doubt, like a contagion, is in the air. Looking uncertainly away from him and then briefly back for a quick uneasy glance into his eyes, Kathryn asks, "Did you see Mother and Jimmie? Did they invite you over?"

"The last night I was there they had me over for dinner. Wild duck. Wild rice. It was very nice."

Kathryn says she'd better go take in the dishtowels. At the

children's low closet she starts to lift out a faded old duffel jacket of Alec's, but then feels awkward, putting it on while he's present, and instead hauls out an old smoky-smelling jacket of her own. Pulling it on as she steps out onto the porch, she breathes in the cool of the smoky, misty air. (Someone down the street is burning a fire in a fireplace). She breathes in the smell of the thaw doing its dark, warm work under the dying, crusty snow. She sniffs at each towel and pillowcase as she pulls it from the line.

When she comes back into the kitchen she finds Alec standing peering at the wall of children's drawings. His hands are locked politely behind his back; he looks like Prince Philip examining the drawings of children in a hospital or at a naval-base school.

After almost deciding not to, she says to his back, "Did Mother say anything? About me?"

He turns toward her slightly. "Not that I can recall." But the air of contained nobility in his eyes seems to suggest there are things he could tell her if he was low enough to have a mind to be cruel.

"You might as well tell me. I know she must have said *some*thing."

"Just how were you—" and here Kathryn could swear she spots a flinch of pleasure in his nearest eye—"and were you still having a problem with your weight."

"Ha," she says bitterly and very low, almost without inflection. "I knew it would be that."

"Why ask then?" he asks her. "Why be forever harping on your mother? The handwriting woman was right about that —about you being obsessed with your past."

From her corner of the kitchen she cries out to him, "Do you honestly feel my mother has been fair to me?"

"*No*. No, I don't. But even your mother might be capable of change one of these days. And maybe it's time you also stopped being such a baby . . . expecting life to be fair every minute." Buttoning up his houndstooth check jacket, he studies her with a stern sadness. "High time," he decides. "And one other thing: if penuriousness really *is* alien to your nature in any circumstance, then it's also high time you considered getting yourself a job."

She says she's been thinking about it.

"You'll have to do more than *think*, my lovely, you'll have to *look*."

"I'll look," she whispers.

There's a moment, then, when she's positive he's going to say, "*Looking* is all very well and good, my lovely, but jobs don't grow on trees," but instead he says, "How will you feel if Deborah ends up having the same feelings about you that you have about your mother?"

"I would feel awful. But we both know that won't happen."

"Then she'll think of some new reason to hate you." And he grabs a milk-fogged glass up from the draining board and with what seems to Kathryn to be enraged vigor, rubs at it with a greyish blue-and-white dishcloth. "Don't you ever clean up around here?" he yells at her over a shoulder. "Don't you ever worry about setting a bad example for Deborah and Tim? This sink is a health hazard." But when she moans, "I know, I know," his mood switches at once, becomes reasonable. "Listen," he says in a regretful voice—the voice of a friend on the run—"I better go."

On the way over to the children's low closet he sleeks a hand over a wet-combed flank of his hair. He lifts out his coat and dark grey plaid scarf, then takes off for the living-room with them hugged to his chest, to kiss Debbie and Timmie goodbye.

While he's with the children, Kathryn dumps his clean socks and shirts into his laundry bag, ties the drawstrings up tight. She is remembering bad things about him, to protect herself. The way, when they were fighting, he used to stand in the open doorway to the back porch, so that when he was howling her shortcomings to her in the kitchen, his voice could still be heard floating out over the patios of their neighbours' back gardens. When he comes back out to the kitchen she hands the bulky sack to him.

"Well," he says. "Thanks very much." He seems to be

bowing to her slightly, in his eyes. Then he says, "*Salut.*"

When Kathryn first came to Montreal she thought *salut* was what people said hello with, but now she knows they use it just as often to say goodbye. "*Salut.*"

She goes out onto the back porch to watch him take off. She watches his car as it dips into the hollow at the end of the street and then swings to the right and is gone.

The year Deborah was born there was a spring like this; Kathryn was in the Montreal General with her on three windy March days with cool hazy nights not unlike this one. Alec arrived late on one of these evenings, just as visiting hours were coming to an end. The nurse had already brought Deborah in for the night's final feeding and Alec, slipping across enemy lines in running shoes and hooded nylon windbreaker, had made like a stowaway—stealthily closing the door to Kathryn's room and comically hiking his knees up like a cartoon man walking on tiptoe to reach her. Then he'd hitched himself up, cold and excited, to face her and Deborah, and while she had continued to breastfeed the baby he had stayed crouched awkwardly side-saddle up on her bed, kissing her deeply, one cold hand held in the clasp of her bed-warmed thighs (she had yelped at the first shock of his night-chilled hand on her skin) while Deborah, papoosed in a pink hospital blanket and frowning with concentration, hadn't missed a beat in sucking her breast.

She can recall it all so clearly; the pleasure of having made it, of having touched down, with an ease that bordered on fraudulence, in the holy land of adulthood. She can remember what nightgown she was wearing even—a silver-grey one, damply mooned with new milk. She can remember her excited sense of the night, above the doctors' parking lot and the high hospital towers—of its windblown cold grey sky and, just within the brick walls of the maternity wing, the other fathers already leaving, hunched up in peacoats and raincoats and hurrying like thieves down the hospital corridors where, here and there, a student nurse was stepping out of a twilit doorway to dip down and set out a marbled plastic vase of cut flowers, like an offering to the gods, for the night.

If Only We Could Drive Like This Forever

Before she even opened her eyes in the mornings she would be warning herself not to think of the mail. Don't think of it, don't pray for it, don't pounce on it when it comes. And don't *not* think of it, either. Wrapping herself in the silky black kimono that had the oriental pattern of oiled-looking green grasses on it, she would remind herself there were worse things than not getting news. Bad news was worse. Or a letter that said, "I hate it here. I want to come home."

She pinned up her hair with pins that one hand skilfully kept feeding the other, like a nurse feeding scalpels and suture needles to the blind but dextrous hand of a surgeon. The dish the hairpins lay in was a big, ugly, ceramic green leaf, bought at a rummage sale to raise funds for the nursery school Billie used to go to. It, too, could make her think of the forest and what was Billie doing at this minute and why wasn't he writing. She tried to imagine what his wilderness camp was like, but couldn't picture more than an aerial view of a canoe-shaped island of cedars riding a deep wind-blown lake. Dear God, she prayed, let him be safe. Let him be safe and happy. Let him write.

Running down the stairs to put on the water for coffee, she felt the pale sun on her silken shoulders. Last morning of her marriage. Miller was already up—down in the basement, rooting around among his possessions, looking for old books and skates. It was hot and muggy. Too hot to be down in the basement looking for things you wouldn't be needing till next December. She filled a saucepan with a blast of cold water and struck a match for the gas.

With his skates yoked around his neck, Miller came up the stairs from the basement, carrying a carton of books. He was perspiring already, even though he was barefoot and dressed in nothing but a pair of pale cotton shorts. He set the carton down on the counter beside the stove where Yvonne had started to scramble eggs and chives. He stood to her left and read the books' titles out to her while she used the spatula to shovel the curdled eggs back and forth, and as they together divided the little basement collection in half, she momentarily felt so swamped by his valedictory male shyness that she had her work cut out for her trying not to think of how beautiful he was—here in his shorts, in the mild summer morning. Their other books—the novels (all Yvonne's) and the memoirs and geology books (all Miller's)—had long since come to a parting of the ways.

While they were drinking their coffee, Miller turned on the news. The announcer was reading a bulletin about a five-year-old boy lost in the bush near Calabogie. He had been on a camping trip with his family and last night had wandered away from his older sister when they were on their way down to a lake for a quick bedtime dip. By the time the frightened girl had confessed to her parents that her little brother was missing, night had fallen on the northern wilderness. The police had been informed, and a large volunteer search party was now being organized by concerned citizens in Calabogie.

Yvonne got up from the table and began to stack the plates and saucers. She wasn't sure how far north Calabogie actually was; she was a Maritimer, and the map of Ontario was still largely unknown country to her. She could picture the lake the little boy and his sister had been on their way down to, though—a prehistoric bowl filled with black water and ringed by tall cedars solemn as druids. In the last of the sun, the light would climb up to the tops of these cedars so that their peaks would be as monotonous and enclosing as a ring of green mountains.

Miller came up behind her and put a hand on her shoulder. His touch made her flinch. He let his hand drop; cast the last of his coffee into the sink. When she reached up to turn the radio down, his glance was the quick, cool glance of a diagnostician, his smile the tenderly, embittered mocking smile of an unhappy husband. He said, "So now you're worried the same thing will happen to Billie."

She stared at him with the coldness of one who has at long last been caught out. "Billie's not *five*," she said.

"Five, eleven ... You'd worry if he was *fifty*-five. You'd worry if he was ninety-*three*."

She hated his triumphant male ownership of her fearfulness. She said, "I just wish he would write." The back of her throat hurt. She thought of a terrible thing she had heard about the bush: how it was a maze, how no matter which way you turned in it, it offered you the same trees, the same lake.

"You can't spend your whole life worrying about him," Miller told her, and he ran back down the stairs to his possessions.

Yvonne was supposed to be typing a thesis for a physics student at U of O. She worked on it at the dining-room table while Miller was in and out, loading the car at the front of the house with old boots and jackets. She made an extraordinary number of mistakes. Miller took off with his last load of small things just before noon. When he had gone, she felt briefly elated.

At twelve-thirty, while she was making herself a tuna sandwich, she turned on the news again. There were no leads in the little lost boy case. The mailman came at two. There was a bill from Ontario Hydro and a postcard from Yvonne's niece Alana, also away at camp. But her camp was a civilized girls' camp, not far from Ottawa, with Jazz Dancing and

Drama. She and Billie had left for their separate camps on the same morning, driven by Miller. Billie had been told his father would be moving out while he was away, so there was no subterfuge involved. When he was smaller and Yvonne and Miller would get into one of their screaming matches, he would butt his way between them howling, "Get a divorce! Get a divorce!" Miller would catch him in a light headlock and call him a billy-goat. Which would lead to Billie butting his head against Miller's thigh because he didn't want to be called a billy-goat.

The little lost boy's tracks were found on the sandy bank of a stream the next morning. More people had joined in the search. Yvonne had not slept well, alone in the big bed. The announcer said that temperatures were very high in the north. High and dry. Forest-fire weather. But by evening the little boy had still not been found.

The next morning there was no change. The weather was even hotter. Yvonne saw the mailman coming up the front walk of her housing development just after two. He looked sweaty and grim. She typed a whole page without stopping, in order not to listen for the sound of letters falling through the slot. If there even *were* any letters. But behind the clatter and bell of her machine she heard a letter fall. She would not permit herself to run out into the hallway to pick it up. This was a trick to make it be from Billie. She went out to the kitchen and plugged in the kettle. When she'd poured out her tea she carried her cup, chattering in its saucer, out into the hallway. The letter was a bill from the gas company.

She climbed the stairs to Billie's room. She stood in his doorway and sipped at her tea. There were two posters on the wall above his plaid-blanketed bed—both blow-ups of the Tenniel illustrations from *Alice in Wonderland*. The left-hand poster was of Tweedledum and Tweedledee; the right-hand poster was of the Cheshire cat smiling his phantasmal jack-o'lantern smile from his perch among the engraved leaves of his tree. Soon he will want these down, thought Yvonne; he will want to replace them with rock stars.

The announcer on Friday morning's ten o'clock news reported that the little boy's tracks had again been sighted. This was the evening before. He referred to the boy as a plucky little lad. A psychic had offered her services. The police had issued a statement saying that if the child was not located by sundown they would be calling in marine police units. It almost always meant bad news when the psychics and divers arrived on the scene. Yvonne imagined them descending on the forest like vultures—the psychic an anorexic, beak-nosed young woman in a black dress that fluttered; the police divers with their webbed feet.

On Sunday night the search was called off. Yvonne had not been sleeping well for several nights, and she sat crouched on the low, pale grey corduroy sofa in her living room, sipping a cup of tea as she watched the evening news. Her eyes welled up briefly, for the little boy's parents. Tomorrow there would be mail again. If there wasn't a letter from Billie she would put in a call him. But then she remembered there was no phone-line in to the camp. There was only a radio link with the seaplane place at Poland Lake.

While she was brushing her teeth for bed, the phone rang, making her jump. It was Miller. He said, "Listen, I meant to call you earlier, but I got tied up. Any news from Billie?"

It was as if someone had thrown a plank of pain against the back of her throat. For a moment she couldn't speak. Then she said, "Nothing yet."

She didn't think her voice had given her away, but Miller—through years of practice—knew she was crying. He said, "It's pointless to worry. If there was anything wrong, the camp would have contacted us."

Half an hour later, when she was turning out her light for the night, she thought, he's worried too. I rely on him to be calm, he relies on me to worry.

On the Thursday before the Saturday Billie was due to come home, two letters finally arrived—one from him, one for him. The one for him was from Alana. The one from him was

dated a week before it was postmarked, and the first words
Yvonne saw when she tore it out of its envelope were "I hope
you won't worry about the antibiotics." She read the letter
where she stood, out on the front porch in the cool late-
August morning—her eyes moving up instead of down. He'd
had a sore throat, he wrote, and had had to stay in bed for a
couple of days. The camp doctor had given him some
needles. But now, today—the morning of the day the letter
was written, which would have to have been last Friday—he
was going to be taken out in one of the boats to join the
people in the canoes. The doctor had given him a bottle of
pills to take with him. (More antibiotics, Yvonne imagined,
feeling depressed.) He was having a good time. He liked all
the people in his tent. "Bobby Hector is here. I knew him
when I was a kid." And then: "Let me know what time Dad
will be getting here. Please write to me right away and tell
me."

Yvonne stuck the letter into the back pocket of her shorts
and sat down on the porch steps; jiggled her knees in anxiety.
She tried to let a decent interval pass; couldn't; took it out
again. "I hope you won't worry about the antibiotics" were
again the first words to surface. She was touched by their
childish gallantry—he knew her well. He knew that she considered antibiotics (and indeed all drugs) dangerous; he knew
it was a matter of pride to her that he'd never had to take
anything more powerful than an aspirin.

Even the cough medicine she gave him when he got colds
didn't have any drugs in it. It was concocted from tree-
balsam, by some monks in a monastery somewhere in
Quebec. Miller had always refused to take it. Mad Monks'
Mixture, he'd called it. He'd said it tasted like a blend of
liniment and gin.

Around the time Yvonne discovered the tree-balsam cough
syrup, she was reading about something called "the doctrine
of signatures" in a book on herbal medicine. The doctrine of
signatures was a system that recognized a plant's therapeutic
value by way of a representative characteristic, without benefit of textbooks or laboratory procedures. It was based on the

theory that a specific plant remedy existed for every ailment. For example, a plant that grew in mushy soil was needed to remove the muck, or—speaking more medically and decorously—mucus, from the human swamp; one that grew in gravelly or sandy soil was needed to remove stone, gravel or hardening accumulations from the vascular or urinary systems. And herbs—with their thorns and prickles—were what were required for pain. To this list she'd added the tree-balsam cough syrup. It pleased her that something that was found on the bark of a tree—that dribbled down tree-bark like a baby's drool—could cure the barklike cough of a baby's croup. It made her see Mother Nature as a good-hearted soul, dreaming up thousands of amazing clues for a great medical treasure-hunt in the forest.

Which was not at all how she'd been seeing her while Billie was away. Rather she'd been dwelling on her more dangerous aspects. It occurred to Yvonne that it could be extremely dangerous to give a child antibiotics out in the bush. Antibiotics were terribly potent; because of this it was vital they be given at regular intervals. A fear that some careless sixteen-year-old would be in charge of dispensing Billie's pills took possession of her then; or maybe the camp doctor would have told the canoe-trip leaders in general (and therefore nobody in particular), "See that the kid gets his pill every four hours." She could imagine these canoe-trip counsellors easily —heedless, deeply tanned girls in shorts or bathing-suits, smoking dope and exchanging flirty insults and elbow-digs with the boy counsellors—as they portaged, as they swam, as they set up camp. Seeing that an eleven-year-old boy got his pills on time would be the last thing on anybody's mind.

In fact she could imagine worse. She could imagine a dark night; she could imagine a flashlight's beam illuminating an outstretched palm that had four capsules on it. She could imagine an adolescent girl (or boy) kneeling beside a sleeping figure in a sleeping-bag and whispering, "Hey, Bill—here's your pills. Somebody goofed, which is why you didn't get them before. Anyway, old buddy, here they be, here they be, and here's some Pepsi to wash the little buggers down with.

You might as well take the whole mess at once." And then Billie, being only a child (and a sleepy child) would swallow enough antibiotic to wreck his liver, his kidneys, maybe even his eyesight. She wished to God she'd never let him go.

When Yvonne got through to Miller in his office at the Department of Mines and Technical Surveys, he said he had an appointment in Smiths Falls on Saturday. He also had to stop off and see someone in Carsonby.

"But didn't you promise Billie you'd go get him?"

"I said I would if I *could*."

Yvonne could picture Miller in his office, swung around in his cobalt blue swivel chair so he could gaze absently out over the wink and sparkle of Dow's Lake.

"So you'll be needing the car, then."

"Unless I can sprout a pair of wings before Saturday morning, yes."

"Then I'll have to check with Voyageur to see what time I can get a bus up there on Friday."

Miller wanted to know if she was out of her mind. He said there would be dozens of parents coming back on the weekend and that it would be the easiest thing in the world for Billie to fit into somebody's car. "I also thought you had to do a rush job on somebody's thesis."

She ignored this. She said she would try Bobby Hector's parents.

But it turned out the Hectors couldn't. They had a full car and were going to be driving farther north on Saturday, for a family reunion at Bobby's grandparents' cottage, north of Kirkland Lake.

Yvonne phoned Voyageur. The woman at the ticket wicket said the trip would take close to eight hours. Six hours to North Bay. A half-hour wait. An hour to Poland Lake. She next put in a call to Poland Lake to see if one of the pilots there could fly her in to Lake Hauser on Friday night around suppertime. "No problem," a cheerful man's voice told her. She asked for a nearby place to stay and this man said, "There's a lodge called The Hermitage." When Yvonne phoned The Hermitage, a shrill woman's voice with a British accent shrieked at her, "Fine, luv! Not to worry now! Lots of vacancies this time of year!" Next she called the physics student whose thesis she was typing. "Listen, no problem," he said. Then she called Miller back.

Miller didn't say No problem; Miller went through the roof. He told her she was acting like a foolish and hysterical woman; he told her Billie could come down by himself on the bus; he told her Billie was eleven years old; he told her she couldn't keep on babying him for the rest of his life.

In a lot of ways Miller astounded Yvonne. He was a generous man with money, for one thing. To Yvonne's niece and nephew—Alana and Roy—he had been more than kind. And when Yvonne's sister and brother-in-law had come into hard financial times, Miller had given them money to help them with their mortgage. He had also bought Roy a new bike. And yet he didn't allow himself to get anything much at all in the way of mileage out of all that he gave. He had paid for Billie's and Alana's camps, and for all the new equipment and clothing they had needed to have with them, and he had given up a Saturday to drive them there, but he had spoiled the adventure and the new gear by his haranguing and pickiness. Even the picnic supper he'd suggested the night before Billie and Alana left had turned out badly; he had so relentlessly corrected everyone's table manners. And after they'd finished packing the remains of the meal in the picnic hamper and were ready to start their trek back to the car, he'd squinted up at the sky and remarked, "It's a good thing Alana's and Bill's camps are in the same direction; this way I'll be able to kill two birds with one stone." Both children had turned to look back at him. It was as if a small fall cloud had passed its quick cold shadow over the park. Yvonne had known it was superstitious of her, that "kill two birds with one stone" was only a figure of speech (the motto of hostesses all over the world), but still she hadn't been able to help herself; the words had no sooner been spoken that she had seen the children as the two birds, Miller's car as the stone.

Her seat-mate as far as Arnprior was a tanned, watchful woman in a pleated, grey worsted skirt and a tailored, long-sleeved white blouse. She was carrying a black raincoat and a black briefcase and she had short, black hair cut in a style Yvonne thought of as typical of a woman athlete. But it came out in their conversations that she was a nun.

The sun shone down on their laps, picked up the gold of the nun's ring. When it dawned on Yvonne that it was a wedding-ring, she glanced up at the woman, puzzled. But then she remembered: bride of Christ. She could imagine her just as easily being the bride of a chartered accountant. She could picture her looking sunburned and gawky in a bleached sundress. She could picture her with a cigarette hanging out of the corner of her mouth as she kicked and collapsed a child's stroller into submission before she yanked it backward up the stairway of a yellow brick bungalow. She could picture her looking unperturbed, although she was no longer under God's official protection. She pitied her, that she would never have children. She also envied her, that she would never have children. No hostages to fate.

It was five to four when the bus turned into the North Bay terminal. There was to be a twenty-minute stopover. Yvonne took off for a nearby supermarket to buy plums and tortilla chips. When she returned to the bus, two mechanics were crouched by one of the wheels at the back. She climbed inside. The nun was gone. She didn't want to move over into the nun's seat. She'd always thought nuns were supposed to be pale. How had this one got to be so tanned? Maybe she did community work. Miller was a fiend for community work; he had the stamina to sit in anonymous rooms and listen to the agenda for next week's meeting and the minutes for last week's meeting. The hours he'd been willing to spend listening to minutes!

Forty minutes into their journey the bus came to a stop. The driver, a fat, balding young man, ran down the short, peb-bled, metal stairway to see what the trouble was. In the middle of a field to the south of the bus a tree that was a leaf-tattered green scarecrow stood guard over a wind-blown mound of winter-pale grasses. The sorrow of the country!

thought Yvonne. It was a thing you never thought of when you were living in the city.

After five minutes had passed and the driver still hadn't returned, she got up and plucked her sweat-dampened skirt away from the backs of her thighs and went stiffly down into the weak sunshine to look for him.

She found him behind the bus, having a peaceful cigarette.

"Are you going to send for another bus?"

"Already did."

"How long will it take to get here?"

"Hard to say. Could be forty minutes, could be an hour."

She sighed sharply.

He pretended not to hear.

"I'll have to hitch a ride, then."

His young man's glance said he had no objections.

The thought of hitch-hiking scared her, although when she was younger she had done it often enough. But only with Miller. It was different when you were two and one of you was male. On a trip down to the east coast the first summer they were married, she had been the decoy while Miller had been obliged to crouch behind bush after bush at the edge of the highway. "Your legs will haul in the rides," he had said. And they had. They were her only spectacular parts. The blaze of hope whooshing from men's faces at the way *her* face, close up, was no match for her legs had depressed her. Every day there was a new crop of faces to be disappointed. Every day her own face was eclipsed by her legs. By the time they reached Nova Scotia she was feeling very ugly. And her face wasn't even all that plain. It was just an ordinary face, really, a girl's face—too much of a girl's face probably—big-eyed, roundly pale; also possibly a little too anxiously hopeful. "*You* look like the moon," Billie had said to her once. They had been sitting on his bed and looking at one of his storybooks when he was two or three. A thieving fox was running at the edge of a smudged charcoal field under a smiling silver moon. She had been pleased to be seen as the benign man-in-the-moon by her baby. But where men were concerned, she would have preferred to resemble the more sexy Mr. Fox.

She wiped her perspiring hands on the sides of her skirt,

stepped out onto the highway. A car was approaching, a high-lit black beetle in the distance. She waited a little, taking deep breaths, then stuck out her thumb.

The car swerved squealingly in. The crazy thing was, it was driven by a woman. In fact, Yvonne had time to catch a glimpse of someone who surprisingly resembled herself: a shoulder-length haze of pale-blond hair, dark glasses, a short-sleeved white blouse resembling the white blouse she had almost pulled out of her closet this morning before breakfast. She ran to catch up with the beetle, breathless with gratitude.

The car's radio was blasting through the front window: Yvonne hauled open the door with a thank-you all ready to be shouted over the music and saw that the woman was a man. The hands on the wheel were a man's hands, the short-sleeved white blouse was a man's summer shirt, the short-nosed tanned face had a two-day blond bristle. She had already ducked a little, to ease herself into the car, but now she hesitated, raised a hand to grasp the top of the door frame. The metal burned her palm so that she had to rub it on the hip of her skirt.

"How far you going?" she shouted in to the driver.

He peeled off his sunglasses and reached over to turn his radio down. His blue eyes, exposed, had a puffy allergic look; she could see the way they were grazing her breasts as she leaned forward to hear him. She was aware too of the way her breasts were lengthening, with their big thumbprints of sunburn on them, above the now partly revealed white V of her bra. "How far *you* going?" he shouted back out.

She felt she had no choice but to yell back, "The Hermitage! Poland Lake!"

"Well, that's okay! I'm going farther than that!"

She got in. She had to get there before sundown. Out of fear, she shouted out her story about having to fly into the bush to pick up her son. Except that she didn't say "son"; she said "one of my children." She was aware of having said this in order to present herself as a person who had a large family; as a person who, should she not arrive at her destination, would be immediately and proficiently searched for. While she was shouting at him, she studied, in anxious brief glimpses, the powerful hands, the pale cloud of womanly hair. Not too many men in Ottawa wore their hair long any more. But she guessed that out there in the country it might still be the fashion, that men out here might cling hard to what they fancied was decadence.

The miles flew by and the only moves her driver made (apart from driving moves) were little hitchings of his shoulders to the music. And one last move: he reached across her to open the door for her at the exact spot she had asked to be let out, under the swinging sign to the lodge.

"This the place you wanted to go to?"

She said yes.

Leaning into the car to pull out her shoulder-bag, she thanked him. Because of his dark glasses, she couldn't tell if his eyes were mocking her—if they were, the mockery hadn't made it down to his mouth. He said, "Sure thing—any time."

She followed the Hermitage road into the rich, leaf-smelling forest. At first she walked through dense woods but after three or four minutes came to a sort of clearing: lush tropical grass together with dead northern trees—a paradoxical combination meaning swamp. Then the road dipped into a leaf-spotted little hollow—how strange, she thought, how wonderful, really, to be walking along this woodland road instead of dying of heat in the city; and then the hollow became a slope—a kind of ramp in the floor of the forest—and then there was a real clearing. Here there was a balding grass common, ringed by nearly a dozen log huts and cabins. And here too, she was struck by how late it was getting—the light was already at the throats of the trees. Supper was over too, by the sound of things; the wholesale crash of cutlery coming from the long lodge at the east end of the clearing was far beyond being the pre-supper sound of tables being set.

The boss of the seaplane place bore an uncanny resemblance to Yvonne's ninth-grade math teacher. He had the same mobile right eyebrow, the same prim jokester's smile. When she told him she wanted to fly in to the camp, he looked astounded. This too was familiar, and she had a sinking feeling that it was something he was going to prove to be skilled at: looking astounded and then saying no.

He did say no, and then said, "No way," and he made a karate-chop at the sun. "See that sun? Half an hour from now it's going to be gone." And he turned his hand horizontal and brought the inner edge of it flush with his throat and then drew it slowly across it. "No *way*."

"How about tomorrow morning, then?"

"All planes booked up for all of tomorrow. Everything we've got's been chartered to fly some gentlemen from down south to a couple of lakes farther north."

"Then how can I get in to the camp?"

There was a silence while he considered. "I could fly you in there on Sunday," he finally said.

She cried out at this. She told him she couldn't wait till Sunday; she told him about Billie's having been sick and the bus breaking down. "The person I spoke to in *your* office promised to fly me in on Friday evening."

"That wasn't me," he said, clapping a solemn hand to his heart. But then he surprised her by going over to the dockside window and shoving it up and calling down to someone below, "Hey, Vernon, there's a lady up here needs to fly in to the camp!"

Yvonne followed him over to the window. Below them, on a sandy track on the wharf, a slight man in windbreaker and jeans with straight black hair down to his shoulders was standing with his back to them, lightly tossing lifebelts and small cartons into the trunk of a beaten-up old car. He snatched a glance at them back over a shoulder. He had a look of grim authority in his face, and pitted skin. Struck by helplessness, Yvonne realized it was a Friday night. He wouldn't be willing to take her, then; he'd be wanting to take off somewhere himself. A few moments later he appeared in the doorway to the office, drying his neck with a towel. When he saw Yvonne, he stopped. He said, "Okay—but we'll have to leave right away."

Buffeted by the wind on the lake, the plane seemed to be bumping its way up an invisible stairway as it made its climb to the sky. Then the world and the turbulence were left far behind. Yvonne's tension made her feel like she was getting menstrual cramps, which she was in fact due for. The pilot started to point things out to her. He was much younger than his boss. He was also quite a bit younger than Yvonne, but there was something about him that suggested a long history of manliness. He was also much more casual than his boss had been about the sun going down, and although almost everything about the way he conducted himself made him seem older than she guessed he must be, his coolness about the sinking of the sun made him seem younger. He said, "We can make it okay—don't worry."

And now that they were quite high in the sky she was sure he was right. There was still plenty of sun up here, so much sun that all of the earth seemed to be bathed in it. Now and then there was a river, now and then a lake, then for miles and miles nothing but evening-lit, cedary green. The only sign of human habitation was a village of silver-roofed industrial shacks, built on the bank of a little river. This river was tan in places, and in places it was pink, and it was flanked by beaches of mud and pink chemical sludge. (Even *it* looked beautiful—a beautiful, destroyed pink-and-tan river.)

It surprised her when the plane started to drop. She had expected to get a view of Lake Hauser well in advance, but suddenly it was right there, on their left, and they were already sinking in over the camp. They could see several small groups of grey huts, and a great, rain-darkened grey barn, and a long, low white lodge, and three orange tents, and a grey dock leading out into the black lake. Little figures were running toward the dock, and some of them appeared to be waving. At this point Yvonne started feeling like the bottom had dropped out of her stomach, she was praying so hard for Billie to be down there and well.

"Billie McCormack!" she shouted, even before she'd jumped down from the plane. "He was on the canoe trip—is he back yet?"

"Who?" someone shouted back, striking dread in her heart.

"Billie McCormack!"

"Get McCormack!" a scrawny boy who had a voice as deep as a man's yelled to a boy who was running down from the field, and the boy in the field spun around and ran off.

A handsome, hawk-nosed, smiling man with woolly grey hair and faded red shorts gave Yvonne a hand down to the dock. But up close his light eyes had a cheerless look. "I have to get Billie right away," she told him. "We have to fly out of here before it gets dark."

"God knows where Billie even *is*," this man said. "The last canoes only got back an hour ago. I don't know if he's even had anything to eat yet."

She ignored him. "Get Billie!" she called to the children who were starting to cluster around her.

"Why don't you stay here yourself, for the night?" the man in the red shorts asked her. "Instead of rushing right off like this? Billie might not even be within calling distance. He might be off in the woods somewhere."

Yvonne turned from him and said to the pilot, "How long can you give me?"

He was kneeling on one knee at the end of the dock. He had rolled up one of his blue shirt-sleeves and plunged an arm down into the warm, dark water of the lake. Or at least she imagined it warm—at least warm compared with the air, which was cooling down fast. "It's okay—we can stay another fifteen minutes, maybe twenty." He looked up at her and she was able to see again how much she preferred his unsmiling face to the smiling face of the cold-eyed gadfly beside her. "I won't leave without you," he said.

She peeled off her sandals and threw them up into the plane and grabbed the wrist of the man in the red shorts and started running up the wharf. He trotted along willingly enough, taking her measure. Or maybe only the measure of her parts. "Stay the night," he panted down at her hair, and then there was an end to the warm wharf-boards under her feet and they were running on bristly dry yellow grass.

"Billie!" she howled over at some children. "Find Billie McCormack and tell him to pack!" The children ran off in every direction, like children running off in a game of hide-and-go-seek. She dropped the wrist of her running-mate. "You go look for him too."

"Wouldn't have a clue where to look," he said, looking at her breasts.

But then there was Billie, rising up over a knoll, seeing for himself she was there. Beneath his bleached-in-the-sun cowlick and bangs, he didn't look astonished by her presence—all his amazement seemed reserved for how she'd got there, as if she'd dropped, without benefit of plane, straight from the sky. He said, "But how did you *get* here?" and somebody punched him in the arm and said, "Man, didn't you hear the air-o-plane?" and he said "I think I must have been asleep." As he reached up a hand to shove back his hair she saw the imprint of some bent grasses on his forearm. From pillow? From field?

She said shyly, "Hey! You look taller." This made him smile—not at her but at one of the boys who was with him, and then this boy boxed at the air all around his hair.

All the green was being leeched out of the forest as they flew back over it, although for the first minute or two the last of the sun setting over the bush made the trees look like a million low cedar hedges, all shoved together. But it was real night by the time the plane was ready to start its drop down to its home-base water. As it came in low over Poland Lake, the wharf rushed up and at them, a long row of lighted little huts up on stilts.

The boss was waiting for them in the uneven boat-lit light of the lower dock. He caught Yvonne by the hand when she landed, and they rocked together for a moment, like dancers. Then Billie jumped down. "In on a wing and a prayer," the boss said to Billie, and Billie looked up at him, puzzled. Now only the pilot to jump, and when he landed they all rocked and jostled together on the little square of a dock, setting off a great gulping and slipping of water around the dock's floats. With the dark a wind had come up; Yvonne drew a scarf out of a slit in her windbreaker, shook it out—it putted like an outboard motor in the stiff breeze—tied it on over her hair. The boss put an arm around her shoulders to steady her, but the pilot was the one who said, "Listen I'll give you a lift back to your cabin."

They drove through a curving wood on their way to the lodge. The tree-trunks were the colour of granite, of highway. Of gravestones. But Yvonne felt like they were a little family in the car, protected against the grey of the wood and the dark of the night, secure in a smaller, darker night of their own. And she was consumed by the thought, if only we could drive like this forever! Just the three of us!

"Do you live around here?"

"About an hour from here. North."

"Close to a city?"

"Just south of Kirkland Lake. Ever hear of a place called Dane?"

"No."

It was a sweet pleasure, watching his mouth toy with the idea of smiling. "Ever hear of a place called Swastika?"

"No."

"Well, I live halfway between Dane and Swastika."

She asked him if he flew the plane much in the winter. He said that in the winter he usually got work as an auto-mechanic—sometimes in the north—"Timmins, Kapuskasing"—but that he sometimes travelled south. "Not really far south, though. Just down to North Bay."

Then he was turning the car sharp right, into the woods, and they were bumping along the road to the lodge over tree-roots and hollows. But surprisingly quickly they were met by a grove of grey tree-trunks, caught in the headlights, and then, after a wrench to the left, the balding-grass common.

"Is this the place?" Billie asked Yvonne.

When she said yes, he got out and started making a prowl of everything within the circle of the car's lights.

The pilot had stretched one arm along the seat behind Yvonne. She didn't mind his pitted skin; she even liked it—it gave him a focussed, ironical look. He was watching Billie. He said, "Looks like he's glad to be back in civilized country."

"Is this civilized country?"

"After a fashion." He turned to look at her, a small smile in his eyes. Then he aimed his gaze out the window again, and after a pause said, "There's a movie theatre two miles from here." This time he didn't turn to her and she could feel the power of his not looking at her even more keenly that the power of his looking. "And a dance hall."

It seemed to her there was an ache in his voice when he said dance hall. It made her heart kick over; it made her wonder if he was going to ask her to go out with him. But she only said —like a fool—"I forgot to put on my shoes."

The overhead light didn't work and so he struck a match for her. When she'd fastened her sandals on, he blew it out. It seemed to her that at that moment they were both toying with the idea of saying something jokey and flirty—that he was toying with saying, "We should have candles, not matches," and that she was toying with saying, ". . . and violins"—but that the moment for saying such things (and just as well) quickly passed. What she really wanted to do was turn to him in the dark and nuzzle the inside of the wrist whose hand was still holding the match. And in fact they did turn to one another just after this, as if they were trying to help each other remember something they'd both forgotten, but then Billie was already coming back to them, frowningly swatting at bushes with a broken-off tree branch. If they went out somewhere, could they take Billie with them? Her little chaperon? Her little protector? He was coming up to Yvonne's rolled-down window. Urgently he plucked at her blouse sleeve. "Mum? I thought you said the dining-room only stayed open till nine o'clock."

When Yvonne got out of the car and leaned in to thank the pilot, he was quiet a moment. Then he said, "Sure thing." And with a "Be seeing you," he turned on the ignition and took off. For a lonely moment after his tail-lights had disappeared into the trees, Yvonne felt aroused, bereft, the way she used to feel after being out in Miller's first car with Miller, a thousand years ago.

After the sound of the car had died away in the woods, Billie said to her, "I had a really good time at camp, but I'm just so glad you came to get me."

Yvonne felt a sting of emotion in her throat. "I'm really glad too," she said, and she kissed him. And he not only allowed himself to be kissed, he even gave her a quick kiss back.

Through one of the gatehouse's windows, they could see the cabins' key hanging on the horned twigs of a pair of deer's antlers that had been mounted on the wall behind a tall, pulpitlike counter. But when they stepped inside, Yvonne saw that the old man who'd been on duty at suppertime had been replaced by a much younger man who had a sleek, unreliable look. His dark brown hair was wet, new-combed. Maybe he'd just been for a dip in the lake. He looked as if he *lived* in the lake. (But secretly, queerly.) When he gave Yvonne the key his eyes slid to Billie. Even his lips had a licked, wet look. "Have a nice stay," he said.

Their cabin sat on a short stony plateau with three other cabins. They had to climb a rocky path to get up to it. There was a light on in the first cabin, and as they passed by one of its front windows Yvonne could see the Roman-soldier white legs of a man in black bathing-trunks who was standing beside a bed, his top half-hidden from them by the beige turtle-necked sweater he was struggling to draw down over his head. The scene reminded her of an illustration in one of her childhood storybooks—of a boa constrictor, part of its body bulged out by its gulped lump of prey. She slowed down, wanting to see what sort of head the sweater-neck would give birth to, but Billie whispered, "Come *on*, don't stare," and pulled her along by the cuff of her jacket-sleeve.

As she was fitting the key into the door of their own cabin he asked her, "What did you think of that guy?"

"Which guy?"

"The one who gave you the key."

"Oh *him*. I thought he looked sort of creepy." She shoved the door open. It creaked drily. The cabin smelled dry too—of its own dry wood and of a pine-scented deodorant. She patted the wall, feeling for the light switch. An old childhood fear that her hand would encounter another hand, not a switch, was activated for an instant, then her thumb hit the switch and the kitchen-part of the cabin was lit up by a low lamp that sat on a small, blond wood table to the left of the door. "I thought he looked like a psychotic otter."

"That's a neat expression. It could be a neat name for a rock group—the Psychotic Otters." He made a tour of the kitchen, touching things: the oilcloth tablecloth, the chipped midget refrigerator. "Except that there's already a group called the Psychotic Pineapples." He went off to explore the rest of the cabin. "It's pretty nice in here", he called from one of the bedrooms. He came back out, looked around. "This is really quite pleasant." He sat down in a tan vinyl armchair. "I'm not sure I know what psychotic means, exactly."

"Strange. Deranged. But the person can sometimes appear quite normal. Or maybe that's a psychopath. Someone without a conscience. I *think*. No—I've got it wrong; someone without a conscience is a psychopath. A psychotic is someone who's out of touch with reality." The words "without a conscience" had made her think of Miller.

"How's Dad?" he asked her.

She turned to him, startled. "Oh, fine. Very busy, though. *As* usual. In fact even busier than usual." She filled a granite-ware basin with water and dumped the bag of North Bay plums into it.

"How's Alana?"

"She's good. She wrote us a funny letter. She wrote one to you too; I should have brought it with me."

"Oh, well. You can't think of everything."

True, but the fact that he should say so made her feel that

their starting to live together, a little couple, was already beginning to take its toll. She wondered if she should say, "Listen, hon—you remembered Dad was moving out, didn't you?" but instead said, "Hey, I meant to tell you—Dad got moved out okay."

He looked up at her, his face drained. He said, "Oh." And then, "What's his new place like?"

"Haven't seen it yet."

Oh, his eyes said.

There was a little round table to the right of the armchair he was sitting in. It was covered with a khaki-fringed vinyl cloth that had a pattern of khaki leaves and ferns on a rose background. The lamp sitting on it had an orange lampshade that, when the light was turned on, gave a deep orange sunset sky to a border of cowboys riding bucking black horses. Billie turned this sunset on. Turned it off. On. Off. He said. "I'll bet it's pretty nice though."

"Oh, it's sure to be," said Yvonne quickly. "It's high up so he'll have a great view out over the park and everything." This was true—Miller had raved to her about the magnificence of the view—and yet, following her saying it, there was an entrenched pure silence in the room, as if she had lied. After a moment or two, Billie got up and took off for the bathroom, and Yvonne, feeling at loose ends and unhappy with herself—why bring up Miller's moving out *now*?—went into the front bedroom and started brushing her hair. The mirror had a frame made out of tiny brown plastic logs. When she heard Billie come out of the bathroom she called out to him, "Isn't this weird, Billie? Here we are, deep in the woods and surrounded by *trees*, and the logs in the frame of this mirror are made out of *plastic*."

He came to her doorway to see. He said, "At camp they gave us Tang for breakfast."

"Tang!" she cried out at him, watching him in her mirror.

"It was the wilderness, don't forget. They couldn't just fly in fresh oranges and stuff. We had banana flakes too. I liked the banana flakes okay."

Back out in the kitchen, Yvonne held out the bowl of

washed shining plums. "Stick in your thumb and pull out a plum," she said, and then worried that this was too nursery-rhymish a thing to have said to a boy his age.

But he laughed obligingly.

A deeper laugh wakened her sometime in the night. (A laugh in slow motion, or so it had seemed from the depth of that moment's dream.) She woke up at once; was sure she could still hear it reverberating in the room; lay desperately still in her bed, stiffly primed to hear it again. But there was only the sound of the wind in the leaves. Unless it was also the sound of a rain. A very light summer rain. She listened intently, trying to hear rain in the rustling, but couldn't be sure of it.

Her body continued to listen for the laugh. She dreaded hearing it again but she also wanted to. To identify it; to dismiss it. Maybe she'd been snoring. Maybe a snore had wakened her up and her mind, trying to work it into the tailend of that moment's dream, had turned it into a laugh. No; it was a laugh. She got up and pulled her windbreaker on over her nightgown, made the rounds of the cabin, checked the door. She peered out through the screen mesh of the front window. There were no lights on in any of the other cabins. There was only one outside light, on the far side of the common, illuminating a triangle of log-wall and an over-turned washtub that had a long, striped beach towel spread over it, like a tablecloth.

After she'd climbed back into her bed she sat up on it, chafing her chilled feet. As she reached up to turn off her light, Billie, on the other side of the thin partition, caused her heart to leap to her throat by laughing aloud—out of the pleasure of some dream.

But it must have rained at some point during the night; the morning air was so sharp and clear they had to wear sweaters to breakfast. There was the smell of damp wood, as well; of damp wood and wood shavings. And bacon frying.

Chilly though it was, a sunbather was already out, lying on the beach towel Yvonne had seen spread over the washtub during the night. He was a skinny, white-skinned man in white bathing-trunks, lying on his back on a patch of lawn near the log-framed entrance to the dining-lodge, reading a bright blue book. He was holding this book high over his head (arms raised straight up) so that it made Yvonne think of a blue roof over a round, stone-walled well. But what she noticed about him most, as they hurried by him in the cold, clear morning, was the way the bulge of his genitals, so pronounced in the white trunks, was twinned by his Adam's apple.

In the dining-hall, a hefty, cockney-talking woman with dull, frizzy hair and a self-confident air was serving the man at the one other occupied table. Yvonne thought she must be the woman she'd talked to on the phone; even without the accent she would have known the woman was British—from the timbre of her voice and from her festive, imperious manner. And couldn't the man be the owner of the turtle-necked sweater? But there was no way of telling; whoever he was, this morning he was wearing an open-necked pale yellow sports shirt. His hair was dark and had a lifeless citified look; his face solemn—sour, even. He gave Yvonne a gloomy once-over, over his newspaper, and very soon after she and Billie had settled themselves, he got up to leave. She watched him walk stiffly out of the dining-hall—he had a self-conscious, constipated walk—took in his new-looking jeans and new hiking boots. It occurred to her that all the parts of his body that had been revealed the night before—if he was the boa constrictor man—were now hidden by clothing, and that nearly everything that had been hidden was now revealed. There were also some people out in the kitchen; she caught glimpses of them some of the times the door was shoved open. The sad girl who'd served them a late supper the night before, still in her plain sundress, eating a banana. A petite, black-haired woman in a mauve waitress uniform and straw-weave slippers. The back of a tall, slim man—was it the otter man?—in a lumberjack's jacket, with the sleeves rolled up to his elbows. (In the quick view Yvonne got of him he was standing at the back of the kitchen industriously, or perhaps even dementedly, scrubbing at something. Then the door was swung shut and the next time it was pushed open he was gone.)

The top half of the back wall of the dining-hall was one long window, and while Billie and Yvonne were waiting for their pancakes to be brought to their table they went over to it and looked out. Or rather down. Yvonne could feel the view in her legs: the whole back half of the building was cantilevered out over forest. "'This is the forest primeval,'" she quoted to Billie and then she said, "We could go for a walk in it after breakfast; the bus isn't supposed to come till after twelve."

It was very hot by the time they came out of the dining-lodge, but the forest all around the clearing still preserved its fine, bowery chill. For a while they walked along a path wedged between the woods and the water, then turned inland and followed an old lumber road that, after nearly an hour's roundabout walking, brought them back to the lake. Unless it was a different lake. There was a little island just off the shore. But when they got closer to it they saw it was not quite an island—it was connected to land by a short, chive-grassed handle of sand. From the sky it would look like a ping-pong paddle. They circled the paddle-part in less than five minutes and then each chose a territory: Billie a beach that was cooled by long and short spotted bibs of shade; Yvonne a beach in full sun.

After ten minutes of pleasant dreaming in the heat, Yvonne decided to go in for a swim. She didn't have a bathing-suit with her but she thought, it's private here, no one will come. The water turned out to be startlingly cold, and for her first few gasps she swam a bobbing, distrustful breaststroke, her face held in a regal grimace. This is how I'll swim when I'm old, she thought, and she forced herself to loosen up a bit— made herself tread water, then get started in on a crawl. Now and then, when Billie stood up, Yvonne's eye (the one that kept flashing wetly from the brief turns of her face up out of the water) would take in the sun glinting on the top of his straight fair hair just beyond the hill of sand at the end of their little island. Then he would disappear again. Out of sight, she could imagine him squat-walking along the strand-line, picking up sticks and stones and talking to himself (keeping himself posted on what he was doing) and sometimes, in a low, contented drone, singing. Picturing him accounted for and busy, she began to revel in the light breeze that was skimming the lake and making it lap at her chin. She rolled over in the water and swam outward, feeling how this breeze was also busy at her back, up in the leaves of her beach's birches and poplars—which seemed to her, in the mood she was in, to be the most cheerful trees in the whole northern hemisphere. Glenview was the name of the camp she'd gone to when she was a kid. How awful the word Glenview sounded *now*—like some boring suburban housing development. But it had been rustic enough—a pioneer-type compound, its tents and log cabins spread out on a sunlit, green clearing among wooded, dark hills. She recalled running from Archery to Canoeing to Swimming, obeying the calls of whistles and cowbells.

"Billie!" she yelled. "I'm swimming and it's great! Do you want to come in?"

"I'm making something!" he yelled back. "I'm digging a harbour!"

She swam sidestroke for ten minutes or so, then floated awhile, then did another froggy breaststroke—an eerily titillating stroke for a naked woman to do in such polar water, finally dragged herself gaspingly up onto the beach, collapsed on the burning marvellous sand.

After she'd been sunbathing for a while, she heard a plane in the distance. It droned closer and closer and was soon clackingly roaring almost over their heads. It was a seaplane. From down below, its pontoons made it look as if its yellow stick-legs were shod in two yellow-painted metal kayaks. Yvonne turned and craned her neck to look up, feeling her hair clinging damply to her sunburned freckled shoulders. Was *her* pilot flying it? Flying some gentlemen from down south to a couple of lakes farther north? And if so, would he spot her down here, small and naked and tanned except for the low-slung, white bikini patch on her buttocks? She'd dreamed about him during the night. Vernon. In the dream she was very happy because they were going to become lovers. But just as he was starting to make love to her she remembered she was married. The man she was married to was Miller and so she whispered to Vernon—in a whisper that was more like a wail—"I can't! I'm married to a man who bakes bread!" Now the plane was banking, turning north, and in less than five minutes had droned itself down to the size and sound of a mosquito. It made Yvonne think of winter for some reason—of a plane seen in the distant sky in winter, long ago.

She woke up startled, convinced they were in danger of missing their bus. She walked one hand along the sand at the back of her head, hunting down her watch. But the watch, when her fingers found it, was burning hot, so that she had to draw her blouse off her eyes and roll blindly over and then use the blouse to retrieve it. Then carry it down to her lap, still gripped in the blouse like some fatal insect—belly up, to show her the time. She saw she'd been right to wake up worried—she'd been sleeping for nearly an hour. "Billie!" she called. "We should think about starting back if we want to have time to get something to eat before we go for the bus!"

He didn't answer.

She staggered up, feeling dazed; hauled on her skirt. Buttoned up her blouse as she made the quick, lopsided run to his beach. But his beach was empty—small, hot, empty, and without even the variety it had had in the earlier morning when it was enlivened by its wind-bobbed bibs of shade. She cast only one glance at the river he'd dug in from the lake, to irrigate his small sand city. She called his name several more times, first tentatively, then sharply, as if her sharpness could make him only be hiding from her. But there was something established about the beach's forlorn look, as if no one had been there for at least half an hour. She was feeling more awake by now—fear had woken her—and she took off at an angry frightened walk, strode all around the little peninsula, yelling his name in every direction, and allowing only a short pause after each yell in which to stand very still and strain to hear him call back. But nothing. The bluffs were silent, impassive, and the rustlings of the leaves in the slim, closer trees now only irritated her, were a rustling interference to the silence she would need to receive a faraway answer.

She drew the map of northern Ontario out of her shoulder-bag (a Greek bag Miller had bought her in the Byward Market two years ago), shook the map open in front of herself, tried to study it while keeping on with her walking and yelling. But seeing that the area Billie was lost in was really very small on the map didn't do a thing to diminish the size of the real woods all around her. All it did was bring back the memory of the sun-hot Sunday spring morning Billie and Roy and Alana, leaning over the map-clad kitchen table, had picked out their favourite place-names. These names, circled by Alana with black Magic Marker, now jumped out at Yvonne like racoons' eyes—Windy Lake, Emerald Lake, Shining Tree, Sultan, Woman River—and this reminder of childhood innocence and happiness made her feel bitter toward the impassive bluffs all around her, and bitter toward fate and nature, and bitter too, that she could not allow herself to take any kind of action., She couldn't even allow herself the relief of running into the woods to look for Billie because he might come back and find her gone and then run back into the woods to look for *her*. Because by now of course he would be panicky too. The thought of his panic raised her own several notches. She could feel it leaping from foothold to foothold inside her. She tried to whip up her anger at him for running off, to stave off total terror, but terror overrode everything. And the terror was of the woods, not the water. She understood that it was the woods that had frightened her all along—all the time she had been yelling and yelling and listening and listening she had also been moving toward the dark lure of an idea that nearly paralysed her. It had to do with their having been followed; it was fed by tabloids and fables and the daily newspaper. Words accumulated in her head—the beginnings of sentences too fearful for her mind to finish: "Here is the spot ..."; "The map shows ..."; "In dense woods, the body ..." Her back had turned clammy, ill-feeling; her mind was useless to her, a panicked vacuum. She could not imagine a life without Billie but already knew it would be one of the future's tricks that she'd be condemned to go on living.

But now her mind, active after all, was trying to figure out who had followed them, was considering: the gloomy man in the new jeans and hiking boots; the skinny sunbather in the white trunks; the man she thought of as the otter man. Terror picked the otter man. She tried to recall what she'd said to Billie about him. She'd said he looked like a psychotic otter; she remembered he'd laughed at that. She'd also said he looked creepy. And then she was *certain* he'd shadowed them, gliding sleekly among the trees. A psychopath. A pervert. A deranged person who knew these woods like the back of his hand. She remembered her conviction, back in the days when she was waiting to get a letter from Billie, that he would be safe once he was safely with her. Which made her know, all at once, what irony was: it was what was lying in wait to trap you when you had too narrow, too particular, too held-to-yourself wishes. When you had too much overbearing pride. Dear God, she prayed, let him be all right, let him be well, let there be some sensible explanation for all of this, let him be fine, let him be well, let him be all right, let him come running now, out of the trees.

Her throat felt painfully on fire. The glimpse she'd had of the otter man at breakfast, standing at one of the sinks at the back of the kitchen and scrubbing at something, was working away at her too. She wished she'd pointed him out to Billie; she wished she'd said, "There's that creepy otter man again— he's scrubbing at something...." The word "blood" might possibly then have floated up into both of their minds and Billie would have been properly alerted.

But she couldn't keep going without some kind of hope, even though to dare to hope seemed dangerous, seemed on the way to being the worst way to tempt fate. Still, she knew that she hoped. Secretly she knew that along with feeling terrified, she was also using feeling terrified as a hedge against losing Billie, out of the conviction that if she could keep frantic enough for long enough—for a required, but unknown, span of time—she would finally, or even soon (but she mustn't think soon because then it would never happen) be given the gift of the sight of him coming running toward her out of the trees. But this was a thing you could never know about hope—whether you'd be rewarded for having it, or punished. The bluffs—the great buffalo humps of densely treed forest, and the massive inhuman tablets of old stone with rusted moss on them, all going straight down into dark and deep water—all seemed to be saying: *punished.*

Her mind was so tied up with its fears, and with its resolves to be a better mind from now on, and also (still) so tied up with its hopes, and with its careful skittishness about admitting to its hopes, and so bent on its throat-breaking cycle of yelling and listening (her panic had tightened her throat to the point where it was hurting as much to listen as it did to shriek), that she didn't even see Billie when he first came running out of the woods. He was less than thirty yards from her when she first saw him. She had no energy left for running to meet him; she had only had enough to grab him when he got to her and to give him a furious parental shaking.

"But I wasn't far away at all! And I only heard you start to call a couple of minutes ago!"

She wanted to know how this could be possible. Her eyes still brimmed but her voice was dry. She referred to its dryness by way of reproach. She told him her throat was all raw from over fifteen minutes of non-stop yelling; she sank down on the sand and said, "You better explain yourself." And then added coldly, teacherly, drily, "If you can."

He said he had followed a little path that ran close to a loud brook and had ended up lying down beside the brook and playing with some stones that he'd pretended were cars that had to do a stunt-driving test on the ledge of a rock. He hadn't known she was calling him until he'd got bitten in the ankle and had sat up to scratch at the bite. He hitched up a pant-leg to show her a little pebble of flesh on his ankle. So it was a mosquito she had to thank for putting an end to her anguish: Billie's sitting up to scratch had happened to dovetail with one of her howls.

About fifteen minutes into the ride to North Bay, Billie sighed and said, "It's a real drag going home in the bus. I wish we had the car." And then, "Hey! How come Dad didn't come to get me? He's the one who said he was going to. He's the one with the car."

Yvonne said that Miller had had some meetings he'd had to go to. Out of town. He'd had to drive to Smiths Falls. He'd also had to stop and visit someone on his way back, in a place called Carsonby. But she could hear how artificial and anxious her voice was sounding.

"I imagine he'll be at the bus station to meet us, anyway," Billie said.

"I imagine he will. I'll give him a call when we get down to North Bay and tell him what time we'll be getting back into town."

This might have brought an end to their talking of Miller, but an image of Miller warmly greeting Billie at the Ottawa bus terminal appeared before Yvonne. He would be wearing his khaki Bermudas and probably one of his grey-striped white shirts—the same clothes he'd worn on the shopping trip he'd taken Billie and Alana on, the weekend before they were to leave for camp. He'd bought piles of stuff for both of them; Alana had even talked him into buying her a pleated tartan skirt and dark green cashmere cardigan for school, but the tallest stacks were of T-shirts, navy sweatshirts, sweatpants, tan cords, jeans. To make sure the cords and jeans weren't too tight, Miller had instructed Billie and Alana to squat in them, in front of one of the three-way mirrors in Youth Togs. (And in front of their salesperson—a girl with a face as white as a Kabuki mask and spiky fair hair.) To demonstrate, Miller had gone into an athlete's bouncing squat, his hands in sporty fists on his hips. The kids didn't want to squat. Miserable, they had stared at their shoes.

Yvonne thought, he'll pay excellent child support, but

he'll exact his price for it. He'd probably be willing to pay her alimony as well. The word alimony sounded to her like a poison, a lethal cloudy elixir a murderer might pour into gin. She prayed to God she wouldn't need it. She had a horrifying image of herself as an old woman: she was in a long black coat with a woollen kerchief tied over her white hair and was walking out to a mailbox in bleak country—the Alberta badlands came to mind—to pick up her monthly stipend from Miller. But the air was wonderfully clear there, with a buoyant sting to it, like champagne. Lonely air. Let it not happen, dear God. Let me *make* something of my life. She said to Billie, "Dad didn't want me to come. He said I was babying you."

"Oh, yeah? Well, he promised me, didn't he? I don't think that that's babying a person, to do what you promised."

"Neither do I," said Yvonne quickly. "Actually, Dad was the one who was acting like a baby. Carrying on. Yelling. And then he had the nerve to say *I* was acting foolish and hysterical."

Billie sat staring darkly ahead, at some unpleasing memory of his father. "That man needs to have his head examined," he said.

Now I've gone too far, thought Yvonne, and she wondered if she should try to make amends. If she should say, "You know Dad. His bark is worse that his bite." If she should say, "You know that your father loves you." But she couldn't imagine saying this without giving in to the temptation to diminish it by adding, "in his way." Instead she said, "Did you tell each other ghost stories in the evenings? Around the campfire?"

"Sometimes. But mostly we talked about women." He adjusted his seat into reclining position. He seemed okay. "Also I learned a lot of riddles. Some of them were really gross. If I can think of one that isn't too gross, I'll tell it to you." And then he did think of one. "What did the elephant say to the naked man?"

"Oh, God—I don't know. Something to do with trunk? I know! If you want to get dressed, there's a pile of old clothes in my trunk!"

He smiled at her with a child's cheerful pity. "Do you give up?"

"I give up."

"Now *you* ask."

"Okay—what did the elephant say to the naked man?"

"How do you breathe through that thing?"

She laughed, surprised. The bus rattled through a short, sunlit forest, then into open country. She said that ghost stories had been all the rage back in the days when she went to camp. "I heard some that really scared me."

"Do you remember any of them?"

"I remember one."

"This is going to be a real drag of a trip—maybe you should tell it to me."

"Okay—it's called 'The Golden Leg.'"

"Dad used to read me a story called 'The Golden Egg,'" he said.

She told the story much better than she'd told it the nights it had been her turn to tell it at camp. Billie sat staring straight ahead so he could concentrate on hearing it. And he made only one comment: when she got to the part where the wife with the golden leg was going in for a swim, he said, "Pretty bizarre. Gold is a heavy metal, man. A person with a gold leg would sink in the river and drown." Except for this he was silent. But when she got to the end and made the wife's ghost hiss *"You* got it!" at the husband who'd robbed her grave for the golden leg, he burst out laughing.

"A good story," he said. "But I wish you'd told it to me before I left for camp. That way I could have told it at one of the campfire nights."

"I considered it, but I was afraid it would scare you."

He said, "No offence, Mum, but your idea of scary is not necessarily my idea of scary."

"True," she said. She looked out the window. The fields were blooming with fireweed. She recalled Miller, years ago, bringing home geological survey maps for Billie to paint on and how odd it had been to see those ladylike pale green and sand-coloured maps backed by the free sweep of navy blue and primary oranges; she recalled a painting Billie had made of a deep blue sea topped by a band of pointed orange waves. The Sea on Fire, he had called it. She turned to remind him of it and saw that he was asleep. She had forgotten to ask him about the antibiotics. But he seemed to be okay. The gratitude she felt for this, and for his safe passage out of the woods, she now felt to be intense but wary—part of the long, precarious balancing act of parenthood.

She wondered where the pilot was now. Still flying north? Or already starting to head back for Poland Lake? Coming back, he would be alone in the plane. She imagined him remembering the moment he'd plunged his arm down into the warm, dark lake. She imagined him recalling the way he'd turned to look up at her with his unsmiling eyes to say, "I won't leave without you."

Miller would be sure to come and meet them at the terminal, if she gave him a call from North Bay. *He* would smile— a welcoming, irritating smile. As she thought this, his smile began to race along beside her, keeping up with the bus. Disembodied, it floated through the leaves of the trees in the little forests as they hurtled south.

PENGUIN · SHORT · FICTION

Other Titles In This Series

PENGUIN · SHORT · FICTION

Other Titles In This Series

Dark Arrows: Chronicles of Revenge
collected by Alberto Manguel

Evening Games: Chronicles of Parents and Children
collected by Alberto Manguel

Inspecting the Vaults
Eric McCormack

Tales From Firozsha Baag
Rohinton Mistry

Darkness
Bharati Mukherjee

The Moons of Jupiter
Alice Munro

The Street
Mordecai Richler

Melancholy Elephants
Spider Robinson

The Light in the Piazza
Elizabeth Spencer

The Stories of Elizabeth Spencer
Elizabeth Spencer

Goodbye Harold, Good Luck
Audrey Thomas